radicalized

CORY DOCTOROW is a science fiction author, activist, journalist and blogger, the co-editor of *Boing Boing* and the author of many books: most recently *Walkaway*, a novel; *In Real Life*, a graphic novel; *Information Doesn't Want to Be Free*, a book about earning a living in the Internet age; and *Homeland*, the award-winning, bestselling sequel to the 2008 YA novel *Little Brother*. Cory has been on the frontline of international debates on privacy, copyright and freedom of information for over a decade.

Also by Cory Doctorow

praise for
cory doctorow

'Doctorow is one of our most important science fiction writers, because he's also a public intellectual in the old style: he brings the news and explains it, making clearer the confusions of our wild current moment. His fiction is always the heart of his work, and this is his best book yet. In a world full of easy dystopias, he writes the hard utopia, and what do you know, his utopia is both more thought-provoking and more fun.'

Kim Stanley Robinson

'A dystopian future is in no way inevitable; [Doctorow] reminds us that the world we choose to build is the one we'll inhabit. Technology empowers both the powerful and the powerless, and if we want a world with more liberty and less control, we're going to have to fight for it.'

Edward Snowden

'The darker the hour, the better the moment for a rigorously imagined utopian fiction. *Walkaway* is now the best contemporary example I know of, its utopia glimpsed after fascinatingly extrapolated revolutionary struggle. A wonderful novel: everything we've come to expect from Cory Doctorow and more.'

m Gibson

cory doctorow

radicalized
four novellas

HEAD
ZEUS

For my parents: Roz and Gord Doctorow, who taught me why we fight, and not to give up. This isn't the kind of fight we win, it's the kind of fight we fight.

contents

unauthorized bread

THE WAY SALIMA found out that Boulangism had gone bankrupt: her toaster wouldn't accept her bread. She held the slice in front of it and waited for the screen to show her a thumbs-up emoji, but instead, it showed her the head-scratching face and made a soft *brrt*. She waved the bread again. *Brrt*.

"Come *on*." *Brrt*.

She turned the toaster off and on. Then she unplugged it, counted to ten, and plugged it in. Then she menued through the screens until she found RESET TO FACTORY DEFAULT, waited three minutes, and punched her Wi-Fi password in again.

Brrt.

Long before she got to that point, she'd grown certain that it was a lost cause. But these were the steps that you took when the electronics stopped working, so you could call the 800 number and say, "I've turned it off and on, I've unplugged it, I've reset it to factory defaults and…"

There was a touchscreen option on the toaster to call support, but that wasn't working, so she used the fridge to look up the number and call it. It rang seventeen times and disconnected. She heaved a sigh. *Another one bites the dust*.

The toaster wasn't the first appliance to go (that honor went to the dishwasher, which stopped being able to validate third-party dishes the week before when Disher went under), but it *was* the last straw. She could wash dishes in the sink but how the hell was she supposed to make toast—over a candle?

Just to be sure, she asked the fridge for headlines about Boulangism, and there it was, their cloud had burst in the night. Socials crawling with people furious about their daily bread. She prodded a headline and learned that Boulangism had been a ghost ship for at least six months because that's how long security researchers had been contacting the company to tell it that all its user data—passwords, log-ins, ordering and billing details—had been hanging out there on the public internet with no password or encryption. There were *ransom notes* in the database, records inserted by hackers demanding cryptocurrency payouts in exchange for keeping the dirty secret of Boulangism's shitty data handling. No one had even seen them.

Boulangism's share price had declined by 98 percent over the past year. There might not even *be* a Boulangism anymore. When Salima had pictured Boulangism, she'd imagined the French bakery that was on the toaster's idle-screen, dusted with flour, woodblock tables with serried ranks of crusty loaves. She'd pictured a rickety staircase leading up from the bakery to a suite of cramped offices overlooking a cobbled road. She'd pictured gas lamps.

The article had a street-view shot of Boulangism's headquarters, a four-story office block in Pune, near Mumbai, walled in with an unattended guard booth at the street entrance.

The Boulangism cloud had burst and that meant that there was no one answering Salima's toaster when it asked if the bread she was about to toast had come from an authorized Boulangism baker, which it had. In the absence of a reply, the paranoid little gadget would assume that Salima was in that class of nefarious fraudsters who bought a discounted Boulangism toaster and then tried to renege on her end of the bargain by inserting unauthorized bread, which had consequences ranging from kitchen fires to suboptimal toast (Boulangism was able to adjust its toasting routine in realtime to adjust for relative kitchen humidity and the age of the bread, and of course it would refuse to toast bread that had become unsalvageably stale), to say nothing of the loss of profits for the company and its shareholders. Without those profits, there'd be no surplus capital to divert to R&D, creating the continuous improvement that meant that hardly a day went by without Salima and millions of other Boulangism stakeholders (never just "customers") waking up with exciting new firmware for their beloved toasters.

And what of the Boulangism baker-partners? They'd done the right thing, signing up for a Boulangism license, subjecting their process to inspections and quality assurance that meant that their bread had exactly the right composition to toast *perfectly* in Boulangism's precision-engineered appliances, with crumb and porosity in perfect balance to absorb butter and other spreads. These valued partners deserved to have their commitment to excellence honored, not cast aside by bargain-hunting cheaters who wanted to recklessly toast any old bread.

Salima knew these arguments, even before her stupid toaster played her the video explaining them, which it did after three unsuccessful bread-authorization attempts, playing without a pause or mute button as a combination of punishment and reeducation campaign.

She tried to search her fridge for "boulangism hacks" and "boulangism unlock codes" but appliances stuck together. KitchenAid's network filters gobbled up her queries and spat back snarky "no results" screens even though Salima knew perfectly well that there was a whole underground economy devoted to unauthorized bread.

She had to leave for work in half an hour, and she hadn't even showered yet, but goddamnit, first the dishwasher and now the toaster. She found her laptop, used when she'd gotten it, now barely functional. Its battery was long dead and she had to unplug her toothbrush to free up a charger cable, but after she had booted it and let it run its dozens of software updates, she was able to run the darknet browser she still had kicking around and do some judicious googling.

She was forty-five minutes late to work that day, but she had toast for breakfast. Goddamnit.

THE DISHWASHER WAS next. Once Salima had found the right forum, it would have been crazy *not* to unlock the thing. After all, she had to use it and now it was effectively bricked. She wasn't the only one who had the Disher/Boulangism double whammy, either. Some poor suckers also had the poor fortune to own one of the constellation of devices made by HP-NewsCorp—fridges, toothbrushes, even sex toys—all of which had gone down thanks to a failure of the company's cloud provider, Tata. While this failure was unrelated to the Disher/Boulangism doubleheader, it was pretty unfortunate timing, everyone agreed.

The twin collapse of Disher and Boulangism *did* have a shared cause, Salima discovered. Both companies were publicly traded and both had seen more than 20 percent of their shares acquired by Summerstream Funds Management, the largest hedge fund on earth, with $184 billion under management. Summerstream was an "activist shareholder" and it was very big on stock buybacks. Once it had a seat on each company's board—both occupied by Galt Baumgardner, a junior partner at the firm, but from a very good Kansas family—they both hired the same expert consultant from Deloitte to examine the company's accounts and recommend a buyback program that would see the shareholders getting their due return from the firms, without gouging so deep into the companies' operating capital as to endanger them.

It was all mathematically provable, of course. The companies could easily afford to divert billions from their balance sheets to the shareholders. Once this was determined, it was the board's fiduciary duty to vote in favor of it (which was handy, since they all owned fat wads of company shares) and a few billion dollars later, the companies were lean, mean, and battle ready, and didn't even miss all that money.

Oops.

Summerstream issued a press release (often quoted in the forums Salima was now obsessively haunting) blaming the whole thing on "volatility" and "alpha" and calling it "unfortunate" and "disappointing." They were confident that both companies would restructure in bankruptcy, perhaps after a quick sale to a competitor, and everyone could start toasting bread and washing dishes within a month or two.

Salima wasn't going to wait. Her Boulangism didn't go easily. After downloading the new firmware from the darknet, she had to remove the case (slicing through three separate tamper-evident seals and a large warning sticker that threatened electrocution and prosecution, perhaps simultaneously, for anyone foolish enough to ignore it) and locate a specific component and then short out two of its pins with a pair of tweezers while booting it. This dropped the toaster into a test mode that the developers had deactivated, but not removed.

The instant the test screen came up, she had to jam in her USB stick (removing the toaster's hood had revealed a set of USB ports, a monitor port, and even a little Ethernet jack, all stock on the commodity single-board PC that controlled it) at exactly the right instant, then use the on-screen keyboard to tap in the log-in and password, which were "admin" and "admin" (of course).

It took her three tries to get the timing right, but on the third try, the spare log-in screen was replaced with the pirate firmware's cheesy text-art animation of a 3-D skull, which she smiled at—and then she burst into laughter as a piece of text-art toast floated into the frame and was merrily chomped to crumbs by the text-art skull, the crumbs cascading to the bottom of the screen and forming shifting little piles. Someone had put a lot of effort into the physics simulation for that ridiculous animation. It made Salima feel good, like she was entrusting her toaster to deep, serious craftspeople and not just randos who liked to pit their wits against faceless programmers from big, stupid companies.

The crumbs piled up as the skull chomped and the progress indicator counted up from 12 percent to 26 percent then to 34 percent (where it stuck for a full ten minutes, until she was ready to risk really bricking the damned thing by unplugging it, but then—) 58 percent, and so on, to an agonizing wait at 99 percent, and then all the crumbs rushed up from the bottom of the screen and went back out through the skull's mouth, turning *back* into toast, each reassembled piece forming up in ranks that quickly blotted out the skull, and the words ALL DONE burned themselves into the toast's surface, glistening with butter that ran down in rivulets. She was just grabbing for her phone to get a picture of this awesome pirate load-screen when the toaster oven blinked and rebooted itself.

A few seconds later, she held a slice of bread to the toaster's sensor and watched as its light turned green and its door yawned open. Halfway through munching the toast, she was struck by an odd curiosity. She held her hand up to the toaster, palm out, as though it, too, were a slice of bread. The toaster's light turned green and the door opened. She was momentarily tempted to try and toast a fork or a paper towel or a slice of apple, just to see if the toaster would do it, but of course it would.

This was a new kind of toaster, a toaster that took orders, rather than giving them. A toaster that would give her enough rope to hang herself, let her toast a lithium battery or a can of hairspray, or anything else she wanted to toast: unauthorized bread. Even homemade bread. The idea made her feel a little queasy and a little tremorous. Homemade bread was something she'd read about in books, seen in old dramas, but she didn't know anyone who actually baked bread. That was like gnawing your own furniture out of whole logs or something.

The ingredients turned out to be incredibly simple, and while her first loaf came out looking like a poop emoji, it tasted *amazing*, still warm from the little toaster, and if anything, the slice (OK, the lump) she saved and toasted the next morning was even better, especially with butter on it. She left for work that day with a magical, warm, *toasty* feeling in her stomach.

SHE DID THE dishwasher that night. The Disher hackers were much more utilitarian in their approach, but they also were Swedish, judging from the URLs in their README files, which might explain the minimalism. She'd been to an Ikea, she got it. The Disher didn't require anything like the song-and-dance of the Boulangism: she popped off the maintenance cover, pried the rubber gasket off the USB port, stuck in her stick, and rebooted it. The screen showed a lot of scrolling text and some cryptic error messages and then rebooted again into what looked like normal Disher operating mode, except without the throbbing red alerts about the unreachable server that had haunted it for a week. She piled the dishes from the sink into the dishwasher, feeling a tiny thrill every time the dishwasher played its "New Dish Recognized" arpeggio.

She thought about taking up pottery next.

HER EXPERIENCE WITH the dishwasher and the toaster changed her, though she couldn't quite say how at first. Leaving the apartment the next day, she'd found herself eyeing up the elevator bank, looking at the fire-department override plate under the call screen, thinking about the fact that the tenants on the subsidized floors had to wait three times as long for an elevator because they were only eligible to ride in the cars that had rear-opening doors that exited into the back lobby with its poor-doors. Even those cars wouldn't stop at her floor if they'd picked up one of the full-fare residents on the way, because heaven forfend those people should have to breath the common air of the filthy commoners.

Salima had been overjoyed to get a spot in her building, the Dorchester Towers, because the waiting list for the subsidy units that the planning department required of the developer was years deep. She'd been in the country for a decade at that point, spending the first five years in a camp in Arizona where they'd watched one person after another die in the withering heat. When the State Department finally finished vetting her and let her out, a caseworker met her with a bag of clothes, a prepaid debit card, and the news that her parents had died while she was in the camp.

She absorbed the news silently and didn't allow herself to display any outward sign of her agony. She had assumed that her parents had died, because they'd promised to meet her in Arizona within a month of her arrival, just as soon as her father could call in his old debts and pay for the papers and database fiddling that would get him on the plane and to the US Immigration checkpoint where they could claim asylum. She'd been a teenager then, and now she was a young woman, with five years' hard living in the camp behind her. She knew how to control her tears. She thanked the caseworker and asked what had become of their bodies.

"Lost at sea," the woman said and donned a compassionate mask. "The ship and all its passengers. No survivors. The Italians scoured the area for weeks and found nothing. The wreck went straight to the bottom. Bad informatics, they said." A ship was a computer that you put desperate people inside, and when the computer went bad, the ship was a tomb you put desperate people inside.

She nodded like she understood, though the sound of her blood in her ears was so loud she couldn't hear herself think. The social worker said more things, and gave her some paperwork, which included a Greyhound ticket to Boston, where she had been found a shelter bed.

She read the itinerary through three times. She'd learned to read English in the camp, taught by a woman who'd been a linguistics professor before she was a refugee. She'd learned geography from the mandatory civics lessons she'd gone to every two weeks, watching videos about life in America that were notably short on survival tips for life in the part of America where they slept three-deep in bunk beds in a blazing desert, surrounded by drones and barbed wire. She'd learned where Boston was, though. Far.

"Boston?"

"Two days, seventeen hours," the social worker said. "You'll get to see all of America. It's an incredible experience." Her mask slipped for a moment and she looked very tired. Then she pasted her smile back on. "Get to the grocery store first, that's my advice. You'll want some real food to eat."

Salima had got good at being bored over her five years in the camp, mastering a kind of waking doze where her mind simply went away, time scurrying past like roaches clinging to the baseboard, barely visible in the corner of her eye. But on the Greyhound bus, the skill failed her. Even after she found a window seat—twenty-two hours into the journey—she found her mind returning, again and again, to her parents, the ship, the deep fathoms of the Mediterranean. She had known that her parents were dead, but there was knowing, and there was knowing.

She debarked in Boston two days and seventeen hours later, noting as she did that the bus didn't have a driver, something she'd missed, boarding and debarking by the rear doors. Another computer you put your body into. Given the wrong informatics, the Greyhound could have plunged off a cliff or smashed into oncoming traffic.

There'd been a charge port on the armrest, and she'd shared it with the seatmates who'd come and gone on her bus, but she made sure she had a full charge when she stepped off the bus, and it was good she did, as she used up almost all of her battery getting translations and directions in order to find the shelter she'd been assigned, which wasn't in Boston, but in a suburb called Worcester, whose pronunciation evaded her for the next six months.

All her groceries were consumed, and everything she owned fit into a duffel bag whose strap broke as she was lugging it up a broken escalator while changing underground T trains on her way to Worcester. She'd spent half the funds on her debit card on food, and had eaten like a mouse, like a bird, like a scurrying cockroach. She had started with nearly nothing and now she had nothing.

The hardest part of finding the shelter was the fact that it was in a dead strip mall, eleven stores all refitted with bunks and showers and playrooms for kids, arranged along the back plane of an empty parking lot that was half a mile from the nearest bus stop. Salima walked past the mall three times, staring at her phone—whose battery was nearly flat again; it was so old it barely held a charge—before she figured out that this row of shops was her new home.

The reception was in an old pharmacy that had anchored the mall. It was unattended, a cavernous space walled off by a roll-down gate, with a row of touchscreens where the cash registers had sat. It smelled of piss and the floor was dirty, with that kind of ancient, ground-in grime you got in places where people trudged over and over.

Only one of the touchscreens was working, and it took a lot of trial and error before she figured out that she needed to tap about 1.5 centimeters south-southwest of the buttons she was hitting. Once she clocked this, things got faster. She switched the screen to Arabic, let the camera over it scan her retinas, and repeatedly pressed her fingers to the pad until the machine had read her. Once it had validated her, she had to tap through eight screens of things she was promising: that she wouldn't drink or drug or steal; that she didn't have any chronic or infectious diseases; that she did not support terrorism; that she understood that at this stage, she was not permitted to work for wages, but that also and paradoxically, she would be required to work in Worcester in order to pay back the people of the United States for the shelter bed she was about to be assigned.

She read the fine print. It was something she'd learned to do, early in the refugee process. Sometimes the immigration officers quizzed you on the things you'd just clicked through and if you couldn't answer their questions correctly, they'd send you back to the back of the line, or reschedule your hearing for the next month, because you hadn't fully appreciated the gravity of the agreement you were forging with the USA.

Then she found out which of the former stores she'd be living in, and was prompted to insert her debit card, which was topped up with credits she could exchange for food at specific stores that catered to people on benefits. As she tapped through more screens, entering her phone number, choosing times for medical checkups, she became aware of a low humming noise, growing closer. She turned around and saw a low trolley trundling through the aisles of the derelict pharmacy, with a cardboard banker's box on it. It steered laboriously around corners, then moved to a gate set into the roll-down cage, which clunked open. The screen prompted her to retrieve the box, which contained linens, a towel, a couple six-packs of white cotton underwear, t-shirts, a box of tampons, and a toilet bag with shampoos, soaps, and deodorants. It was the most *functional* transaction she'd had in... *years*... and she wanted to kiss the stupid unlovely little robot.

She couldn't carry her box and her duffel bag at the same time, and she didn't want to let either out of her sight, so she staged them down the face of the strip mall, moving the box ten paces, setting it down and getting her duffel and carrying it ten paces past the box, then leapfrogging the box over the duffel. Her pile of papers from the kiosk included a map showing the location of her storefront, near the end (of course), so it was a long way. At the halfway mark, a woman came out of the store she'd just passed and regarded her with hands on hips, head cocked, a small smile on her face.

The woman was Somali—there'd been plenty in the camp— and no older than Salima, though she had a small child clinging to her legs, gender unknown. She wore overalls and a Boston University sweatshirt and had her hair in a kerchief, and for all that, she looked somehow stylish. Later, Salima would learn that the woman—whose name was Nadifa—came from a long line of seamstresses and would unpick the seams on any piece of clothing that fell into her hands and re-tailor them for her measurements.

"You are new?"

"I am Salima. I'm new."

The woman cocked her head the other way. "Where are you staying? Show me." She walked to Salima and held out her hand for the map. Salima showed it to her and she chupped her teeth. "That's no good, that one has bad heat and the toilet never stops running. Gah—here, let us fix it."

Without asking, the woman hoisted her box, and led her back to the office, Salima trailing after her alongside the little child, who kept sneaking her looks. The woman knew which screen worked and could land her finger at the exact south-southwestern offset needed to hit the buttons. Her fingers flew over the screen and then she had Salima stand before the retina monitor and put her fingers on the scanner again, and new paper emerged in the kiosk's out tray.

"Much better," the woman said. Salima felt confused and a little anxious. Had this woman just moved her in with her family? Was she to be a babysitter for the child who was staring at her again?

But she didn't need to worry. Single women stayed in one of three units, and families in two more. Salima's new home—thanks to the woman, who finally introduced herself—had once been a nail salon, and its storeroom still had a few remnants from those days, but it was now hung with heavy, sound-absorbing blankets made out of some kind of synthetic fiber that turned out to be surprisingly good at shedding dirt and dampening sound. The woman and her kid left her there, and she pulled the fabric corners shut and tabbed them together and spent a moment in the ringing silence of the tiny curtained roomlet, a place that would truly be hers, shared with no one, for some indeterminate time.

Later, she'd discover all the ways that the other shelter-dwellers had decorated their little spaces, which most of them called cells, with heavy irony, because every one of them had spent months or years in literal cells, the kinds with concrete walls and iron bars. She'd decorate her own room, and Nadifa's children would come to poke their heads in without warning and demand stories or someone to play a game with or ideas for pictures to draw. She wasn't exactly roped into being a babysitter, but she wasn't exactly *not* roped into it, either, and she liked Nadifa's kids, who were just as bold and fearless as their mother, who was also a lot of fun, especially when she found a bottle of wine and sent the kids out to play in the common room, and they'd perch at opposite ends of Salima's narrow bunk, telling lies about men, and sometimes the odd truth about their lives before the shelter would slip in, and there'd be a tear or two, but that was all right, too.

Nadifa already had her work papers and she showed Salima how to get papers of her own, which took months of patient prodding at the one working kiosk to get it to emit pieces of paper that she'd have to bring to government offices and feed into other kiosks, sneaking the trips in between her work details. The irony of being too busy working to get a work permit did not escape her, and oh, how she laughed at the irony as she scrubbed graffiti and picked up trash in the parks and cleaned city buses in the great bus-barns in places even more out of the way than her Worcester strip mall.

Getting her work papers wasn't the same as getting a job, but Salima was smart and she'd spent her years in the camp pursuing different qualifications by online course—hair braiding and bookkeeping, virus removal and cat grooming—and she felt sure there'd be something she could do. She searched the job boards with Nadifa's help, enrolled with temp agencies, submitting to their humiliating background checks, which included giving them access to her social media and email history, an invasion that was only made worse when she was later quizzed on the messages she'd saved from her parents, videos and picture-messages sent after they'd been separated, but before they'd both died.

Work trickled in, a few hours here and there, shifts dwarfed by the long commutes on the bus to and from the jobs, but she cherished hope that taking these shitty jobs would build her rep with the agencies that were sending her out, that she'd pay her dues and start getting real shifts, for real money. She bought a couple external batteries for her ailing phone so that she could work on the bus rides. She and Nadifa had divided up the entirety of New England and every day they ran hundreds of searches to look for new high-rise approvals that came with subsidized apartments and then made a note of the day that the waiting list for each would open. They knew the chances of either one of them getting accepted were vanishingly small, and if they were both accepted, it was pretty much impossible that they'd end up in a place together.

Which is why the Dorchester Towers were such a miracle. It was bitter December and the shelter hadn't ever gotten its promised shipment of winter coats, so everyone was making do with multiple layers of sweaters and tees, which didn't read as "professional" and had cost Salima a very good week-long bookkeeping job for a think tank that was closing its quarterly books. She'd been worried sick about losing the job and, worse, getting a black mark with the temp agency, which had got her several other great bookkeeping jobs that had fattened her tiny savings account more than a dozen cleaning jobs.

Rattling around the strip mall with the other denizens trapped by the weather and the inadequate clothes, she pondered raiding her savings for a coat, trying to figure out how much work she'd have to lose before it would be a break-even proposition and estimating the probability that the long-delayed winter-coat shipment would finally arrive before too much work was lost. Her phone let her know she had a government message—the kind that she would have to retrieve from the kiosk in the shelter office—so she put on three sweaters and stuffed her hands into three thicknesses of socks and fought the gale-force winds to the office.

Standing in a puddle of her own meltwater, she logged into a kiosk—they'd fixed them all, including the one that sort of worked, and now all of them were equally unreliable and prone to falling into an endless reboot cycle—and retrieved the message. She was just absorbing the impossibly good news when Nadifa staggered in from the cold, carrying her smallest one close to her for body heat.

"Does that one work?" She pointed at Salima's kiosk and

Salima smiled to herself as she wiped the screen and stepped away from it.

"It works!" Her joy was audible in her voice, and Nadifa gave her a funny look. Salima stifled her grin. She'd tell Nadifa when—

"Oh my God." Nadifa was just staring at the screen, jaw on her chest. Salima peeked and laughed aloud.

"Me too, me too!"

The message was that Dorchester Towers had approved Nadifa's residency, with a two-room flat on the forty-second story that would be ready to move into in eighteen months, assuming no construction delays. The rent was income-indexed, meaning that Nadifa and her kids would be able to afford to live there no matter what happened to them in the future. Nadifa was sometimes loud and pushy, but she was never squeaky, so it amused Salima quite a lot when Nadifa threw her hands into the air and bounced up and down on her toes, making excited noises so high-pitched they'd have deafened a dolphin.

She didn't even stop bouncing when she hugged Salima, pulling her along as she jumped up and down, laughing with delight, and Salima laughed even harder, because of what she knew.

She logged Nadifa out of the kiosk and logged herself in and quickly tapped her way into her official government mailbox, and simply pointed wordlessly at the screen until Nadifa bent and read it. Her jaw dropped even further.

"You're on the thirty-fifth floor! That's only six floors below us! We can take the stairs to each other's places!" Nadifa's smallest child, confused by all the shouting and bouncing, chose that moment to set up a wail, and so Nadifa pulled him out of his sling and twirled him around over her head. "We're getting a place, a place of our own! And Auntie Salima will be there, too! We'll have a kitchen, we'll have *bedrooms,* we'll have—" She broke off and cradled the boy under one arm, used her free hand to grab Salima and shake her by the shoulder. "We'll have bathrooms. Our own bathrooms! Our own bathtubs! Our own toilets!"

"Our own toilets!" Salima shouted, and the little one said something that was almost *toilets* and that set them both to laughing like drains, laughing until tears streamed down their faces, and the kid laughed with them.

The coats arrived after dinner that night, too.

SALIMA AND NADIFA clubbed together to rent a van the day they moved out, and they filled it to the ceiling with the detritus of Nadifa's years and Salima's months at the shelter— kids' toys, clothes, shampoo bottles with enough left inside for three more careful washes, drawings, picture books, scrap paper for drawing and paper dolls painstakingly cut out of old printouts from the kiosk. The car inched its way through the Boston traffic, which they could only glimpse intermittently through the tiny bits of windscreen that weren't covered in shopping bags full of possessions.

The van pulled into Dorchester Towers' back alley two hours later. It was a hot June day and the kids had needed two toilet breaks and several water breaks, which had blown up their plans to beat rush hour traffic, landing them squarely within it. But the two women were stoic. They had been on journeys that were much, much longer and far, far more difficult.

The poor-doors for Dorchester Towers weren't finished yet, and so they had to go through a temporary plywood tunnel to enter the building. The lobby was in the same condition as the doors—raw drywall, open electrical receptacles, rough concrete floor with troughs cast into it for conduit. They lugged their things into the lobby in stages, leaving Nadifa's eldest to stand guard and watch the kids as they went back and forth to the van, trying to get everything out before the sixty-minute mark, when they'd be billed for another hour's rental. They squeaked in.

There in the lobby, sweating and humid, they met the Dorchester Towers elevators. The touchscreen asked you for your floor, then tracked the passage of the cars up and down the shafts. Cars would touch down in the lobby and they'd hear the doors on the other side sigh open and shut, but the doors facing them never opened.

They debated what to do. Eventually, they decided that the doors on this side must not be working at all, that it was yet another thing that had to be completed, along with the lobby and the doors and please god, air conditioning.

Kids, belongings, themselves—somehow they got them out of the doors again, down the alley and around the building's circumference to its lobby doors, which, they couldn't help but notice, were finished, chromed, shined, smudge-free and guarded.

The guard on the other side of the door buzzed the intercom when they tried the handle. He was white and wearing a semi-cop outfit, some kind of private security, which was unusual because that was the kind of job you saw brown people in, most of the time. They noticed this, too.

"Yes?"

"We live here, we're moving in today. On the…" Salima waved down the road. "On the other side? But the elevators aren't working there yet. We can take the stairs, after we move in, but she's on the forty-second floor, and I'm on the thirty-fifth, and we have all this—" The pile of bags and clothes and drawings and children and themselves, all so disreputable, especially contrasted against the shining chrome, the unsmudged glass, which now had two of Nadifa's kids' faces and hands smearing slowly across it. Oops.

The security guard tapped his screen. "Elevators are working."

"Not on that side. The elevators came down, but the doors didn't open."

"Step aside please." He said it so sharply that even Nadifa's kids snapped to attention. There were some people trying to get in, pressing their thumbs to a matte place on the doorframe that didn't smudge. The doors gasped open and let out a blessed gust of air conditioning that almost brought them to their knees. The beaded sweat on their backs and legs and faces and scalps spilled as much of their heat as it could in the brief wind. Then the fine people were through the door, not having looked once at them. They were preppy, a look Salima had come to understand since moving to this city of colleges and universities, with floppy blond hair and carefully scuffed tennis outfits and sweaty, shining faces. The security guard greeted them and chatted with them, words inaudible through the closed doors. They were amiable enough, and waved good-bye as they stepped into the elevator. As the doors closed, Salima saw the doors on the opposite side, the doors that opened into that other lobby.

The security guard gave them an irritated look and shook his head like he couldn't believe they were still hanging around, blocking his doorway. "Your entrance is around back."

"The elevators don't work," Salima reminded him. "We waited and waited—"

"The elevators work. They just give priority to the market-rent side. You'll get an elevator when none of these folks need one."

Salima grasped the system and its logic in an instant. The only reason she'd been able to rent in this building was that the developer had to promise that they'd make some low-income housing available in exchange for permission to build fifty stories instead of the thirty that the other buildings in the neighborhood rose to. There was a lot of this sort of thing, and she knew that there were rules about the low-income units, what the landlords had to provide and what she was forbidden from doing.

But now she saw an important truth: even the pettiest amenity would be spitefully denied to the subsidy apartments unless the landlord was forced by law to provide it. She had spent enough time as Auntie Salima, helping to raise Nadifa's three kids, to recognize the logic of a mulish child who wanted to make their displeasure known.

"Come on," she said, as she picked up a double armload of bags and slogged back around the building to the poor-door.

THE APARTMENT WAS *wonderful*. The promised luxury of a private shower and a bathtub she could lie down in if she squinched her legs and put her chin on her chest (but it was *her* bathtub!) and a single bed with a good mattress that no one else had ever slept upon, and when she folded that up, she could fold down the sofa slab with its bright cushions. Raise that slab up a little higher and twist the coffee table so that its legs extended and it became a dining table and you could seat three, or four if they were all very good friends. The walls had good insulation, and what little sound leaked in from the units around her was inaudible so long as she ran the fan in the HVAC at the lowest setting, something she could automate with the apartment's sensors so it just happened whenever she was home.

The kitchen had "all major appliances," just as advertised: the toaster, the dishwasher—a small thing that would hold all the dishes from a meal for one, along with a mixing bowl or one of the toaster's baking pans—the fridge. They all started working once she'd input her debit-card number, and they presented her with menus of approved consumables: the dishes that would work in the dishwasher, the range of food that would work with the toaster, from bread to ready-meals. The washing machine would do a towel and sheets, or two days' clothes, and there were dozens of compatible detergents she could order from its screen. The prices all included delivery, or she could shop for herself in approved stores, but there was always the risk that she'd pick up something that was incompatible with her model, so it would be better for everyone concerned if she'd do her shopping right there in her kitchen, where it was most convenient for everyone.

It was only a short walk to the T, and the stairs weren't that bad going down in the morning. Coming back up was another story: thirty-five floors was seventy flights of stairs. She braved them about once a week and told herself that she was making herself healthy with such an intense aerobic workout.

Having a place to live that was truly hers made a huge difference in her life. Something about the stability, the confidence—hell, just having a reliable place to do laundry every night—it all added up to the sense that she was finally exiting the endless limbo she'd lived in all her life. Her earliest memories were of being on the move with her parents, one camp and then another, then an uncle's house for a while, then another camp, then temporary apartments, then the crossing to America, the camp, the shelter. All that time, she'd had the sense that her life was on hold, that she was floating around like a leaf in the breeze, sometimes snagged on a branch and sometimes lofted up to the clouds, but never touching down, never coming to rest. It meant that she never really thought about her life more than a few days in advance. Now, in her own home, she was thinking about what her future held.

Some combination of luck and self-confidence was with her, and within a month she'd landed a full-time job as a bookkeeper for a company that serviced little mom-and-pop shops. She had half a dozen clients and she'd try to see each of them once a week, even if she could have done most of the work from home. She preferred setting up in the back room of a dry cleaner or a convenience store or a little ice-cream parlor and going over the logs from the registers and the invoices, scheduling payments and chatting with the staff and the owners. She learned that people liked to be warned of impending cash-flow crunches and other potential snags she could see in their books and within a few months she was more like a trusted advisor than a contractor. She remembered their birthdays and brought them cards, and then when her twenty-fifth rolled around, the owner of a vintage clothing store surprised her with a gorgeous Japanese satin jacket from the previous century, the back embroidered with a tiger that had faded beautifully over the years, with a patina like a Persian rug.

Nadifa's kids got into school and Nadifa even started to fill in; the breathing room of time to herself meant that she could get a decent meal, could take care of her hair and clothes. She'd always had a regal bearing, but it warred with a natural overburdened-mother's shoulder-slump, the exhaustion lines, the hands always full of kids or toys or laundry, the stains on her beautifully tailored clothes. With some stability in her life, Nadifa's underlying nature asserted itself. Her clothes were impeccable, the lines in her face made her look serious, and then when she'd crack a wicked joke and her eye would gleam, the contrast between the seriousness and the humor was like something you'd see in an old painting.

Nadifa's kids never lost their mischief, but school was good for them, gave them some structure to work within and fight against. They were behind, especially Abdirahim, the eldest at twelve, and Nadifa rode his ass, making him work through his remedial homework assignments on his phone or even the big screen in their living room provided the littles could be tamped down to mere chaos. Nadifa's place had two rooms, one for the kids and the living room, which was exactly like Salima's, turning into a bedroom by folding down the table and folding up the sofa and folding down the bed, a magic trick that had to be done in the right order or everything snagged everything else in the middle of the room in an unholy knot that had to be carefully worked to loosen it.

Things were good, until the appliances started to disobey her.

SHE DID THE washing machine just because she *could*. Once you had a kitchen full of devices that would obey you, the one that wouldn't loomed ever larger and grew less and less tolerable. Besides, she was single, had no interest in swiping right on randos who never failed to disappoint. She had become an obsessive watcher of jailbreaking videos, especially since she'd followed a breadcrumb trail of ever-more daring videos, until she found the one that told her how to download the darknet tools that would get her to the real-deal sites where you could download new firmware images, swap tips and complaints, and jolly along with thousands of lawless anarchists like herself who were toasting any damned thing they felt like.

The washing machine was the hardest yet and involved uncoupling a lot of water hoses. She kept messing up the ring clamps, which she'd never had to use before, but she bore down on it with a bookkeeper's resolve, methodically trying one variation after another, keeping a pan beneath the join to catch the leaks when she tested it out by turning on the water. While she worked, she switched to bread-making videos because that was her new passion, and now every time she saw Nadifa's kids they begged her for whatever her latest creation was. She was making braided loaves now, an egg bread called challa, basting the rising dough with egg whites to give the crust a high gloss.

A week later, she made two important discoveries: first, shopping for detergent in the grocery store was a *lot* cheaper than buying it through her machine's screen, and second, that her persistent eczema was actually an allergic reaction to something in the authorized laundry soap. Spring was springing and she'd been dreading sweating out the hot days in long sleeves to cover her flaking, itchy arms. She bought three vintage short-sleeved blouses and asked Nadifa to alter them to fit her as beautifully as all of Nadifa's clothes.

She stopped short of jailbreaking her thermostat. For now. The thermostat was integrated with the building's sensor grid, including the camera over her door, the cameras sprinkled around her apartment. It recognized her even before she entered, and spun the HVAC system up to speed before she'd even closed the door behind her, giving her just a moment of the claustrophobic, gasping air of the shut-up apartment before the white noise of the fan whisked a soft air current around and around. What's more, it would watch her place while she was out at work and send her a video stream if it detected anyone in her place when she wasn't there. She liked that, it comforted her. She'd been robbed twice in the shelter in Arizona, and had gotten used to carrying everything she owned of any value with her at all times. It was such a relief to be able to amass more valuable goods than she could easily carry.

The elevator was another matter.

When she'd moved into Dorchester Towers, the building had only been in service for a few weeks and was at less than half occupancy. As the apartments had filled up, the number of market-rate people using the elevators had increased to the point where it could take a full forty-five minutes to get a ride up to the thirty-fifth floor, and when the elevator finally came for the poor-door's lobby, there were so many people waiting that she'd end up riding in a squash of people, face in someone's sweaty armpit, and if she was lucky she'd be pressed against a wall behind her and not up against some strange man. She was nearly certain that the times it had seemed like she was being creeped on it had been an accident of the press of bodies and not actually creepiness, but she couldn't be sure, and anyway, it still *felt* creepy.

One day she was sitting in Nadifa's living room, drinking tea and watching Nadifa's eldest do his extra homework. She and Nadifa had been complaining about the elevators for a good twenty minutes—it was a well-established subject among all the subsidy tenants and they could really work themselves up about it—when Abdirahim, Nadifa's eldest son, looked up from his math.

"Mama, why don't we just use elevator captains?"

"Do your homework." Nadifa operated on pure reflex when

it came to her kids and homework, but after a moment she added, "What's an elevator captain?"

Abdirahim's smile was luminous. "It is so *cool*. If you're the first person in the elevator in Japan, you're the elevator captain. You have to hold the door-open button until everyone boards, and then you have to press the door-close button and all the floor buttons. If the elevator captain gets out before the elevator is empty, the next closest person has to do it."

"Where do you hear this?"

"We did a unit on unspoken rules in social studies. I'm doing an extra-credit on the unspoken rules of refugee detention in America. The teacher loves that, she gets all solemn when I talk about it. The other refugee kids think it's hilarious."

"I don't think it's hilarious." Nadifa was deadpan. "I think it's very respectful." She turned back to Salima, opened her mouth to start talking again, and then turned back to Abdirahim. "Why would we use an elevator captain?"

His smile was twice as big. "We could just take turns staying in the elevator in the morning and the afternoon, during the busy times. It won't stop for a poor if there's a rich who needs it, sure, but if there's a poor in it, it won't stop for a rich until the poor is out."

Nadifa mouthed *a poor* to Salima and rolled her eyes. Salima covered her smile. The kids knew what was what and they told it like it was. Meanwhile the plan was dawning on Salima and Nadifa. It was weirdly elegant: simple, so there weren't many things that could go wrong. Plus, it used the fact that the rich people didn't want to have to ever see one of them against them.

"Do your homework." Nadifa used her stern voice, but her smile to Salima was the twin of Abdirahim's. Salima mouthed *smart kid* and Nadifa nodded.

*

THE TWO WEEKS of the elevator captains were the best in the building's short history. From 7:30 to 8:45 in the morning and 5:15 to 6:30 at night, there was effectively one elevator exclusively reserved for the use of the poor side of the building, serving the ten floors out of fifty-six. That left fifteen elevators for the rich people to use, and so at first they may not have even noticed that their unseen neighbors living in their building's off-limits spaces were getting up and down in a matter of minutes, rather than waiting an hour or trudging the stairs.

But someone figured it out. Nadifa called Salima at work, using anger to mask her worry. "They were waiting in the lobby. Three security guards! Three! And of course it had to be Abdirahim who was elevator captain." It was Abdirahim's idea and he was the most enthusiastic captain in the building. Salima had even bought him a little peaked military cap from her vintage store client's stock, and he wore it at a jaunty angle during his shifts, looking almost indecently cute.

He'd just brought the elevator back down to the ground floor and was mashing the close-door button with the lightning reflexes of a thirteen-year-old raised on video games when the *other* door opened, the rich-person door, the door that never, ever opened while any of them were in the car.

The three security guards demanded Abdirahim's name and papers—and when he told them that they were in his home, on the forty-second floor, they refused to let him go get them. Instead, they took him down into the basement, using their security-guard fobs to override the elevator's controls. They locked him in a windowless room with a reinforced door and conspicuous cameras in each ceiling corner and slammed the door on him.

After a long time, they came in to question him. He knew that he was late getting home and that his mum would be getting worried, though not frantic, because Nadifa didn't do frantic. Furious, yes. Frantic, never. Furious was a lot more worrying, honestly. That was the thought that was in his head when he explained the whole elevator captain business to the security guards, who questioned him and denied him water or the use of the toilet until it seemed that every drop of water in his body was in his bladder and trying desperately to escape.

They went over the story again and again, and he began to cry, because it reminded him of the questioning they'd had in the camps, when he was tiny, and again when they got to America, when he was small. Those had been hard times, with his father dying and refusing to show it, sitting up ramrod straight and answering question after question, praying they wouldn't detect his illness and use it as an excuse to turn away the family.

The memory of that time overcame him and he sobbed and couldn't answer their questions anymore, and that's when they called Nadifa, finally, and she was *furious*, but not at him; she yelled at them about re-traumatizing a child and demanded their names and their badge numbers and even got out her phone and recorded it all, even him crying, which made him ashamed, but still, he couldn't stop.

There would be a reckoning, Nadifa swore, and Salima thought she was probably right, but that they would get the worst of it.

They did.

The elevators had cameras in them, of course, and it took the face-recognition software all of ten seconds to produce a list of all the poor-door residents who'd used the elevator captain system, with times and dates of each ride. It took a day for the building management to merge those records with form letters informing everyone who'd participated that they were in violation of their lease, which forbade "tampering with, reverse engineering, disabling, bypassing, disconnecting, spoofing, undermining, damaging, or subverting" any of the building's systems. Further violations would result in eviction proceedings. Be warned. Be told.

It was humiliating to be addressed in this manner. Even for Salima, who had been subjected to the most humiliating of depredations over the years—strip searches and confiscations, collective punishments, and scouring of her most private data and memories to find an excuse to deny her humanity— it burned. After years of spinning in place, she had finally started her life in earnest, with a place and a job and friends who were nearly family. This was a reminder that her current life was a tissue-thin surface covering the world she'd lived in before.

For her whole life, the world had been divided into the people around her, people who knew her, and who she was. Most of those were people who wished her well and supported her and she supported them back. Some of those people were bad people and meant her harm—the camps were not paradise— but even for them, it was personal.

But there was another world, vast beyond her knowing, of people who didn't know her at all, but who held her life in their hands. The ones who thronged in demonstrations against refugees. The politicians who raged about the scourge of terrorists hidden among refugees, and the ones who talked in code about "assimilation" and "too much, too fast." The soldiers and cops and guards who pointed guns at her, barked orders at her. The bureaucrats she never saw who rejected her paperwork for cryptic reasons she could only guess at, and the bureaucrats who looked her in the eye and rejected her paperwork and refused to explain themselves.

Now there was a new group in that latter class, distant as the causes of the weather: the building management company and its laser printer, blasting out eviction threats to people whose names they didn't know and whose faces they'd never seen over transgressions so petty and rules so demeaning.

The elevator captains had been a good chuckle, a way for everyone from the poor-doors and the poor-floors to feel like they were mice outsmarting the cats. The letters put them in their place: roaches, facing exterminators.

THE ELEVATORS WEREN'T any better programmed than the Disher or the Boulangism or the thermostat or anything else, really. The big difference was access. She could take her Disher to pieces in her kitchen without having to explain herself to anyone, but let her try that in the hallway, in sight of the cameras and her neighbors, and the situation would be very different.

To take out the elevators, she'd need to take out the cameras, and then work in the very small hours, and still she would risk discovery, so she'd need a disguise, a maintenance outfit, and maybe she could also take out the lights and replace them with working lights—she began to visualize the tableau: her down on one knee in shapeless coveralls with a hard hat pulled way down, the lights out and illumination from floodlights that would shine right into the eyes of anyone who tried to snoop. It was a fun daydream, and she enjoyed the game of thinking of how someone might catch her and how she might avoid being caught. It was an especially good way to recover from the exhaustion of trudging thirty-five flights up, or the frustration of waiting for forty-five minutes with a cooling pot of tagine from the corner deli in her hand, the smell driving her crazy.

She pushed around the wreckage of her tagine with a glass of cheap and delicious retsina—a favorite among so many refugees who'd made the passage through Greece, and now a staple of refugees who hadn't, thanks to its popularity in the camps—and looked out her tiny window at Boston far below her, the Charles swollen to its levees, the ant-like people swarming home under the streetlights as autumn's early night fell swiftly upon them. She daydreamed about hi-viz and work lights, about the tools she'd use to remove the firefighter's override panel to reveal the USB port beneath, the subtle ways in which she would alter the building's algorithms so that the faceless people would never discover her intrusion.

There was a ding at the door and the screen showed her Abdirahim, weirdly distorted by the camera's autofocus on his face, which was a good foot below the adult-height camera mounting. She waved the door unlocked and he let himself in, looking from her to the tagine to the wine and then back to her.

"Have you eaten?" It was a phrase she remembered her mother saying to everyone who came through their door, even when there was no food to share. It had irritated her once, and now she said it automatically on those rare occasions when someone came through *her* door.

"Yes." Abdirahim said it too quickly.

"But you're still hungry." It wasn't a question. She remembered being a thirteen-year-old: hungry all the time. She got him a plate and spooned some tagine onto it and then found a pita and popped it in her toaster to warm it. When it was done, he looked at her with wide eyes.

"Yours works?"

It took a moment for her to figure out what he meant. The

toaster. "It works," she said. "I fixed it." Then, with a little pride: "The dishwasher, too. And the thermostat. And the fridge."

"Show me."

"Eat first."

The food barely touched his throat on the way down. She felt like she should probably make him eat slowly in her capacity in loco parentis, but she was as eager to show him as he was to be shown. When he said *show me* it made her realize that she'd been bursting with secret knowledge that she'd wanted more than anything to share.

When he was done, she put his dishes in the dishwasher and gestured him over to her so that she could show him the boot screen as she put the Disher through its paces, with the fanciful graphics she'd installed, of anthropomorphic dishes with bad attitudes showering angrily in the trademark Disher spray. He clapped and laughed and demanded to see the rest, and then to be shown how to do it.

They say you don't really know how to do something until you can teach it to someone else. As Salima looked up the instructions again, she realized how much of it had just been recipe-following the first time around and how much she'd come to understand since, so that the steps made *sense*. She was able to explain to Abdirahim the *why* of each step, nearly as much as the *what* and *how,* and her heart beat and her blood sang with the experience of mastery.

This was the antidote, she realized, to the feeling of distant people whom she'd never meet who held the power of everything over her. To be able to control the computers around her, rather than being controlled by them.

"You see," she said at last, as a realization came out of the blue to her and left her wonderstruck and thunderstruck, feeling like a revelating prophet. "You see, if someone wants to control you with a computer, they have to put the computer where *you* are, and *they* are not, and so you can access that computer without supervision. A computer you can access without supervision is a computer you can change, because all these computers are the same, deep down. When you get down to the programs underneath the skin, a toaster and a dishwasher and a thermostat, they're all the same computer in different cases. Once you can seize control over that computer, all of them are yours."

As the words left her mouth, her messianic fervor was replaced by nagging self doubt, the knowledge that she was shouting triumphantly at a small boy who had only gotten out of temporary refugee housing a few months before, and she felt foolish and small. But then she saw the gleam in Abdirahim's eyes, and it was the same as the gleam in *her* eyes, and she knew that the two of them were sharing the vision.

"Our dishwasher and toaster haven't worked in weeks," he said.

"Oh, dear." She hadn't even thought of that. She had reflexively kept her work a secret from Nadifa, because she was doing something potentially dangerous and she didn't want Nadifa to point this out. But that was before her vision. "We should do something about that." She held out her hand. "Let's go see your mother." She remembered to take the retsina with her on her way out the door.

PERHAPS NADIFA WOULD have been upset at the idea of hacking the family's appliances, but that was before she had spent two weeks parenting without a toaster or dishwasher. The hardship of eating everything cold or shelling out money she didn't have for takeaways had softened any concerns she might have had, and as she watched Abdirahim show his sisters how to jailbreak all the apartment's major appliances, she radiated motherly pride.

"He's good at it," Salima said. "I only showed him once and now—" She gestured.

"Do you think we'll get in trouble? With the building, I mean? They own the appliances."

Salima shrugged. "They were getting a share of the money we spent before, for the special bread and soap and so on. But with both companies bankrupt, they won't be expecting any new money. Now, if the companies do ever come back from bankruptcy and still no one here is using their products..."

Nadifa nodded. "That would definitely be trouble." She watched her kids, who had the cover off the thermostat and were avidly watching a video on the big screen next to it, where a person whose body had been mapped to a giant animated rabbit was explaining how to get it to fall back into a debug mode from which it would accept commands that let you override central commands to it. "But if it's just the two of us, will they even find out?"

Salima shrugged again. "If the system is designed well, then yes. It would be very weird for our apartments to generate much lower revenues than any of the others. I once did a job where I saw that two of the self-checkouts at a pharmacy were generating twenty percent less money than the rest. At first I thought it was that they were broken, but even when they were serviced and even moved, they were always twenty percent down from the average. They got sent away for analysis and they'd been hacked and were being skimmed."

"But you are good at your job, and you care about that sort of thing." Unspoken: no one good at their job, who cared about anything, was involved in the poor-floors of Dorchester Towers.

"I'm sure they care about money. But perhaps they're not so well designed." She pondered it. "I don't know. They certainly care a lot about making money, so the parts that help them make as much money would probably have the most attention. I'll search for it. There must be other people in this situation."

The kids successfully tested their modifications to the thermostat and closed it up, looking this way and that for something else to attack.

"Don't forget the refrigerator," Nadifa said. "That's a fun one. Very tricky."

They raced to the screen and started typing, sending Idil, the eldest girl, to read the model number off the label on the inside of the fridge door.

SALIMA KNEW THAT the kids wouldn't stop at their own apartments, of course. She'd pass them in the hallways, sometimes, rushing from one apartment to the next. The feeling this gave her was hard to pin down: pride and excitement, but also trepidation and a sick, impotent sensation, the echo of the slow roll her stomach had done when she came home to find that laser-printed threat stuck to her door, to all their doors.

On the elevators, Salima heard whispers: *Have you done your place yet? It's so easy. I'm baking bread again! We found some beautiful dishes at a thrift shop, such a treat to be able to wash them in the machine. My little boy did it so easy!*

Then one night, a knock at her door, urgent and low. She opened it and found Abdirahim, wide-eyed and stressed, and her pulse quickened, her armpits slickened and she thought, *Oh no, this is it.*

"Tell me," she said, bringing him in.

"I did the same as always," he said. "A toaster. I've done so many of them. But something went wrong and now it won't even turn on."

She whooshed out a sigh of relief. He'd bricked some poor person's toaster, but he hadn't gotten them all evicted. "Let's go see."

There were message boards for this eventuality, of course. Abdirahim wasn't the first person to brick an appliance. There were tricks to get it to boot into an emergency shell from which the original factory operating system could be laboriously reinstalled, and then they could start over. She used Abdirahim as her helper, reading her instructions and searching for help when they got unexpected error messages.

The toaster's owner was an old Serbian man, who'd never spoken a word to her, though they'd shared elevators and waited in the lobby together often enough. She had assumed that he was a racist, because that was usually the reason that white people didn't speak to her. She didn't take it personally. Some people were just ignorant.

But it seemed that he was painfully shy and awkward, and not (necessarily) racist. He offered them tea and served them biscuits he counted out carefully from a packet that he took from a nearly empty cupboard in which she spotted a huge jar of food-bank peanut butter and not much else. He excused himself to use the toilet four times while they worked, and she heard the painful dribble of an old man struggling with an enlarged prostate.

At one point, she was ready to give up. The toaster wouldn't even show her a bootloader screen—it was in worse shape than when she'd started. But the old man looked so concerned, and she knew he wouldn't be able to afford a new toaster—she imagined the cold meals of biscuits and peanut butter he'd been surviving on since Boulangism had shut down.

So she and Abdirahim went back to step one, checking everything, *everything,* very methodically. Finally, they noticed that the toaster was actually an earlier model than the ones that everyone else had in the building—cosmetically identical, but with a model number that was a single letter off, and when she searched on that, she found a completely different set of instructions, and these worked. It was after 1:00 A.M. when they finished, but she still went down to her place and came back up with the makings of grilled cheese sandwiches on homemade bread, and they had a midnight feast that gave her heartburn, but it was worth it.

The next time, it was a kid she didn't even know, tapping at her door and asking for help with a bricked screen. Abdirahim had apparently told his army of Dorchester Towers Irregulars that she was a reliable source of level 2 emergency tech support.

The third time it happened, she realized she needed to get ahead of the phenomenon if she ever wanted to have another moment to herself.

"Abdirahim." She stared intently at the kid until he met her eyes. Nadifa's presence helped.

"Yes, Auntie?" He only called her that when he was in trouble. The rest of the time it was "Salima," or, with learned American familiarity, "Sally," which was a new one on her that she wasn't entirely happy about.

"The way you are doing this, you and your friends, it's dangerous. You're going to get caught and you're going to get the people who live here caught, too. Do you remember the elevator captains, and what happened?"

"Yes, Auntie."

"We don't want that again, do we?"

"No, Auntie."

"We don't want to get everyone here thrown out onto the streets, either."

"No, Auntie."

"So I want you to get all your friends to come to my place, tomorrow, after school. Five p.m. Tell them, anyone who doesn't come is not allowed to jailbreak anything ever again."

He registered surprise. "You mean that if we come, we can still jailbreak?"

She smiled and met Nadifa's eye. "Oh yes, my boy. We're not going to stop breaking the rules. We're just going to be *smart* about it."

SHE BOUGHT SNACKS for the kids, more than she thought she'd need, but it wasn't enough. They just kept coming, scratching at her door until she just propped it open, and still they came, cramming into her flat. Ten kids. Twenty. Forty. Then she lost count. They stood in the bathroom and passed around bags of sweets and pretzels, filled her kitchen and stood on the counter. One of them sat in her kitchen sink.

"Quiet please, quiet." They shushed each other. She turned to Abdirahim. "Is this everyone?"

He made a show of craning his neck around the room, nodded. "I think so."

She shook her head at him. "Close the door, please, and some-one turn up the air conditioning?" The smell was that goaty, musky smell of many children at various stages of puberty in an enclosed space, a smell that brought her back to the kids' dorms in the camps she'd lived in.

"I want to start by saying that I'm very proud of you all. You've taught yourselves some important skills, you know, and you've helped your neighbors when they needed it. But you know that what you've done—what I did, too—is against the rules, and now that it's happening so often, it's going to be harder and harder not to get caught. Getting caught is not an option. Can anyone tell me why?"

A forest of arms shot up and the smell buffeted her again. She pointed to a young girl, chubby, with a face full of clever mischief. "Because we'll all get thrown out of the building?"

Salima nodded. "What else?"

The girl thought for a moment. "Also, everyone we've helped will get thrown out?"

Salima nodded again. "Very good." It was good to hear that the kids knew the stakes. It was also scary to hear them uttered aloud, and scarier still to think of the level of reckless-ness the kids had exhibited, even though they'd understood those stakes.

"I've been researching this, because I don't know any more about this than any of you. I learned by watching the same videos and reading the same message boards as you. But we're not the only ones going through this and there's been a lot of talk about it. The companies that made Disher and Boulan-gism have been bought up by new owners who say they'll be back online soon, and so we need to figure out how to stay safe once that happens."

She checked to see whether they were following all this. It was pretty esoteric, this idea of bankruptcies by distant companies. What did these kids think about the appliances they jailbroke? Did they see them as just weirdly nonfunctional gadgets they had to work around, like the bad touchscreens at the shelter? Or did they see them as the enemy, something that they were at war with, the weapons of a distant adversary who wanted to subjugate them to its will?

"The truth is that no one seems to know exactly how the companies will monitor what we do, especially after they have new owners. A lot of the original programmers were fired and some of them are on those same message boards, or at least they claim to be those original programmers, and there's a real race on to see who can come up with a reliable way to trick the monitors into thinking that we haven't been jailbreaking. We're definitely going to have to change peoples' appliances so that they generate *some* billings for the companies, because they'd notice if no money was coming from Dorchester Towers, right?" There was nodding. They were following along. They were bright kids, she thought, kids who'd spent their whole lives outsmarting gadgets that were designed to control them.

"Here's the assignment: we're going to read *all* those message boards and bring back what we find, figure out which people seem to know what they're talking about, then we're going to go back to every apartment and tweak all those appliances so that they're safe.

"That's assuming we come up with a decent plan. If we decide that no one knows what they're talking about, we're going to restore every appliance to its factory defaults, unjailbreak everything." That prompted groans and even a few cries of protest, but she held her hands up. "I know, I know. But better to have bad appliances than no home. There are millions of people around the world in the same situation as us, anyway, and they're all trying to solve this problem, so perhaps it won't be so hard as all that. I know that reading message boards isn't as much fun as messing about with gadgets, but if you want to be able to keep jailbreaking, you'll have to do the research, too."

It was too crowded for much Q&A, but Abdirahim put his

hand up anyway. She called on him. "Auntie, there's one thing I can't figure out."

"Only one?" She smiled and he smiled back.

"For now. When I bring a notepad to school, I can write anything I want on it. I don't need to ask the company that made the pen or the store that sold me the notebook how I can use it. I can tear out the pages and make paper airplanes, or doodle, or copy down what the teacher says. When I put on a pair of shoes, I can wear any socks I want. I can walk anywhere I want to go on my shoes. I can wipe myself with any sort of toilet paper—" That got a laugh. "But I can't toast any bread I want in my toaster."

She waited. He was struggling to find the words. "What's the question, Abdirahim?"

He shook his head, shrugged. "I guess I don't know. I just want to understand, how can it be against the law to choose your bread but not your socks? What makes a toaster different from shoes?"

She opened her mouth to answer, but discovered she didn't know the answer. Right up until that moment she'd felt like she had some intuitive sense of which things were objects-with-rules and which ones were objects-without-rules, felt it so readily that she hadn't even named the two categories until just that instant. Now that she tried to come up with a rule to explain the difference between the two, she found she couldn't.

"That is an excellent question," she said at last. "Why don't you research the answer and tell us all what you find out."

He rolled his eyes and let out a showy groan but he looked excited by the challenge. He really was a bright little fellow. She chased the kids out of her flat, buzzing with conversation, joking and shoving and posturing in the way of kids. The smell lingered after they were gone and she turned up the HVAC to

140 percent of its nominal capacity, a feature whose purpose had mystified her when she'd jailbroken the thermostat. But now she was thankful for it.

She tried to go to sleep, but Abdirahim's question nagged at her, so she raised her bed until it was a sofa and worked on the big screen for a couple hours, discovering to her relief that reading about technology law was better than a sleeping pill.

THERE WAS SOMETHING about the woman standing over her on the T that snagged her attention. She wasn't anyone Salima knew, but *something* about her seemed *so* familiar. She kept sneaking glances, and then it hit her: the logo on the woman's ID badge, dangling from a lanyard at eye height. Salima knew that logo, though she hadn't seen it in months: it was the Boulangism logo, a stylized slice of bread in a single continuous line, three squiggly heat lines radiating off it.

The woman caught her staring, and they made eye contact. She was young and white and had messy brown hair and those contacts the computer people wore to help them stare at screens all day without messing up their sleep schedules. The light from the ads lining the top third of the car cast a rainbow sheen over them.

"Boulangism?" Salima said.

The woman nodded enthusiastically. "That's right."

"They're in Boston?"

"They are now. They got bought out by a fund on Route 128, and then they recruited a bunch of us MIT kids to bash them back into shape and get them stood up again." The woman was younger than Salima had thought—an undergrad, or maybe a young grad student. Salima tried to picture the kids who crammed into her apartment as a classmate of this young woman, getting tempted away from their studies by a deep-pocketed company. They were smart, but were they smart enough? How smart did you have to be? She suddenly wanted to know more about the woman.

"Do you have a Boulangism?"

Salima nodded. "Do you?"

The woman snorted. "God, no. I mean, that business model, authorized bread? I wouldn't put one of those in my house if you paid me. Why'd you buy one?"

"I didn't. It came with the apartment."

"Unplug it and put it in a closet. Get a real oven."

This had literally never occurred to Salima. She had no idea how much a toaster oven cost. She could probably afford it. Not that she had any closet space. And then there were all the other people on the poor-floors, the old ones, the ones with kids, the ones who didn't have her skills or who couldn't speak English. She couldn't buy ovens for all of them—let alone dishwashers and all the other appliances.

"You don't seem to think much of them."

The woman rolled her eyes. "It's a good job, and the technical challenges are interesting. Hell, even the basic units do a good job, as far as that goes. But the lockdown is ob-nox-ious."

Salima couldn't help herself. "I think so, too."

"They've brought in a whole team to find people who're jailbreaking their units, a snitch squad. Now *that's* a job I wouldn't do. A girl's gotta have standards."

They'd gone past Salima's stop. She didn't care. She could always ride back the other way. The conversation was too good to end. "I'm Salima."

"Wyoming," the girl said, and shook. Her hands were slim and clever, typist's hands.

Though they were in a very public place, Salima felt a bubble of inattention around them—that urban thing, where you pretended you couldn't see the people pressed up against you. It was something she'd gotten good at in the camps, where there were so many times when the skill was necessary to keep her sanity.

"When do you think you'll have the servers up again?" Salima said. The guy next to her stood to debark as they pulled into a station. How many more stops would they have? Salima thought she'd stay on one stop past Wyoming, get off and cross to the opposite platform and ride back. If she got off at the same stop, she'd seem like a creepy stalker.

Wyoming startled at the question. "Oh, shit! I didn't even think of it. This must have *sucked* for you. How long has it been? Four months? Five? With no oven? You must be *so* sick of waiting for us, huh?"

"Five months," Salima said. "It certainly has been a long time."

"You poor thing. I would have just jailbroken mine. There's been so much of that, honestly, it'll be months before they sort it out. I don't blame the users, either. I mean, *ugh*."

"I agree." They both laughed. The car was mostly empty now, and there were only two more stops left before they reached the end of the line. Where did this girl live? With a fancy coder's salary, she could afford a beautiful place in the middle of Cambridge, not a place out here in Needham.

Salima took a risk. She liked this woman. "Is it hard, jailbreaking?"

"No, it's not hard at all—I mean, how could it be? Look, it's just basic security, basic math. You want to run a program on your toaster that lets you override the bread-check. We don't want you to run that. So we have something in the operating system, it checks to see whether the program you're running is one that we've approved. To check that, we look at a cryptographic signature, we check to see whether the program has been signed by a private key that we keep secret.

"Let me back up. In crypto, we have this idea of private keys and public keys. They come in pairs. Anything the private key scrambles, only the public key can unscramble, and vice-versa. If the public key unscrambles it, it must have been scrambled by the public key. If the private key can unscramble it, it must have been scrambled with the public key. Do you get it?"

Suddenly, so much of what she'd read on the message boards made sense. Public keys and private keys, coming in pairs. What one does, the other undoes. "I can code a message with your public key and my private key, and only you can read it, and you know only I have written it." It came out slowly, but understanding was flooding through her. It was so elegant.

"That's exactly right. Well, a Boulangism ships with the company's public key, and all the code updates that get sent out are signed with the private key. If the public key can unscramble that signature, then the toaster knows to trust the update, because it has to have been signed by someone using the company's keys." More understanding, like the final act of a murder mystery, where all the clues slot together and the confusion is transformed into an orderly series of events. She almost jumped in to say something, but stopped herself, because she thought she knew where this was about to go and she didn't want to tip this stranger off by knowing too much. She was a nice lady, sure, but she worked for the enemy.

"That would work a hundred percent of the time, because the math really works. Something that's been scrambled with one half of the keypair can only ever be unscrambled with the other half. Like, it would take billions of years to fake it, even with all the computers in the world working on it together. But there's a weakness."

Salima's heart pounded. She *knew* what Wyoming would say next, because the mystery was in its final act and she was frontrunning the detective as he revealed the killer and the details of the crime.

"The public key that your Boulangism checked is stored on your Boulangism itself. It's buried in a secure chip that's not supposed to be changeable, but there are so, so many ways around that. Sometimes there's a mistake in the secure chip, something that lets you change the key. More often, there's the boot-up sequence, where the computer in the Boulangism learns what kind of computer it is and where it needs to look for public keys. That's also in a secure storage, but there has to be ways to update it, because programmers make mistakes and when we do, our stuff can be hacked by bad guys, so we want to be able to send you new code for your appliances.

"So a Boulangism owner goes online, figures out how to change the key, or change where the computer looks for the key, and swaps in a key that the owner has a private key for, and now they can sign any code and get the Boulangism to run it. Boulangism hired skilled engineers to spend years locking down their products and they get defeated in hours by teenagers with amateur equipment. It's not that those coders were stupid, but they were sure *doing* something stupid."

Salima smiled. "But you don't do the stupid part? You work on something else?"

Wyoming smiled back. "That's right. I'd rather eat glass than do that stupid shit. I work on the adaptive cooking—you know, using sensors to make sure the food is perfect. It's super-satisfying, and delicious, because I get a test bench where I actually cook stuff from time to time."

"That's a nice perk."

"Yeah, and there's a gym, too, which is a good thing because it's only two weeks in and I've gained three pounds."

The train pulled into a station and there was an incomprehensible garble from the PA as the conductor announced something. With a start, Salima realized that he was telling them they'd pulled into the end of the line and everyone had to get off. She stood up and tried to figure out how she could remain on the platform and ride back without tipping off Wyoming that she'd stayed on the train just to pump her for info.

Wyoming shrugged into her backpack and Salima slung her purse and put it under her arm, and they stepped off the train and drifted toward the escalator up to the surface level. Salima resigned herself to wasting a subway fare by going up to the street level and walking around the block and then heading back into the station.

At the foot of the escalator, Wyoming put one of her clever, long-fingered hands on her arm and drew her to one side. "I have a confession." She was blushing.

"Oh?"

"My stop was about eight back. I was just enjoying talking with you, so I stayed on the train. I, uh, don't really get to talk about my work much. And you're a good listener."

Salima couldn't help herself. She laughed. "My stop is also several back. Green Street. I was enjoying our talk so much that I—"

Wyoming's eyes widened and she put her hand to her mouth. "You're not serious—" She giggled, and that set Salima off, and their laughs fed one another until they were both gasping as the conductor announced that the train they'd just debarked was ready for boarding and they staggered right back to the seats they'd just vacated.

On the ride back, Salima learned that Wyoming had come from Cincinnati, that she'd done an undergrad in electrical engineering and computer science at MIT and then started a master's in applied math when the Boulangism recruiter had offered her a huge signing bonus, stock in the new company that the hedge fund was spinning out, and a big monthly paycheck.

Salima told a little of her own story, cautiously, because she'd met lots of very nice white people who were not very nice at all when she said the word "refugee." By the time they reached her stop, Wyoming had texted her a set of messaging addresses and her number and offered to help Salima any time her Boulangism was "acting up." They shook hands when she got up to go, and Salima looked back at Wyoming—Wye, she'd said, call her Wye—and found her looking back at her, and they smiled one last time and waved good-bye.

Riding up the escalator, she had a brief bout of paranoia. Their conversation had been so easy and warm and pleasurable, could it be a setup? Did Boulangism have spies who tried to entrap suspected pirates, befriending them on the T by positioning themselves with prominent ID badges at eye height?

She shook her head and lined up for the crush at the turnstiles. It was absurd. The world was merely a small and odd place, and there was no disputing that.

WAITING IN THE lobby that night, she ran into three of the kids she'd lectured in the crush of her apartment, along with assorted parents, sweating in the unexpectedly warm early spring thaw, coats draped over their arms with wooly hats and scarves poking out of the pockets.

The kids called her "auntie" and she smiled at them and introduced herself formally to the adults, two moms and a grandfather, familiar faces she'd seen in the elevators and corridors but never had cause to chat with. The adults knew who she was, that was clear, and they treated her with an odd reverence as the bringer of technological freedom. She recognized the relationship from the camps, where there were always fixers and hustlers who could get things done, lay hands on special food and liquor, get you a phone voucher or fix your phone after it gave up the ghost. She had never thought of herself in those terms, but with her newfound understanding, it made perfect sense, even to her.

The small talk with these neighbors seemed like a continuation of the chatter with Wye on the train, part of a long conversation about the subject that had taken over her life: taking charge of the technologies around her, the ones that were used by those distant and faceless forces to take charge of *her*. Wye had made a big deal out of the hopelessness of trying to control someone with a gadget that they could take home and abuse in private, and that made perfect sense to her now, and it was a revelation. The sense of hopelessness at being surrounded by sensors and devices that were designed to push her around was transformed into a sense of inevitable triumph over the fools who thought they could make that work. What had Wye said? "It's not that those coders were stupid, but they were sure *doing* something stupid."

That newfound confidence sang in her as she heated a bit of goat curry and jolof rice in her Boulangism and sat down in front of the living room's big screen to poke around for a way to keep all their gadgets under their control without tipping off the manufacturers. She didn't find any immediate solutions, but that didn't matter: she was reveling in her new expertise, rereading message-board threads she'd puzzled over before, chasing down references and learning more, and more, and more...

The ding at her door brought her out of her reverie, and she glanced up at the corner of her screen to see Abdirahim at her door; the clock read 8:45 P.M., nearly his bedtime. She let him in and got him an apple from her fruit bowl. He was always hungry.

"I found out how a toaster isn't like a pair of shoes," he said around a mouthful of apple.

She sat back and made a go-on gesture.

"It's copyright law, you know, like the warnings at the start of movies?"

That didn't sound right to her, but she tried not to let it show on her face. If he was wrong, they could figure it out together. In the meantime, he was a thirteen-year-old boy who'd gone off and read a bunch of boring explanations of technology law because she'd told him to, and that deserved a respectful hearing.

"I know them."

"A long time ago, in the last century, they made it a crime to"—he scrunched up his face as he struggled with an awkward, memorized phrase—"to 'circumvent an effective means of access control.' If there's a copyrighted thing, you know, a movie or whatever, and there's something else that controls access to it, you can't remove that control or do anything with it. Not even for a good reason. They can send you to jail for doing it, five years and a $500,000 fine! For a first offense!"

"OK, that sounds like it could be true, but what does that have to do with toasters? Is there copyright bread?"

He shook his head. "That's where I got confused, too. But it's not the bread that's copyrighted, it's the software in the toaster, all the stuff we change when we jailbreak it. The part where you have to reset it and do something weird and complicated to get the fix to work, that's the cir-cum-vent-ing"— she could tell he'd practiced the word—"and the copyright, that's the code we're changing. So if it has code in it, and there's an access control, you're not allowed to change the code. Even if it belongs to you!"

Another huge piece of comprehension was sliding into place for her now, more of the half-understood posts from half-remembered threads slotting themselves into orderly procession. She nodded vigorously. "Abdirahim, I think you're right —that sounds exactly right. You did very well, you should be proud of yourself."

He beamed around a mouthful of apple. He was down to the core and was gnawing away at every bit of flesh on it with the practice of someone who'd grown up hungry. What a strange world, where this boy was teaching her about copyright law from another century.

"Just talking about it is a crime, which is why you can't find anything on the regular net, why you have to use darknet tools to find out more. Telling someone how to jailbreak a device is the same as jailbreaking it, it's called 'trafficking,' like with drugs, and it's the same, five years in prison for a first offense!"

Her guts did a slow roll. How many people had she taught to jailbreak? How many five-year prison sentences had she amassed? She missed her old ignorance, just a few hours ago, when none of this had occurred to her and the forums were all a mystery. From the joy of comprehension to terror, in minutes.

"What was the name of that law?"

Abdirahim consulted his phone. "It's Section 1201 of the Digital Millennium Copyright Act of 1998."

She made a note. "Thank you, Abdirahim. I'm going to do some more reading."

He let her give him another apple on the way out of the apartment. She made herself a cup of coffee—just regular drip, though she wished she could go up to Nadifa's for a pot of strong, gritty Ethiopian coffee in tiny cups—and started to read about the law.

SALIMA WAS GLAD when Nadifa came down the next night, after she'd come home from a day at a little sandwich shop, going over their books and dragging her thoughts back, over and over, from their endless loop of worry about the risks she'd subjected all her neighbors to.

Nadifa brought down a bottle of retsina and a plate of little kaymak-filled pieces of baklava, dripping with honey. Salima's earliest memory was of this flavor, a pure sense-memory from a time when she was a very little girl, maybe even a baby just starting on solid food. It was a taste she'd forgotten in her years in the camps, and the first time she'd encountered it in Boston it had been a revelation, a shock that had her crying and thinking of her parents, so long lost. It was so easy for an old normal to make way for a new one, so easy to blot the memories of that old normal. That was a skill that had served her well, but in that bite and its honey, she'd counted the cost for the first time.

Nadifa knew about this, but she also knew how much Salima liked the cakes, because she understood what it was like to embrace the unthinkable parts of your past, that had made you who you were. It was a bond the two women shared.

"I haven't seen you in so long, I have to hear about you from Abdirahim."

She used a swallow of wine to sluice away the honey, the tartness and sweetness mixing. "He's such a bright boy, you know."

"I know. Too bright. Always, since he was small. Asking why, why, why all the time, and never being satisfied with 'because I said so.'"

"It's a sign of good character. I was that way, once."

"Once?" Nadifa snorted. "You've spent the past six months reprogramming all our apartments, Salima. You've never stopped, girl."

She shook her head. "I think I made a mistake."

"Yes, I know you do. That's what Abdirahim told me. He thinks you're scared."

"I never told him that."

"Yes. He's a smart boy, remember?"

"I am scared." She tapped her screen, showed Nadifa her search alert. "Two weeks ago, Boulangism got restarted. Today it was Disher." She tapped again. "Look at this: Compliance Assurance LLC, a new company, received twenty-eight million in funding for a product to discover hacked appliances. That's just *today*'s news."

Nadifa nodded and looked thoughtful. "I don't pretend to understand all of this, but I know some of it, enough to appreciate why you'd be scared. The question is, what will you do about it?"

Salima stared at her screen. She didn't want to meet Nadifa's eyes "I've been trying to find a solution. There are so many people in the same situation as us, people who jailbroke everything after the companies started to go under and now don't know what to do. I could tell the kids to go around and put everything back the way it was."

Nadifa snorted again. "No, you couldn't."

"I could tell them to. But they might not do it."

"They wouldn't do it. They're kids. If they understood risks, they wouldn't join uprisings and march in the streets and the world would be a simpler place. Not a better one, of course. But simpler."

"Then I'd better keep searching for a solution. Those Assurance Compliance LLC people are coming for us."

Nadifa patted her shoulder. "You'll find something."

She did, an hour later, and it wasn't good.

"HELLO?"

"Is this Wye?"

"Yeah." She sounded tired, though it was only 9:00 P.M. Weren't techies all supposed to be night owls? "Who's this?"

"It's Salima. We met on the T?"

"Oh! Uh, hi. Sorry. Rough day and I was just dozing on the couch. What's up?"

Salima had known that if she'd planned this call out she'd have chickened out before she could make it. She opened her mouth and nothing came out.

"Salima?"

"It's—it's kind of an emergency."

"Are you OK?" She was much more awake now, anxious.

"I'm OK. But—" She broke off. "Can you meet me somewhere? I can come to you. Maybe a coffee shop?"

A pause. It stretched. Then: "Yeah, OK. I'll text you a place, OK?"

"OK. I'll let you know when I get off the train."

"Perfect. It's just around the corner from me."

Salima didn't really think that enforcement agents for Boulangism or Disher were listening in on her phone, but she still instinctively thought that it would be better to have this talk with as little technology in the loop as was possible. She fretted on the T, and texted from the escalator.

The diner was fully automated, which meant that there weren't any humans around to eavesdrop on them, but it also meant that there were cameras and mics everywhere. She grimaced and tried not to stare at them as she waited for Wye to show up.

She came in wearing a jean jacket over a faded t-shirt with a picture of an anthropomorphic baseball with arms and legs and a big C on its jacket, which Salima deduced had something to do with Cincinnati. Salima didn't have any tees with logos from back home. Was there a Libyan baseball team? The Benghazi Bengal Tigers?

"Hi there," Wye said, and tapped out a quick order on the table with long-practiced ease, and the conveyor that snaked around the backs of the booths lurched into life and started juddering towards them with a squeak.

"Thank you for coming."

The hot-box on the conveyor reached their table and gasped open, lid yawning wide. Wye extracted a cup of tea with a packet of cookies balanced on its pressed-cornstarch saucer. "Sure. Have you ordered anything? The grilled sandwiches are good, if you're hungry. They've also got really good boba." Was this how MIT students ate?

"Thanks," Salima said. She quickly scanned the menu and jabbed at a celery soda, which sounded vile but cost exactly the minimum-per-person amount noted at the bottom of the menu. The hot-box closed itself and the conveyor started to move again. "And thanks again for coming, I mean it."

"Like I said, it's no problem. Normally I'd be wide awake at this hour but my sleep's been screwed up from work stress lately and I had a bad night last night. It was good to hear from you again, honestly." She smiled. It was pretty, with good white teeth and a lopsided dimple. She was so young, even if she was a year older than Salima.

"I called you because I didn't know who to talk to. I—" She breathed. "I helped my neighbors jailbreak their things."

"Their things?"

"Everything. Dishers. Boulangisms. Thermostats, fridges, TVs, phones. Everything." She checked herself. "Not the elevators, though."

She laughed—laughed! "The *elevators*?"

"I live on a poor-floor—low-rent. The elevators only stop for us if there's no one from the regular floors waiting or riding. It can take a very long time."

She stopped smiling. "And that's why all your appliances needed jailbreaking?"

"They came with the apartments. We're not allowed to touch them, it's in the lease. We could get thrown out. I mean, all of us."

She stared at Salima with wide eyes. She opened her biscuits and ate one, still looking at Salima. "That. *Sucks*."

It was Salima's turn to smile. "We think so, too."

"So, what, you want to revert everything before you get caught?"

"We don't want to get caught."

"Oh. *Ohhh*. You want to keep doing it. Huh. I know there's some stuff out there that's supposed to work."

"I've been looking. There's a lot of advice, and it all contradicts itself. I can't tell what works."

"Yeah, that sounds like online tech advice all right." She sipped her tea. Salima tried the celery soda, prepared to discreetly spit it back down the straw, but it wasn't bad. Wye had a faraway look and she said, "Gimme a sec." She got a screen out of her pocket and poked at it a while, showing it her retinas after a few seconds, then tapping some more. "I think I have an idea."

"You'll help us?"

She snorted. "Why wouldn't I help you?"

"You could lose your job."

She shrugged. "I wasn't gonna last there anyway, I can tell that already. There's other jobs."

Salima had never been fired in her life. She couldn't imagine it. When things were hard at work, she worked twice as hard. She felt gratitude to Wye, who was risking a job for her, but there was a slithering serpent of disapproval of Wye's breezy attitude towards her career. Did she even understand how lucky she was? Perhaps if she did, she wouldn't be so quick to help. Salima kept her face carefully neutral.

"What about getting arrested? It's a five-year prison sentence for jailbreaking."

"Only if it's commercial. If I don't charge, all they can do is sue me. I'll cover my tracks…

"I have an idea, anyway. Do you know what a virtual machine is?"

Salima didn't, and she could tell that if she just said no, then Wye would explain something to her and that would lead to Wye doing something to help her, and wasn't that what she'd hoped for? But she couldn't just go along.

"Please stop," Salima said. "It was a mistake. I can't ask you to risk yourself for us. There's—" She blinked hard at the tears that had sprung up in her eyes. "The kids in my building, I showed them what I was doing and they took it up, and now they could all be punished, along with their families, because I wasn't careful about letting other people take my risks. This is a bad situation, but 'I'll cover my tracks' isn't going to save you. Everyone who ever got in trouble thought they'd covered their tracks. *I* thought I'd covered my tracks. I'm sorry, Wye, I really shouldn't have called you."

She picked up her jacket and started to stand. Wye put her hand on her arm and squeezed, stopping her. "Please don't go, Salima. I *can* cover my tracks. It won't be hard. At the very least, I can help you figure out how to restore everything so that you won't get into trouble. Look, I'm a grown adult, and I can decide what risks I take."

The tears were going to breach any moment. Salima firmly pulled her arm free. "Thank you, Wyoming. I'll call you when it's all sorted out and we can have a drink to celebrate, all right?"

She didn't give her a chance to answer. The tears came out when she reached the street, and she wished she'd grabbed some napkins on her way out of the diner. She never cried, never. Not since her parents had died, anyway. Why was she crying now?

SHE WAS ALMOST asleep when she answered her own question: she cried because she had something to lose, for the first time since she'd lost her parents. It was a terrible realization, like she'd been betrayed by her own happiness. Everything she'd attained was something she had to lose.

If she had only not tried to make a life for herself, she wouldn't have anything at stake. If she hadn't made friends, she wouldn't have any friends to have betrayed with her knowledge-drunk recklessness. If she hadn't basked in the admiration of those kids, the kids wouldn't have put themselves and their parents in harm's way.

She wasn't almost asleep anymore. She went back to her screen, dug into the darkweb, and got the recipes to put everything back the way it had been. She practiced on her own kitchen, making sure she had it down cold. Once she'd mastered it, her whirling brain finally decided to let her sleep, but the sun was already rising. She set an alarm for one hour later, and when it went off, she made four pods of dried-out, nearly undrinkable coffee she found at the back of a drawer, and drank it as a penance. The sour, acid liquid scalded her tongue and roiled her guts all the way to her first job of the day.

When she got back that night, there was a crowd of kids and their grownups waiting in the lobby, as usual. They called out to her and she hustled past them and climbed the stairs, sleeplessness weighting her legs, sweat coursing down her neck and back, down her face and into her eyes. The exhaustion was like a dead thing on her back as she staggered into the apartment, flopping down on the sofa and letting her eyes close, just for a moment that turned into an hour as she crashed, only to awaken with a guilty start. She had work to do.

She walked up to Nadifa's apartment. After the thirty-five floors she'd climbed on her way home, another six should have been easy, but her legs and butt were sore and tired and she had to drag herself by the handrail. She realized that she'd forgotten to eat dinner and then realized she couldn't remember if she'd eaten lunch. It had been a long time since she'd missed any significant amount of sleep. She was out of practice.

Nadifa took one look at her and led her into the apartment and plied her with mint tea and small cakes that she'd have sworn she had no appetite for, but which she couldn't stop eating. Abdirahim was nominally doing his homework, but Salima could tell that he was burning with curiosity and eavesdropping, so after her second cup of tea, she called for him to join them. He turned around on the screen seat and raised it up to table height.

"Abdirahim, I've made a decision and you're not going to like it."

He had a good poker face. Kids who grew up in the camps got good at controlling the information they transmitted to the people around them. She could tell he knew what was coming, though, and that he didn't like it.

"When I started jailbreaking, I didn't know what I was doing. I didn't understand the risks. But now I do, thanks to you and my own reading. And Abdirahim, the risk is just too great. There is no way to know for sure what the companies will do to catch us, and if they do, we could lose everything. Even if we could fool the companies, the management of the building will notice when they don't get their share of the money, now that the companies are being restarted. The people your friends have helped out didn't appreciate what they were being signed up for, none of us did, but now that we do, we have a responsibility to help them out."

His poker face was slipping. His bottom lip was trembling. His knuckles were white where he gripped the table's edge. Nadifa gave him a warning look. Salima's heart broke for him. After all he'd been through, he'd found a way to take charge of a world that had never given him the tiniest amount of control, and she was going to make him undo it all. She wanted to cry, and she could only marvel at his self-control. She put her hand on Nadifa's arm.

"I'm sorry, Abdirahim. You have a right to be angry. It's not right, but it's necessary. That's the most difficult kind of situation." She took a deep breath. "I can't do it without you. That's not me trying to make you feel good. You are the one who taught the other kids, and only they know which apartments they worked on and what they did. I couldn't get the other kids to even listen to me without your help.

"Abdirahim, will you help me?"

She could tell Nadifa wanted to order him to say yes, and she squeezed Nadifa's arm gently but firmly. *Let him make up his own mind.*

He stared at his hands for a long, long time. His breath was ragged. She wondered if he was going to cry after all. But then he raised his head and blinked his wet eyes at them. "I'll do it, Auntie."

She knew he'd taken the time to really think it through and had come to the right conclusion after that careful deliberation, and not because an adult had told him so, not even because his mother would never have tolerated refusal.

"I knew you would, Abdirahim." She squeezed Nadifa's arm one more time. "You should be very proud of this one."

"I am," she said. She patted her son's hand. She knew what this had cost him, too.

Suddenly, Salima was so very tired. She'd been tired before, but this was an all-new height, or maybe depth. For a moment, she literally couldn't stop her eyes from closing. She fought them open again. Nadifa was looking at her with concern.

"We'll take you downstairs."

They each got a shoulder under her arms—Abdirahim was as tall as his mother already—and drunk-walked her to the elevators and pushed the button. Time wavered. It felt like an hour before the car arrived and sighed open, and it smelled of expensive perfume from someone from the parallel universe of non-poor-floors who'd finished their ride and freed the elevator for a grudging ride for the likes of them.

Nadifa sent Abdirahim back upstairs once they were in Salima's apartment, then helped her change into a nightie and adjusted the sofa to bed configuration, screwing the table down and dropping its leaves so it became a bed table. She brought out the comforter and draped it over Salima, and in her half-conscious state, Salima recovered a memory long buried, of a time before time, when she lay in her crib and her mother had tucked her in. The memory was so sweet, without any of the sorrow that usually went with memories of her mother, and she drifted away into dreams with a smile that was still with her when she got up a few hours later to pee and swipe at her teeth to clear the rotten taste from her mouth before falling back into bed.

A SENSE OF purpose is a wonderful tonic for anxiety. Now that Salima knew what she had to do, the helpless fretting was replaced by a boundless energy. After an early breakfast, she rang Nadifa to confirm that Abdirahim was awake, and she bounded up the stairs two at a time and showed him how to reset the factory defaults on everything in their apartment. Just as she'd done in her own place, she made him run through it twice to make sure he had it and then made him write out the procedure from memory on a notepad. He was a quick study, as she knew he'd be.

"Now you need to spread the word. Can you have the children come to my place again tonight, after school and before supper, say six p.m.?"

He wasn't happy about it. "They will hate this."

"I know. I hate it. It's like giving up. But giving up is smarter than fighting a battle you can't win. That's as important a lesson as any, you know."

Nadifa nodded. "There are much harder ways to learn that lesson." She got a faraway look.

Abdirahim looked miserable.

"I know this is very hard," Salima said. "You were a hero when you taught your friends, now you're going to be that frightened boy who made them put it all back. I'll take the blame. I'll explain it to them. Just bring them to my place, all right?"

A night's sleep had done her so much good. Her day went so smoothly it might as well have been oiled. She found some small systematic errors in the books of the dry cleaner's that explained why his profits had been consistently down and he confessed that he'd been about to fire his sole employee for stealing, and was so relieved that he hugged her. She got a seat on the T both ways. Spring had finally stopped oscillating between freezing and basting and settled on a sunny, breezy happy median that scudded the fluffy clouds overhead like a screen saver, and the new buds on the trees all seemed to have burst open overnight.

She bought a much bigger bag of snacks for that night's meeting, mindful of the previous meeting's shortcomings. She had to shop in the Boulangism aisle of the corner market for bread, and she bought coffee pods and dishwasher soaps in the adjacent sections.

That brought her down, making the last block home a slow march. She thought back to her first meeting with Wye, about Wye's horror that anyone would use a Boulangism. Salima was earning well now, even saving money every month—a savings that had grown for the months when she'd been able to choose her groceries from anywhere in the shop. There were places to live that weren't Dorchester Towers. Places where she could choose which appliances she used. They were more expensive—so many of the rental ads had fine print notifying prospective tenants that their lease prohibited alteration of the landlord's revenue-earning appliances. But they existed. With a roommate or two, she could afford one.

But Dorchester Towers wasn't just where she lived, it was a little community, a place where she fit, where she had friends and people who were something like family, like Nadifa and the kids who called her "auntie." People who understood what she had been through. Imagine living in a house full of Wyes, girls who seemed so young, with an unbridgeable canyon between their life experiences and her own.

The kids in the elevator lobby asked her excitedly about the meeting that night, and she understood that Abdirahim hadn't given them any hints about the agenda. She couldn't blame him.

They crowded in and ate all the snacks. There may not be enough snacks in the world to fill all those little bellies.

"This isn't going to be easy to hear." The whispering and grins and fidgeting ended in an instant and every eye was on her. So much for her perfect day.

"Since our last meeting, I've learned some things. Important things." She told them, about the law, about the prison sentences, about the new companies that had been formed out of the remains of the old ones, and the teams they'd hired to catch cheaters like them. The risks to them and their families. Eviction and worse. She watched their faces go grave and then graver.

The chubby girl, the bright one who'd put up her hand last time, was the first to speak when Salima finished. "How do we solve it?"

It was a terrible moment. The worried faces brightened and the whole room's attention was intensely fixed upon her. These kids were bright enough to understand the risks, but not bright enough to figure out that she couldn't do anything to fix it.

"We can't. We have to put it all back the way it was. Undo

it all. Factory defaults for everything." Before anyone could
say anything, she said: "It's over."

The kids' faces said it all. Shock, then disbelief, then defiance. Muttering. The word *no,* quietly and then louder and
then racing from kid to kid.

"Yes!" she shouted, holding her hands up. "I'm sorry—I'm
so, so, so sorry—but *yes.* We have to do this. It was a mistake."
She held her hands higher. It was getting louder. "I mean it.
We'll find something else. You can help me. But first, we have
to do this."

Some of the kids were leaving. She saw Abdirahim shake
his head.

"It has to be this way." More of them left.

"Please."

Abdirahim was the last one there.

"I'm sorry," was all he said, before he, too, left.

SHE WOULDN'T SURRENDER, of course. She started with
the people she'd serviced, working from the upper floors down-
ward, doing two or three per night. Abdirahim came along
sometimes and helped, but he was clearly unenthused about
the work and he made mistakes that set her back as often as he
helped. She didn't think it was exactly on purpose, but it certainly wasn't exactly an accident, either.

Many times, she was tempted to text Wye and set up a meeting to pump her for information about the state of Boulangism
and how long she had before they were up and running again.
She had reasoned that the building's owners wouldn't expect
full revenue straightaway after the toasters started working
again—it would take a while for people to notice that their
appliances were working again and switch from whatever

arrangements they'd made during the outage—but there would come a time when it would be obvious that it had all been fiddled, unless she put it back.

Working in her neighbors' apartments, she saw their kids, kids who had watched her jailbreak their apartments and gone on to do the same for their neighbors. The kids who'd walked out on her when she told them they'd have to put it all back the way they'd found it. Kids who watched her out of the corners of their eyes, pretending to do their homework. She made a point of describing the consequences of getting caught for their parents in a loud voice and in eye-watering detail.

It took her five nights and all weekend to work through the apartments she'd personally jailbroken. On Monday night, she came home from work, bolted a humiliating prepackaged, approved dinner from the microwave, and headed out to the top poor-floor, seven floors above. She waited briefly for the elevator, then admitted that the only reason she'd tried for an elevator was that she knew it was a prime time and she might kill half an hour or even forty-five minutes waiting for a car to come, putting off what would come next by that much.

She took the stairs, and knocked on the first door beside the stairwell after carefully noting its number in a little notebook she'd brought with her, in her neat bookkeeper's hand.

The woman who answered was a little familiar, someone she'd shared an elevator with once or twice, Salvadoran or Honduran she'd thought. "Yes?" She was a little older than Salima.

"Hi." She had rehearsed this, but her mouth dried up and the words wouldn't come. "Hi. I live in the building and—" That was wrong. "Did some of the building's kids help you with your kitchen appliances? Or maybe your thermostat?"

The woman looked suspicious. This wasn't how it was supposed to go. "I don't think so."

Salima's cheeks and ear tips burned. "I'm sorry to bother you, honestly. But, look, the day the toasters stopped working? I figured out how to get mine to work again. Then I showed some of the kids and they went all over and did it for everyone else. But then I found out that the manufacturers can tell who's done this, and they can come after us for it. The landlords, too—they got a cut of the money we spent. So I've come to put it all back, before you get in trouble, and before we all get in trouble." She gave her best, most trustworthy smile.

The woman shook her head. "I never had any kids around here."

Salima was sure she was lying—the quickness of her answer, the way she looked around as she said it. "Look, if I don't do this, you *will* get caught. You could lose your home. Worse— they can send the kid who did it to jail." That wasn't quite true, based on what Wye had told her, but it was nearly true. The kid could get in trouble, she was sure, and of course, so could she. "Please."

"I told you, no kids."

"Can I see then?" The woman looked angry. "I mean, maybe you forgot. Can I check, just to be sure?"

"I have to go." The door clicked shut before she could get another word in. She was conscious of the camera on her, so she kept her face neutral as she made a note in her notebook and then took a deep breath and moved on to the next apartment.

It was going to be a long night.

WORK BECAME A kind of dream, or waking nightmare, in which she returned over and over to the real job, racing through the floors of the building, knocking on doors, begging near-strangers to let her make them poorer and make their lives worse. Word had gotten around and she got curious stares and sometimes hostile ones in the elevators, and Abdirahim wasn't even pretending to help her anymore. She didn't complain to Nadifa because she didn't want to have to confess all her sins to the last real friend she had.

She got better at pitching her case at the door, anyway, and almost everyone let her into their places to do her business, which she'd also gotten better at, working through appliances with a quick, practiced hand.

In private moments at night, searching for elusive sleep, she admitted to herself that some of the kids were probably going around undoing everything she'd done, with the complicity of the adults who should have known better.

Every time she rode home from the dry cleaners, she looked for Wye on the T, not sure if she would be happy or frightened to see her. She never found her, but then one afternoon as she was trying to find her own errors in the work she'd done closing the quarter for an ice cream shop, numbers swimming before her eyes, her phone chirped.

> I need to talk to you-Wye

She opened her little notebook and looked at the apartment numbers. She'd gotten through more than three-quarters of the places, and most of them had let her work. Some would have been reverted by kids, but perhaps it was still enough. Maybe Wye had found a trick that would let them keep their jailbreaks after all, something foolproof.

(But only fools believed in foolproof tricks)

> I finish at 5. I'm on Mass Ave today, near Harvard Square
> I can meet you. 515 at the cannon in Cambridge Common?
> Kk

A foolish hope grew in Salima despite her best efforts. She'd never forgotten the excitement that Wye had spoken with when she'd started thinking about how to help them all beat Boulangism, the absurd certainty she'd radiated that she could outsmart the whole industry. Perhaps she could, though of course she couldn't.

Summer was in full roast and it was hot and sticky, with few students left this late in the year. She fanned herself with a folding Chinese fan she'd bought from a cart a few days before, when the heat came on and the humidity soared. She'd thought that Arizona was hot, but this humidity was trying to strangle her from the inside out, a feeling that called to mind dark and buried memories of the Mediterranean crossing when she'd been a small child, sense memories of thirst and nausea and stink.

She fanned herself and looked around but she didn't see Wye until she was right there, because she'd cut her ash-blond hair sensibly short for the heat and put some pink tint in it. She was thinner than the last time they'd met, too, and paler. Long hours, Salima guessed.

"You came," Wye said.

"Hi," Salima said. "I came." She was still embarrassed by their last meeting. "I'm sorry about before. It was very nice of you to offer, but—"

"Yeah. I know, the risk. I understand it. Sort of. I mean, I know I can't really understand what you've gone through, but—" She armed sweat from her forehead. "I mean, I get it. Sorry, too. And don't be sorry." She was really sweet.

"I've been putting it all back, everything reset to factory defaults. No one wants to help me though. The kids hate me for it."

"That sucks."

"It does."

"Look, I wanted to meet with you because there's something happening at Boulangism I thought you'd be interested in, but you can't talk about it because I'm not supposed to be telling anyone without getting a nondisclosure first. Is that OK? I mean, can I tell you and you'll keep it a secret?"

She nodded. "Of course."

"So, we were almost ready to relaunch and then the new owners bought two more of our competitors and folded us all together into a single platform. Now we're a *lot* bigger and they have all these plans, like, letting people buy jailbreaks by the day or the week, so they can cook anything they want. They've been watching the darknet boards, they know that everyone's been figuring out how to jailbreak their shit while we've been getting restarted, and they figure all those people could be customers, but instead of paying for food we sell them, they'd pay us to use food someone else sold them."

Salima almost laughed. It was a crime if she did it, a product if they sold it to her. Everything could be a product.

"It's weird, I know. But here's where you come in. They've got this research unit, anthropologists and data scientists and marketers, and they want to talk to people like you, find out what you'd pay for different kinds of products. They want to see if you'd sell the package to your neighbors, if you could get a cut of the money from them, like a commission? They've got one plan, you could teach those kids you were working with to sell paid unlocking to the people in your building, and they'd get a commission and you'd get a commission because you recruited them."

"It's a pyramid scheme?"

"It's an affiliate program. The kids wouldn't be allowed to recruit people to work under them—we'd handpick the affiliate recruiters and they'd be the only ones who'd get the double commissions. Leaders. It's still just an idea, but when I heard about it, I immediately thought of you. I mean, it solves all your problems, doesn't it? Your kids get to go legit, even make some pocket money. You get to use your skills and the respect of your neighbors to help them out and earn some money for yourself. Oh, and of course, you'd get to permanently unlock everything that we make, so you could demonstrate it for your neighbors. Like I say, it's not a sure thing, but I thought you could come in and meet the team, talk it over, make a call…" She trailed off, searching Salima's face for a clue about her reaction. Salima carefully maintained a neutral expression.

"Wye," she said. "It's so kind of you to think of me. Really."

"But?"

Salima slumped. "I don't know. There's a *but,* but I can't say what it is, exactly."

"It's a weird idea," Wye said. "I know. But maybe you could think about it for a while? I don't need an answer right now."

Salima wanted to just say no, but she didn't. Even as something inside her was recoiling at the offer, another part of her understood that Wye might be right, this could be the very best option.

"How long do you think we have?"

"Until you have to decide?"

Salima had thought of Wye as her ally, every bit as offended by the locked-down world of Dorchester Towers as she was. But Wye had been working long hours for Boulangism and its new sister companies. She thought the problem was that Salima didn't want to get into trouble. Salima had been thinking that, too. But that wasn't the problem. Boulangism itself, that was the problem. The whole rotten business, that was the problem.

"Until Boulangism finds out what we've been doing and gets us evicted."

Wye shook her head. "Didn't you hear me? That won't happen—they're trying carrots these days, not sticks. They want to treat people like you as customers, not crooks."

"OK, sure. But how long until that happens?"

Wye looked hurt. "I don't know. Soon, though. A week or two. They're really excited about the unlock upsell, but they want to do a little research on the price point before they roll it out so that'll delay things a while. But the owners aren't going to keep paying everyone's salaries forever without any money coming in."

"A couple weeks." She could get through the places she'd missed, then start over again on the top floor and work her way down again, impressing on people that it was essential that they tell her if they'd let one of the kids fiddle their stuff again.

" Yeah. Look, Salima, I think you should really consider this. It's a good plan, good for everyone."

"I will." Her voice sounded unconvincing, even to her own ears.

Wye looked even more distraught. Salima felt bad. She'd only wanted to help.

"Salima, have you had dinner? I'm crazy hungry. Do you like fish? There's a fish place near here that's amazing, the kind of place where visiting parents take their kids for a good meal during the school year. Ever since I started taking home a paycheck, I've been meaning to go back, but I've been too busy. Would you join me? I'll pay. I don't want to have to eat alone."

No, she wanted to say. No, I have to go home and get back to work. No, I can't afford your charity, because you might have to testify against me. No, I don't need to be friends with anyone from your world.

"Yes," she said. "That would be very nice." She was too hungry to say no, and she was sick of overpriced prepackaged microwave meals.

SHE GOT HOME after ten, much too late to ring anyone's doorbell and have an awkward conversation about their appliances. The elevator had been blessedly responsive, which was a good thing, since between the wine and the stress of the recent weeks, she wasn't going to be able to climb the stairs or even stay awake very long in the lobby.

The elevator smelled of expensive hair product, telling her that it had been recently vacated by someone who'd gone out the other doors on the way to a nice date night, or maybe on the way back, relieving the babysitter and making a midnight snack in an oven that cooked anything you told it to.

The smell lingered in her nostrils, citrus and tobacco, as she trailed her hand down the corridor wall to her apartment. She was about to open her door when she saw the words scrawled there in fat, permanent marker: FUCK OFF. The letters were large, angry, and yet uncertain, like they'd been written by a child, or perhaps by someone who was just learning English.

She was so tired.

She licked her finger and rubbed at the ink. It didn't even smear. She let herself in and went to the camera feed for her door, and discovered that it was blank, perfectly erased. So, maybe it was a kid who'd written it, a kid who'd learned to search the darknet for ways to control technology designed to control them. A kid who was outraged at being asked to forget how to do that and go back to being meekly controlled.

Would a kid like that ever work on commission, installing official unlocking codes in the poor-floor apartments of Dorchester Towers? Was there enough money in the world?

And if there was, did she want to be the one who used that money to convince a kid to give up on that uncompromising ferocity?

She'd buy some solvent on her way home from work the next day.

SHE RAN INTO Nadifa on the stairs the next morning, struggling with a stroller, chivvying Idil, the older girl, and carrying Yasmiin, the toddler. Salima took the stroller and Idil, leaving Nadifa to sling Yasmiin around on her hip and hold the handrail with her free hand. Nadifa sighed and thanked her.

"You look terrible," Nadifa said, three flights down.

"I didn't sleep very well."

"You haven't been by in so long. The retsina is starting to pile up in my refrigerator."

Her eyes welled up and she blinked hard. She'd missed Nadifa, and missed the days when she'd overflowed with the excitement of mastering the building. The rearguard action of putting everything back had filled her with a buried and unspeakable shame, and just thinking of showing her face to Nadifa made her feel sick.

But it was so good to see her again.

"I'm sorry. It's been… hard." She swallowed. Then she told Nadifa about the words on her door, using careful euphemisms in front of the kids. She told Nadifa about the cameras. She stopped short of telling her about Abdirahim abandoning her. She wanted a friendly shoulder to lean on, not retribution for a thirteen-year-old.

"That's terrible. I'll come by when you get home from work and we'll clean it together."

"It's OK, I can do it." She thought of telling Nadifa about the offer from Wye, but she didn't. Nadifa might tell her to do it. Or tell her not to.

Her arms and back were on fire when they reached the ground level.

"Thank you so much," Nadifa said as she unfolded the stroller. "Normally I wouldn't try to leave until the rush was over, but Idil has to see the dentist this morning." Idil smiled up at her, showing cute gaps in her teeth. Nadifa strapped the baby into the stroller and then she swept Salima up into a fierce hug. "It will be OK. You've been through so much worse than this. You're strong."

Salima embarassed herself by snuffling up snot, but the alternative was leaking it all over Nadifa's shoulder, and Nadifa had the manners to pretend not to notice anyway, so she was able to salvage a little dignity, at least.

She didn't get a seat on the T that morning, and as she hung from the strap, rocking back and forth with the train's motion, she stared idly at the ad over her head, eyes unfocused with sleepiness, and it was only as she got off the train that she realized it had been an ad for the new Boulangism.

She got a text from Wye on the escalator.

> Affiliate program is go. I can hold a place for you in it. You in?

She marked it unread so she'd remember to reply to it later. Every time she looked at her screen that day at work, she saw the alert for it. It was very hard to concentrate. She made a mistake early on and ended up spending an hour unraveling it.

It wasn't a good day.

*

"I THINK I need to talk to Abdirahim."

Nadifa looked puzzled. "Then talk to him."

Salima swirled the wine in her glass. "The problem is that he hasn't been very eager to talk to me. He's angry."

"Adi! Come here!"

He came out of his room wooden faced. "I'm doing home-work."

"Auntie Salima would like to talk to you."

"All right." (Said in a tone that made it clear it was anything but.)

He got the idea of the pay-to-unlock as quickly as she laid it out for him, quicker than she had. "It's like my schoolbooks. I can read them at school or home, but if I want to study in the park, I have to pay to unlock them."

"I didn't know they worked that way."

He shrugged. "It's OK, I don't need to study in the park."

She told him about the affiliate program. "So you could make money for your family, to help out around the house. Your friends, too."

"And Auntie Salima would make money, too," Nadifa said. "So she can save to get a place of her own."

She looked sharply at Nadifa. "Why would I want to leave Dorchester Towers?"

Nadifa snorted. "Who wouldn't want to leave if they could? Move somewhere with a proper elevator, with real appliances? A place where you were wanted?"

Nadifa, trapped in her apartment every day until the elevator rush ended, or having to drag her stroller and the baby and a small child down forty-two floors' worth of stairs. Of course she wanted to go. But how would that ever happen?

She'd been a tailor in Somalia, but she hadn't worked in a shop in more than a decade, and by the time Yasmiin was in school for full days, it would be nearly twenty years. Even if she could find work, a seamstress's salary wasn't going to pay full rent in Boston and support three kids.

Salima was careful with money, careful like a bookkeeper. She lived on her own and had saved up some real money, especially when she'd been able to cook any food she wanted and could buy ingredients instead of ready-to-eat meals. She could move out now if she wanted to find a housemate, and if she signed up one or two more bookkeeping clients, she'd be able to get a place on her own within the year. But she never thought of leaving Dorchester Towers. It was where she belonged.

"I wouldn't go. I want to see your kids grow up."

"Don't be ridiculous. We'd come and visit. As soon as you can go, you should."

Abdirahim watched the two grown women politely argue and Salima wondered how much of the subtext he was getting. She wondered how much *she* was getting.

"It's not right to charge your neighbors to use their own things," he said, breaking in.

Nadifa was about to say something to him about respecting his auntie, but Salima cut her off.

"Do you think so?"

"Of course." He said it so quickly, so firmly, that she knew there was no room for argument.

"Why?"

"Because it's *their* homes. Why should they have to pay to use the things in their homes?"

"I agree with you, but the company would say it's because they chose to live in a place where the rent was lower because the landlord thought he'd make money from their appliances.

It was a deal, and that's their end of it, and they can pay more somewhere else if they want that choice."

"Can we pay more?"

Nadifa snorted. "Not until you graduate from college and get a good job, Adi."

He looked at Salima.

"I know. I didn't say I agreed with it. It's just what they'd say. There are lots of deals you can make and the deal here is that you have to use their products the way that makes them the most money or pay to unlock them. They'd say that you're getting *more* choice, because they'll let you buy an unlocking."

"But we already have that choice."

She looked sharply at him. "No you don't. Not if you've restored your appliances to defaults."

He looked guilty for an instant, then said, "OK, we *had* that choice, and we can get it for ourselves again. For free. You showed us."

That slow roll in her guts again. He'd unlocked it all, everything in their home, and they were going to get caught. Everyone was going to get caught. If Abdirahim wouldn't do as she asked, who would?

She took a deep breath. "What I'm about to say isn't how I see things, but it is how the company sees them. They say that you don't have that choice, that *they* have that choice, and they'll sell it to you. But if you take it without paying, that's stealing. Again, that's what *they* think."

He was fast. "But you'd be able to unlock all your things without paying, right? So why isn't that stealing?"

A sharp little boy, with the smarts of someone who had to think fast all the time, with bad consequences for getting it wrong. "Because I'd be working for the company."

"Against your neighbors. But you say you wouldn't leave here because you belong here. But you get treated like you're better than us!" He was losing his cool. Still a boy, after all. She didn't let herself get angry. Sneaking a look at Nadifa, she saw her friend was very thoughtful, forgetting to tell off her son for disrespecting his elder.

"I don't think I'm better. The company just saw my skills and offered me a job. Like your mother getting money when she sews someone's clothes. They'd pay you, too, remember."

"I wouldn't take their money." He looked at his mother. "I have homework to do."

"Do your homework."

He got up and went into the other room. They didn't look at each other. "What will you do?" Nadifa asked.

Salima shrugged. "I'll have to think about it."

WYE SENT HER two more texts before bed, which she didn't answer. She fell asleep, at last, with the hum of the air conditioning and the fridge compressor in her ears.

Her phone rang while she was brushing her teeth. Wye. She spat and rinsed and didn't answer. It rang again.

And again.

"Hello?"

"I'm sorry to be such a nag, but it's all kicking off here. The board loved the affiliate ID and they've pressed ahead with it, throwing tons of engineers at it. They want to do a big release next week, press conference and everything, with the affiliates, in eight countries. They love your story, and want to feature you. You'd even get some money for the publicity work, you know, to help you out with missing work. I've been at the office since six a.m. It turns out I'm the only one here who knows a real-life jailbreaker and that makes me the resident expert." She giggled nervously. "I'm sorry, it just happened. But we need to move, everything is waiting on you."

She couldn't think of anything to say.

"Hello? Salima?"

"Wye—"

"Salima, I know it's crazy, but this solves everyone's problems. Please say you'll come down, at least, and talk to them?"

"I have to work."

"Where? We can come to you."

She felt trapped. "I'm working at home today." She got to do that, every week or two, when there were a lot of little reconciling jobs to do.

"Perfect! That's just perfect! I'll text you when we know our arrival time, OK?"

"Wye!"

But she'd already hung up,

AFTER THAT, SALIMA couldn't concentrate at all. She listened to the sounds of her neighbors leaving for work, then the mothers with little kids moving through the halls, heading to one another's places accompanied by piping children's voices for playdates and friendly commiseration.

The numbers swam on her big screen, refusing to cohere. She paced the tiny apartment, then the corridor. Her little notebook was in her pocket, the apartment numbers and the dates and her notes. She'd been in so many of these places.

> ETA 15 mins. OK?

She sighed.

> OK

She went back into her place to listen for the downstairs buzzer. At least they were arriving after the morning rush, so they wouldn't have to wait too long for an elevator. Indeed, they were at her door just minutes after she buzzed them in, Wye and two guys, one white and one Indian, both in Boulangism tees, both with youthful haircuts and big, polished, straight-toothed smiles.

"Thank you for seeing us," the Indian one said. He was called Paul, but his business card said "Pritpaul." He'd refused tea and water, as had the white guy ("Rog"), but Wye had accepted a coffee and watched intently as Salima fed a pod into the machine and put a cup beneath, then ejected the pod and threw it out.

"It's OK," she said. "Wye was very excited about it."

Wye had the good grace to look a bit chagrined.

Paul didn't notice. "She's been very excited about you, too. We've heard a lot about you and honestly, you couldn't be more perfect for what we have in mind. We think it could be very big." He held his hands up, arms spread as wide as he could in her crowded room. "*Very* big. Good for us, good for you, and good for people like you."

"People like me?"

"People who fall between the cracks—people who can't afford to pay full price for everything, but who sometimes want to splurge on more features for a special occasion. It's really the best of both worlds, a new kind of flexibility. The old Boulangism owners were blind to that, but we're totally energized about the possibilities of working *with* our customers, not against them. We hope you'll be a part of that."

There was a space in the conversation here where Salima

would say something positive. Everyone in the room wanted her to say something positive. The conversation had a shape, or maybe a direction, and she could pat it on the back, give it a little push in that direction, and the next stop would be something glad from Paul or Wye or the white guy, and then back to her, push and push and push, until it had picked up enough velocity that no one could stop it.

It seemed petty to refuse then, but she could see that a positive word here was a ticket on an express train with no more stops.

"That sounds very nice, but I don't think I'm the right person for you."

Wye looked shocked. Paul and the white guy looked wooden for a moment and then pasted on smiles. "Of course we respect your decision, but I wonder if you could tell us why? We've come a long way to talk about this with you, after all. Maybe if you explain your reservations we can learn something from you that will help us do better in our next meeting?"

She didn't say that she hadn't asked them to come over. "I just don't feel right about it. I understand your idea here, that you're selling us more freedom. But that's only because our appliances take away so much freedom to begin with, and then sell it back."

"But no one forced you to choose Boulangism. You chose a product that came with restrictions, and in return, you got a deal on your rent."

"Do you have a Boulangism toaster?"

"No, I don't."

"Why not?"

"It's not the choice we've made," the white guy said. "We chose a different deal. That's the great thing about freedom: we all get to choose the proposition that suits us best."

Salima managed a tight little smile. "You keep talking about choosing. This is the only place I could get into, and it took months. How is that a choice?"

"You were living somewhere before this place, right?"

"A refugee shelter."

"You could have chosen to stay there, right?"

She wanted these people gone. "I don't think that is much of a choice."

He shook his head. "The point is that you *had* a choice, and that's because appliances like ours made it economical for landlords to build subsidy units."

She didn't say anything. She was getting angry and she didn't like to be angry, didn't want to show these people that she was angry.

"We want to help you people, let you get more out of your lives, give you more choices."

What about the choice to jailbreak my things? She didn't ask it.

"Honestly, I can't understand your decision here."

Choice is good, so long as I don't choose not to help you? She didn't say it.

"Can't you see we want to help you?"

I can see that you want me to help you get more money from "people like me."

She still didn't say it.

"Maybe we should go," Wye said. Unlike the two men, she was paying attention to Salima's reactions.

"We're just having a friendly conversation," the white guy said. "We don't have to be back at the office for an hour, anyway. Salima, can you just tell me what the problem is?"

She heard herself say: "I would rather help my neighbors save their money than spend it."

"What is that supposed to mean? Unlocking your toaster could save tons, if you're smart about bulk groceries and what you cook."

Again, her voice said, "We'd save more money if we didn't have to pay to unlock our toasters."

"I don't see what that—" He stopped. "Oh. Yeah, sure, but you know what happens if you get caught doing that."

"I would rather help them not get caught."

He snorted. "Everyone gets caught."

"How would you know? The people you never caught would be people you never knew about." She met his eyes. He was angry now, red-flushed, a vein showing in his forehead.

"Yeah, maybe so, but that's not going to be you, lady. We know what's going on here, you know. You're on our radar. I mean, I hope you've got all your shit right, because if there's anything out of order here, we'll see it. We'll know who to talk to first, too."

Wye opened her mouth, shut it. She gave Salima an apologetic look. She was also flushed. Paul stood up. "I think we'd better be going. Thank you very much for your time, Salima."

She watched them leave; then, after the door closed, opened it silently and put her eye to it to watch them call the elevator, wanting to be sure they left without talking to her neighbors. Moments after they pressed the call button, the doors opened and there was a surprised-looking woman already in the car, a woman she'd never seen before, dressed in a smart summer-weight suit, smart makeup, smart little haircut. Someone from the other side, whose elevator should never, ever open on a poor-floor.

The three Boulangism employees nodded at her as though nothing was amiss and stepped into the car. When they turned around, she caught Wye's eye for a moment, and Wye shrugged and grimaced in an eloquent expression of ambiguous apology. Was she sorry for the way her boss had spoken, for the threat, for the fact that the elevators came for them when they called them, but not for Salima?

Salima climbed six floors to Nadifa's floor and rang her bell.

THEY ONLY HAD to wait a few minutes in the school office before Abdirahim appeared. "Mama?" He looked worried, and then, when he saw Salima, confused.

"Come on, we'll talk about it as we walk," Nadifa said, giving him a complicated look that silenced any questions. That was a look that they must have had a lot of cause to use over the years, though not for some time.

When they were out on the street and hustling towards the bus stop, Salima said, "We need to restore everything in the building to factory defaults."

He shook his head. "I thought you'd already done that."

"Yes, and you and your friends have undone it."

He started to deny it. She cut him off.

"I'm not a fool, Abdirahim. I don't even disagree. But I turned them down today, told them I wouldn't help them sell unlock codes to our friends. They're angry with me and they're going to try to punish me for it. They're going to watch us all *very* closely, and they're working with the owners of Dorchester Towers." That was a guess, but it was a good one. After all, the landlords were getting a commission from them, so they had to have some kind of relationship. "So we need to get everything put back, before they catch us."

He walked several steps in silence. Then: "It won't stay that way. Too many people know how to jailbreak."

"I know that," she said. "But we need to invent a better way."

*

WYE HAD TALKED about virtual machines, and there was a clue in there. The message boards were, as usual, full of disagreements, speculation, insults, boasts, spam, and obscenity.

Abdirahim had grudgingly gone through Salima's notebook and pointed out the apartments that he knew to be jailbroken, including a few that she'd never been able to get to admit to it. Working together, they'd gone door to door again, bringing along Nadifa for moral support, ringing doorbells long after any decent hour, working until they were so tired that they started making foolish mistakes. They'd take turns working in each apartment, one of them reverting devices and the other one talking to the people there, especially the kids, about the importance of leaving everything as is, just for a little while, until they could come up with a better solution.

Searching for "virtual machines" on the message boards made things a little clearer, but it also sent them down a rabbit hole of reading about computer science ideas neither of them really had the background for. Thankfully, there were a lot of Boulangism and Disher owners around the world who were also unqualified to understand virtual machines, but nevertheless insistent that someone explain them, and they were able to piece together something like comprehension. It helped that between them, Nadifa, Salima, and Abdirahim could read seven languages.

Computers, it seemed, were in some important way all the same. Every computer shared a common heritage, an "architecture" that let it run any program that could be written in computer languages, in software code. Some computers were faster or had more memory than others, and some of them expected the instructions to be written in different ways, but even the slowest computer could run the most complicated programs, though it might take years to accomplish a task that another computer could complete in an eyeblink.

But you didn't need to translate computer code to get it to run on a different computer. Instead, you could write a computer program that was, in effect, *a computer itself*. You could write a computer program that could run on a Disher, whose purpose was to run Boulangism programs. Yes, you could convince your dishwasher that it was a toaster. When the toaster inside your dishwasher gave the instruction to turn on a heating element or take a picture of the food in its bay to test its doneness, the dishwasher running its computer could send it any data it wanted, and it would blindly trust it.

This was the "virtual machine," an imaginary computer inside another computer. As if that wasn't weird enough, you could run a *Boulangism* virtual machine inside a Boulangism, making the toaster pretend to be *another toaster*. Which seemed like a kind of flourish or game to Salima, until Abdirahim got it in a flash and explained it.

"If you have a toaster that has been jailbroken, you can run a virtual toaster inside it. Then you can run a regular, factory version of the toaster software on the virtual toaster. Whenever the factory contacts your toaster, it sends the communications to the virtual toaster. The virtual toaster tells it how to answer to seem like it's unmodified. It's like taking an enemy hostage and making him tell you what to tell his commanding officer so he won't get suspicious." He rubbed his hands together.

"Does it work?"

He shrugged and pointed at his screen. "They say it does. But they wouldn't know for sure, would they?"

"I wish I could ask Wye," she said. "She would know."

"You said she told you about virtual machines—"

"Yes, but she was just thinking out loud. Maybe she thought it over and found a flaw in the plan."

He didn't even look up from the screen where he'd been avidly reading about virtual machines. "You could ask her."

"It wouldn't be fair to her."

"Nothing is fair." He said it so nonchalantly that it shocked her. Such a small boy, such a big thought.

She went so far as to look up Wye's number, but she didn't dial it. Instead, she got her Boulangism and helped Abdirahim install a virtual machine on it. They were going to have to get very good at this.

THE DAY THAT Boulangism relaunched, every virtual machine in every toaster and Disher dishwasher chimed awake and announced the new, exciting unlocking offer. These alerts loaded in little windows they had to tap to upsize and read, before dismissing them.

They all spent the day with tight shoulders and quick movements, jumping every time they got a buzz, sure it was someone at home telling them they'd been raided or that everything had stopped working, or that the landlords were at the door telling them to get out.

But the day passed, and then the next, and the next.

Cautiously, one muscle at a time, they relaxed.

SALIMA WAS VERY good at baking. She had discovered Nordic breads and made four little cardamom buns every morning, dusted with cinnamon. She ate one and gave three to the first three people she met in the stairwell on the way down, still warm, leaving behind a smell that was better than the nicest whiff of perfume you might encounter in the elevator after it had been vacated by someone from the other side.

She was waiting for the Boulangism to chime when her screen rang. She almost didn't answer it—blocked number and early hour, almost certainly a spammer—but she slid her finger across it.

"Salima." Wye's voice was tight, a little out of breath. Salima's shoulders wound themselves as tight as tennis rackets. Somewhere in her mind, she'd always expected this call.

"Yes?"

"The virtual machines you're using aren't fooling them anymore. They sent out an update that is designed to break on VMs. I just checked your building. You're just *hanging* out there now. There's no way they'll miss it."

"Oh." She squeezed her eyes shut. The Boulangism chimed and its door swung open. The smell of cinnamon and cardamom and fresh bread. The sound of her blood, thundering in her ears. "Oh."

"But there's a fix."

"A fix."

"The VM I use for testing. It's undetectable. Has to be, or I wouldn't be able to do simulations in my lab. I've packaged it and—"

"No, Wye."

"*Yes*, Salima."

"You aren't going to risk everything for me."

"You aren't going to get caught because I didn't help you."

Salima hadn't thought of it like that. The people in her building would get caught if Salima didn't help them. That would destroy her. Salima would get caught if Wye didn't help her. So—

"Yes, Wye."

Wye actually laughed, a tiny and tight sound. "I'll send you something." She named a darknet site, one that Salima had an account on, though she'd never discussed it with Wye. She wondered how much Wye knew about what she'd been up to, in the weeks since they'd spoken.

ABDIRAHIM HADN'T LEFT for school yet and Nadifa didn't even hesitate when Salima said she'd need him for the day. Her notebook was scuffed and dog-eared from being carried from apartment to apartment so many times.

"You trust her?"

She nodded. "If all she wanted to do was get me in trouble, it would be so much easier than this."

The new VM and its control software was much tidier than anything they'd downloaded from the darknet. It hid itself very well unless you knew the multitouch pattern to swap your screen from the real, jailbroken controls to the sham controls of the VM. The notes with it promised that it would also be perfectly hidden from Boulangism's network tools. It was easy enough to install, just an update to the settings that they already had in place, but it was also morning, when so many people were heading out for the day, leaving their appliances exposed to the company's snoopy probing.

They worked out a system. She'd knock on a door, explain things quickly to whomever answered, and send in Adi to start working. Then she'd go on to the next door and the next, talking urgently, begging people to leave their doors unlocked for them. Adi finished one apartment and then the next, letting himself into the unlocked places. They'd get to the old people, the disabled people, the stay-at-home moms, but they had to get to these places before their occupants left. She raced from one place to the next, and managed nearly all of them and got phone numbers for the four she'd missed and trekked up the stairs back to Adi, frantically dialing them, getting two and leaving messages for the other two. She'd call them back.

It was a good thing that Wye's software was so slick and easy to install because Salima was a wreck, though Abdirahim was all teenaged cool and bravado, making short work of each place, chest puffed out and an easy smile playing over his lips as he concentrated.

But they were doing it. By lunch they were more than half-way through, and they knocked on the door of the old Serbian man, and he insisted on giving them peanut butter on crackers, which they both gobbled, surprised at how hungry they were. Salima remembered that she had four cardamom buns in her toaster and ran to get them and they each ate one and left the extra for the Serb. He smiled and waved at them as they walked down the hall to the next place.

Just as they were descending the stairs to the next floor, Salima's screen rang.

"Nadifa?"

The voice was an urgent whisper. "The landlords are knocking on the doors."

"Where?"

"Starting on forty-one. They were just at our place, inspecting the appliances." They'd done their own apartments first, partly to make sure they knew what they were doing, partly because they thought that the landlords might start with them.

"OK."

"They didn't find anything. Whatever you did, it worked."

"OK."

"They're getting in the elevator."

"OK."

For a moment, all she could hear was the whoosh-thud of blood in her ears. She realized she was staring at her phone blankly. Abdirahim was looking at her with alarm.

"How many left?"

He pulled out her notebook, tattered, with annotations in both their hands, ran his finger down the columns, moved his lips as he counted.

"Twenty-four," he said.

She closed her eyes and took a deep breath. Twenty-four. The landlords in the elevators. Her place was safe, and that's where the landlords would go next. The remaining places were scattered among the seven poor-floors. There were four floors above them, three below.

She took the notebook from Abdirahim and tore out the pages for the four floors above and folded them and put them in the back pocket of her jeans. "Do the bottom three," she said, "Be careful. Check before you go into the hallways. Don't let the landlords see you. If they catch you, don't let them get the notebook."

He had gone a shade paler, his teenaged bravado drained. He swallowed audibly. He looked at the remaining notebook pages, scanned down them. "OK."

"OK," she said. He turned, but she caught him and gave him a fierce hug. "Go," she whispered, and turned on her heel and raced up the stairs.

A CALM DESCENDED on her as she stepped out onto the next floor. There were three unlocked apartments on this one, no person she'd have to talk to, and so she stepped into the first one, eyes moving around to take in the appliances, matching them to her list, one-two-three. She pulled the USB out of her pocket—she hadn't remembered to warn Adi to ditch that if he was in danger, but he would know that (wouldn't he?)—and stepped to the toaster and lifted it with sure, economical motions.

One apartment. Two. Three. Stairwell. Two more here. People in them. Ring the first doorbell, exposed and anxious, the hum of the elevators in their shafts a few yards away. Heart thudding. Armpits slick. USB gripped so tight in her fist it hurt.

The woman who answered was old, but she stood tall and clear eyed, thin and wrinkled and brown. Salima remembered that she'd been a pediatrician in Damascus. She had once played violin, but the arthritis that had swollen her knuckles took that from her.

"Landlords in the building," Salima whispered as she slipped past the woman. The woman stepped to one side and let her get to work. When Salima was done, the woman stopped her and clutched at her hand, fingers brittle and dry and bent.

"Thank you," she said and gave a small squeeze. The feeling lingered on Salima's hand as she consulted her notes and rang the next doorbell.

SHE DUCKED INTO the stairwell and her phone buzzed. She checked it.

> Landlords in the stairwell

Oh.

She could hear stealthy movement now, the soft tread of a shoe, someone ascending and trying to keep it silent. There was another stairwell at the other end of Dorchester Towers, reserved for emergencies, with an alarmed door. The steps drew closer. She opened the door again and went back into the hallway.

She could knock on someone's door, try to get rid of the notebook and the USB before the landlords came. And if she failed? They would all be in trouble.

She and Adi had nearly done it. Perhaps half a dozen apartments remained. Too few, she thought, for the landlords to be able to evict them all for conspiracy.

She could hear the steps from the stairwell now. They weren't bothering to be quiet. They must have heard the door shut behind her.

The elevator hummed. She was trapped. She crossed her arms over her chest, spread her feet apart, and waited.

The elevator doors opened before the stairwell door. She turned to face it, not letting any fear show. A cool mask, that's what she'd show them.

Abdirahim was inside.

"Get in!" he hissed.

The doors closed and the elevator lurched into motion.

ABDIRAHIM PUSHED THE lobby button. "They're in the lobby, too," he said. "So we can't go there."

The elevator was descending rapidly. The floor counter hit thirty-five and then displayed the two hyphens—"--"—it showed as they raced past the full-price floors. They'd be in the lobby in seconds.

"Adi—"

He smiled and pressed a rapid sequence on the elevator panel, fingers racing and sure. The elevator slowed, stopped. The doors opened.

The *other* doors.

The doors that opened into the rich floor.

"Come *on,* he said.

They stepped into the hallway. Its carpet was a rich, purpley brown, and it had neat lines from a robot vacuum that had swept its nap into a uniform direction.

"Adi—"

He smiled again. "I figured out the elevators the day after they stopped the elevator captains. It wasn't hard."

On the poor-floors, the elevators' infographics only showed the positions of the cars when they were traversing the floors they were allowed to stop at, seeming to vanish between forty-two and the penthouse, thirty-five and the lobby. Here, the infographics showed it all. A car stopped at thirty-seven, went up to thirty-eight. No resident of the poor-floors would waste their time calling an elevator for a single floor's ride. That was the landlords, with special fobs that would summon an elevator directly, even to the poor-floors.

"Now what?" she said. She was still making sense of what Adi had done.

He showed her the notebook, with tick marks beside every entry. "Now we finish your list."

Two more floors to go. Thirty-five and thirty-six. She handed him a sheet, took one herself, and then he summoned another elevator and pressed another fast sequence, then thirty-five and thirty-six.

When the doors opened, he sprinted into the hallway, all recklessness, not even checking to see whether the landlords were waiting for him. She was more careful when the doors opened on thirty-six, peering around the door before stepping into the hall, then she, too, sprinted for the last door on her list.

*

> Another VM for you-update's going in next week. That
enough time?

Salima tapped her screen and replied.

> You are a very bad employee, Wyoming
> I suppose I am
> But you are a good friend
> I suppose I am
> Thank you, Wye
> Any time.

Salima stretched and stood. She had to go to work now.
The ice cream parlor. They were doing a roaring trade now,
thanks to an unusually warm spring. They had a new flavor
she adored, too: black olive brittle and goat's cheese, which
was the weirdest ice cream she'd ever tasted, but also the best.
She collected her cardamom buns and checked her hair in
the mirror. The screen buzzed.

> Send me the cardamom bun recipe please!

She did, and left for work.

model
minority

THE AMERICAN EAGLE was just crossing Interstate 278 when he heard the sharp crack of a baton rapping on a car window, then the voice, loud, commanding, a cop voice, full of rage, north of I-278, the Mason-Dixon line that separated white Staten Island from Black Staten Island.

"Open the fucking window!"

Even with his superhuman hearing, he couldn't tell exactly where the voice had come from, not until the rapping came again, three more nightstick bangs, then the sound of a car windshield shattering. He got a bead on the sound, tuned in to the sounds of the scuffle, and tilted his body towards it, spilling altitude and cutting a swathe through the drizzle, which fantailed behind him in his turbulent wake. With his arms out before him, his cape crackling behind him, he was a blue-and-red missile, arrowing down and towards the sound.

The man on the ground was Black, the four cops around him were white. The Black man on the ground was slender, mid-thirties, with close-cropped hair and a small, neat mustache. His car was as neat as the mustache, shining even on this damp, gray day: an older car, but one that was well looked after. The man was on the ground, and above his smart little mustache, his face was bleeding. There were little cubes of safety glass embedded in it, but also a bruise on his high cheekbone the shape of the tip of a nightstick.

The four cops around the Black man on the ground had their nightsticks out. They were hitting him. They'd be hitting him harder, but he'd been dragged out of his parked car and into the narrow space between it and the next car, and they were getting in each other's way. A baton landed on his head with a crack that the American Eagle felt deep in the small alien bones of his inner ear. He winced and adjusted his angle to make a more direct, faster approach to the scene.

The cars made the Black man's body hard for the cops to reach with their batons, but his legs protruded into the parking lot where two of the cops could swing on him at once. They went at it like men driving in fence posts, big overhand swings that were aimed for the bones, the joints.

The man on the ground moaned and cried out, while the four officers shouted. They shouted, "Stop resisting," and, every two or three blows, broke off from the beating to pan around with their body cams, catching each other shouting "Stop resisting" as they swung and swung.

The American Eagle swooped over their heads close enough that his tailwind pulled their hats askew while he caught two of the batons in his two hands, yanking them clear so forcefully that one of the cops fell on his face. The other one caught his balance just as the American Eagle settled to the ground. None of the cops were hitting the Black man anymore. They were looking at him, all of them, even the Black man, who had blood streaming out of his nose and a scalp wound.

"What?" the cop who had hit the man in the head said. "Motherfucker had drugs on the center console, in plain sight. Wouldn't open his window. Obstructing government adminis-tration."

The American Eagle peered inside the cop, saw his blood pressure, took the measure of his pulse. The man's eye twitched, his gaze roved over the American Eagle, then his baton twitched, all too fast for a human eye to follow.

The American Eagle didn't say a word. Watched, in silence. He was hovering, soles of his boots just a few inches off the wet parking lot pavement. It was intimidating to face down someone who could hover. The cop wilted.

"Cuff him," he said.

"Hey, Officers, the cuffs on my ankles, they're too tight," the Black man said. "I can't feel my left foot. Something's wrong."

He had no cuffs on his ankles, but his left foot and ankle were visibly broken, bent at a sickening angle by multiple blows from the two batons.

The cop who'd said "Cuff him" radioed for an ambulance. The Black man said, "Did anyone get a video of this? I'm going to sue you all the way to hell." The cuff-him cop—a sergeant, name tag BIANCHI, a 'roided-out little man with biceps that bulged around his vest and a neck too thick for his uniform collar—looked like he was going to kick the Black man in the head. His foot actually twitched a little, but you'd need the American Eagle's alien perceptual apparatus to see it. But he restrained himself, and boarded the ambulance with the Black man when the EMTs rolled up. He'd got a bit of safety glass in the face when he'd smashed in the windshield and it had given him an infinitesimal cut on one cheek. The EMTs gave him a very thorough checkup and put a dressing on it.

The other cops looked around sheepishly once Bianchi and the ambulance had departed. There was an administrative task that fell to them now, gathering evidence, taking photos, impounding the vehicle. Compared to the beating that had been under way when the American Eagle arrived on the scene, it was dry and bureaucratic, for all that they were photographing blood spatters and making serious notes about the drugs they'd found on the Black man's center console.

"What's a center console?" the American Eagle asked, eavesdropping on a whispered conversation from twenty feet away.

The two cops who'd been chatting looked even more embarrassed. "That, that's the console," one said. He pointed at the armrest that separated the driver seat from the passenger seat.

"He had drugs in plain sight there?"

"In a bag." The cop held up a large bag of weed.

"But it's got a curved top. Anything you put on there would fall off."

"Maybe it was on the passenger seat."

The cop's partner said, "No, center console. I saw it."

The American Eagle stared at him. He was hovering again.

"Listen." It was the other cop, the one who'd been talking to the tow driver on the phone. "Listen, Eagle. About Gioff, you know, Bianchi? He's not a bad guy. He's good, his dad was career, NYPD. He volunteers with the Little League."

"Guy was a literal Eagle Scout," Center Console said. "Literally."

They both looked pointedly at the American Eagle's emblem.

"Which hospital are they going to?" the American Eagle asked.

They told him, after a sullen pause. He took off and his super-hearing caught Not a Bad Guy tell Center Console that only a fag or a pervert would run around in tights, it was disgusting.

HE TOUCHED DOWN in the ambulance bay and found the EMTs who'd worked on the Black man sipping coffees and waiting for a callout. They watched his approach warily. That wasn't normal; most people had grown up on the American Eagle: the comics, the newsreels, the radio dramas, the cartoons, the toys, the novelizations, the interviews, the educational films, the stage show, the musical, the movies, the reboots, the theme park rides. Even criminals who were going to end up in prison because the American Eagle had just showed up tended to get a little starstruck even as they were cursing their bad luck.

"Hi guys," he said.

"Yo." The EMT was white, jacked, tall, with short hair and really, really good athletic shoes.

"About that guy you just brought in, the one the cops worked over, with the leg?"

"Yeah."

"I want to make sure everything's okay with him. Could you tell me if he got checked in and triaged okay? Do you have his name? It was pretty bad back there and I wanted to check in with him, let him know he's got legal options."

"You a lawyer or a superhero?"

The American Eagle had testified in literally hundreds of criminal trials, not to mention a couple genocide trials in the Hague. He had more than a century of practical legal experience, knew more than half the faculty at Yale. He also knew that this guy wasn't idly curious about his professional credentials.

"So do you have his name?"

The EMT drank some coffee. "Hospital policy. HIPAA. Can't give it out. Sorry, Eagle." He spread his hands. It was okay, because the American Eagle had already read the name off a smudgy carbon in the shadows of the ambulance's interior: Wilbur Robinson, who'd had strong vitals when he was passed off from the EMT to the triage nurse. The Eagle also read Sergeant Gioffre Bianchi's paperwork, which was next to Robinson's. He also had good vitals, and a small facial cut described as "superficial."

"Thanks for your help anyway. I'll just go ask at the ER desk." He headed for the swinging doors, but the EMT stopped him.

"Staff only, that door. Front entrance, *please*," with a wicked little barb in its tail.

The American Eagle drew stares when he entered the hospital, of course, and he felt bad that he was disrupting the work of the nurses and doctors. But he also got intense looks from the two uniformed cops who flanked the reception desk: glares, really. One of them swore under his breath, loud enough for the Eagle to hear, but too quiet for anyone else to hear. The American Eagle memorized his badge number in an eyeblink.

"I'm here to check in on a patient," he told the receptionist, who was legit starstruck, and smiling like crazy.

"Wow," she said.

"He came in an ambulance. Wilbur Robinson." She started typing.

The cop who'd cursed him said, "Wait a sec." He loomed over the ER receptionist. "That patient is a criminal suspect. No information to be released without permission from NYPD."

The American Eagle frosted him. It wasn't a look he was often photographed with, but there were plenty of criminals who'd wilted under that glare. "You are not a hospital official, Officer."

"I'm a law enforcement officer," he said and tapped his badge.

"I'm a deputized federal marshal, as it happens," the American Eagle said. "What is the patient's status, please?"

The receptionist resumed typing. She looked at her screen,

at the Eagle, at the cop. "I'll page the supervising physician to brief you," she said, which was a smart way of getting off the hook without being a dick to a bona fide superhero. Working in an ER had taught her some fast-footed diplomacy.

"Thank you," the American Eagle said.

The cop glared at both of them.

The doc was Asian, and her surname, Farooqi, made the American Eagle guess her parents were Pakistani. The cop started talking before he could say a word: "Your patient has been placed under arrest by the New York Police Department and he is not allowed to have any visitors."

"I didn't ask to see him. I asked to speak to his doctor."

The cop squared up to him, which was brave and stupid, since the American Eagle could have literally punched him so hard that he'd put his fist through his chest, body armor and all. There'd been an early boxing class in Anytown where he'd turned the gym's punching bag into a ripped tatter with an embarrassing explosion of sand all over the floor. It hadn't been easy to be an eight-year-old extraterrestrial with a secret identity in Anytown, Ohio.

The cop was about to say something, but the doctor broke in. She had an ER doctor's knack of literally not being surprised by anything. A cop arguing with a superhero is only interesting if you have slept in the past thirty-six hours and if you haven't been called upon to improvise a means of removing an odd-shaped foreign object from an embarrassing orifice.

"I'm Doctor Farooqi." Small, neat, baggy-eyed, short glossy black hair, skin paler than any Pakistani the American Eagle had ever met—someone who spent a lot of time indoors. "I can confirm that NYPD policies are not relevant to my capacity to discuss or withhold information about the status of a patient." She gave the cop a dead-eyed look that gave exactly zero fucks.

The Eagle liked her. "The relevant rules are to be found in HIPAA and the rules of this hospital. Both of which say that I may not communicate his condition with a federal marshal unless there is a court order or a compelling, immediate law-enforcement need, or unless he consents. Mr. Eagle, do you happen to have a court order?"

The American Eagle shook his head. The cop looked smug.

"I see. And I can see no compelling law enforcement need. Is that right?"

The Eagle nodded.

"Thank you. I will now ask my patient if he consents to my sharing his details with you."

The cop jolted. "Wait—" But the doctor was already gone. The cop looked like he wanted to chase her down and tackle her, but the American Eagle wouldn't let that happen.

When the doc came back, she said, "Come with me, please," to the American Eagle, and led him down the hallway. The cop took two steps after him and the doctor turned and said, "Please wait there." The doc led the Eagle into a consulting room and closed the door.

"Mr. Robinson has suffered extensive injuries to his left leg that will require multiple surgeries and years of therapy to address, and he may never walk without discomfort again. He is mildly concussed and has a fracture to the orbit of his left eye. Thankfully, no bone fragments were driven into his eye. His nose is broken and he has lost two teeth. All of the fingers on his right hand are broken and have been put in a cast. He has one broken rib and less serious contusions and abrasions across much of his body."

The American Eagle had seen a lot of man's inhumanity to man in various war zones across the decades, had even had to clean up after one of the "good guys" had lost his shit and did something not so good. But this affected him differently. This hadn't happened on a battlefield in the fog of war, this had happened in a little private parking lot in Staten Island in broad daylight, committed by a group of guys who could have stopped each other, but instead shouted "stop resisting" for the benefit of one another's body cams.

He unbunched his fists and the doctor relaxed a little. He didn't mean to scare the doc, who'd done him a solid.

"Can you take him a message?"

The doc nodded.

"I'll testify on his behalf."

The doc nodded again. "Is that all?"

"Yes. No. Wait. Tell him it was wrong and I'll testify on his behalf."

"All right."

He left by another exit, coming out in the ambulance bay without passing the cop again. He did a vertical takeoff and used his x-ray vision to watch the elevator ascend with the doc, then followed the doc's progress through the corridors of the seventh floor until she went into Wilbur Robinson's room. The Eagle noted the room and then flew up into the clouds to get away from the prying eyes of the people in the parking lot, who were staring up and pointing at him.

THE LATE WINTER sun set early, and he came back down out of the clouds and hovered above the hospital's west wing, scanning Wilbur Robinson's room before landing on the roof and using his cold breath to freeze the lock mechanism on the roof door, then twiddling the latch with a thin piece of metal so that it clicked open. Once inside, he warmed it up again with his heat vision and ensured that the latch clicked back into place. He leapt over the stair railing and slowly floated down to the seventh floor, avoiding the CCTVs trained on the stairs themselves. Once on seven, he blurred too quickly for the human eye to follow down to Wilbur Robinson's room, snatching a handful of pens out of a nursing-station pot on the way. He scattered these in front of the NYPD officer standing outside Robinson's room, executed a fast turn that sent a sudden gust of wind down the corridor, and as the cop bent down to look at the pens in bewilderment, he blurred back down the hall and past him, into Robinson's room.

Robinson looked at him out of one eye and smiled a sardonic, bruised smile. "You, huh?"

"Did the doctor give you my message?" the Eagle said, taking in the weird twists of Robinson's neat little moustache, now humped over his swollen lips like a stepped-on, rainy-day-sidewalk worm.

Robinson nodded. "Very nice of you, thank you."

"It's not right." There was a hitch in the Eagle's voice.

"Nope, but it's not unusual, either. Why me, Mr. Eagle?"

The American Eagle knew what he meant. He watched the news, read Twitter. He'd seen the camera-phone videos. "Gotta start somewhere."

"Can I make a prediction, you know, with no offense intended?"

The American Eagle nodded. "Of course."

"Right now, you are white, but that's a wholly contingent proposition. I mean, no offense, but you aren't a white man because you aren't a human. You aren't even a man, are you?"

This was not new territory for the Eagle: supervillains often taunted him with cruel speculation about his gender identity and species. But whether or not he was white had never really been part of it. It jolted him, twice: first when he realized that he'd never thought about it, and again—jolt—it really seemed weird that it never came up.

"I'm not really a man, I suppose, not in the sense of being terrestrial or human."

"You're also not white. You ever hear those heritage-not-hate types, that myth that the Irish were the first slaves in America? They're an interesting bunch. They're so close, you know, so close to understanding that whiteness is a thing that other people choose for you. People are white if whiteness is endowed upon them by the wider whiteness. It starts before birth and carries on after you're dead. And what whiteness gives, it can take away. You don't understand that, I bet, but you are only white by courtesy, Mr. Eagle, and you are really only a little green man clothed in whiteness. You won't believe how quickly you can be dewhitened. You're the original illegal alien."

"Mr. Robinson, what happened to you is inexcusable. I'll do whatever it takes to help you get justice."

Wilbur Robinson snorted, then winced. "I have to be honest, Mr. American Eagle, I have a feeling that if you try that, you'll get us both in a lot of trouble."

The American Eagle used his heat vision to melt the seal around the window, carefully lifted it out, then melted the seal back into place while hovering outside the seventh floor. Then he flew home and made himself some dinner.

THE AMERICAN EAGLE didn't need to sleep much. Four hours a night was plenty, and in a pinch, he could go five or six days without sleeping. His planet of origin had a much longer diurnal cycle than Earth. He was used to flying patrols in those long hours, but tonight he sat in, laptop open, VPNed into an anonymizer in the British Virgin Islands that was favored by extremely successful financial crooks and thus probably pretty good against U.S. law enforcement and espionage agencies.

He read what the message boards and social media were saying about him. This was never a good idea, and yet he was drawn to it like a moth to a flame. Soon he'd opened dozens of tabs, and he'd reload them all and shoot through the line, looking for new messages.

No one was impressed with him. The Blue Lives Matter crowd were saying that he'd sold out and taken the side of "thugs" over law enforcement. Anti-racist activists said that no amount of token gestures could undo his generations' worth of assistance in the causes of white supremacy and American empire. Even the people who were sympathetic to him thought that he was being naïve, believing that he could "solve racism by beating it up."

He was powerfully tempted to leap into the fray and anonymously defend himself, but he tamed the urge. He had spent more than a century keeping his identity secret from the increasingly sophisticated intelligence apparatus of the U.S. government and its adversaries and allies, and in the age of mass surveillance, he was keenly aware that there were lots of ways to draw an arrow pointed at his secret identity and a line connecting it to the American Eagle.

He kept on reloading, treasuring the people who took up his cause, even as he recognized their arguments weren't very good: they mostly summed up to "But he's a *superhero*!"

It was dawn when he saw the post showing Wilbur Robinson being moved by ambulance to the Tombs. He hit the buttons that powered off all his devices and sprinted two miles, dodging the CCTVs before taking to the sky. He never took off from the same location twice, and he had a randomizing program that directed him to the day's launch point, avoiding any kind of constant distance from his hideout. He ascended out of the troposphere and broke the sound barrier with a crack that made the clouds behind him ripple. He was over Staten Island five minutes later, tracing the route the police ambulance would have taken to get to the Tombs. He caught up with it a block from the jailhouse, and touched down noiselessly on the roof, training his super-hearing on the transfer as the wheelchair was maneuvered down the ambulance's ramp and into the jail. Bianchi was pushing, and the Eagle heard him cursing softly under his breath in a steady monotone, a recital of all the ways in which Wilbur Robinson was to be made to pay for his transgressions.

The monotone stopped when a sheriff's deputy stepped out to meet them and take over pushing the chair. Wilbur Robinson's face was a blank mask, either bravely stoic or too terrified to speak. The American Eagle felt that spike again, the sense of urgency and wrongness. He used his x-ray vision to track the wheelchair's progress into the jail's intake, watched as Bianchi stepped into some kind of break room and got himself a coffee, then flicked his attention back to Wilbur Robinson just as he went sprawling on the floor.

Without a conscious thought, the American Eagle leapt down to the entrance and pulled the door open so hard its lock went flying off with a noise like a rifle shot. In an instant, he was standing over Wilbur Robinson, who was facedown on the floor, still stoic, leg and cast stuck out behind him at a twisted, awkward angle.

The guard who'd just tipped him onto the floor was skinny, young, and white, and red-faced with fury, which was quickly turning into shock.

"What are you doing?" the Eagle bellowed, thinking *dumb question*.

The guard gawped twice, then found his words. "Prisoners have to be searched. It's a safety policy. This prisoner was noncompliant."

"I wouldn't stand up," Wilbur Robinson said mildly from the floor. He patted the large cast on his left leg meaningfully.

"He has a broken leg," the American Eagle said.

"The prisoner was noncompliant." The guard swallowed. "You are not authorized to be here. Please leave."

"See?" Wilbur Robinson said. "From 'can I get a selfie to show the kids' to 'please leave' in minutes. Watch out, Eagle, non-whiteness is catching. It's all downhill from here."

The American Eagle stared at the guard. The guard wilted.

"You can search him with me present," the Eagle said.

The guard looked like he was going to go for help, but then he pursed his lips, shook his head, and knelt by Wilbur Robinson and searched him.

"I was in a hospital," Robinson said as the guard felt him up. "I'm wearing a hospital gown. Where do you think I'm hiding my contraband?"

As if to answer, the guard drew out a small flashlight and put it between his teeth—it was dented with many small toothmarks—and lifted up Robinson's gown. The Eagle pulled the gown down so fast the breeze ruffled the guard's short hair.

"That won't be necessary. Mr Robinson is not violent."

"It's procedure," he said around his flashlight. The Eagle thought about the likely problems arising from holding a tool used in cavity searches in your mouth and revised his opinion of the guard's intelligence even lower.

"It's not necessary," the American Eagle said, and stood the guard up. "Let's get Mr. Robinson transferred to the jail hospital, shall we?"

Another staring match. The Eagle was good at these. His

species didn't use gazes the way humans did, after all, so he could stare in ways that were arbitrarily unsettling. Nictitating membranes helped. The Eagle won.

The guard knelt to drag Robinson into the wheelchair. The American Eagle took Robinson up like an infant and placed him gently in the chair, then walked with the guard all the way through the jail's many internal turns and twists. Prisoners and guards alike stared after them and the Eagle listened in on their whispered conversations because anyone who whispers around an alien with legendarily superhuman hearing has no reasonable expectation of privacy. It's not like they were saying anything interesting.

He saw Robinson through a medical intake exam, stepping out of the room for part of it to give him privacy while he was nude, using his super-hearing to figure out when to go back in. He waited until Robinson was settled into a hospital bed, and then he said good-bye to Robinson and told him not to worry, that he'd be back. Robinson rolled his eyes.

The American Eagle made sure he ran into Bianchi on his way out of the jail. Bianchi jerked to one side when he saw the Eagle, like he was ducking a punch. He looked terrible, bags under his eyes, unshaved, rumpled.

"Why is Robinson being held?"

Bianchi pretended like he hadn't heard, so the Eagle took another step towards him—another flinch—and Bianchi pulled himself together.

"Why is Robinson being held?"

Bianchi tried to shoulder past the Eagle, who moved to block him. "You're not leaving until you tell me why he's being held." Technically, this was obstruction, but the Eagle was a federal marshal and this guy was a local screw. He had rank.

Bianchi glared at him.

The Eagle shrugged.

"He's being held for obstructing government administration, unlawful possession of marijuana, assault in the second degree, assault in the third degree, blocking pedestrian traffic, and loitering."

The American Eagle had once flown into the heart of the Earth's sun, where light that was born 50,000 years ago began its slow fight against immense gravities to reach the star's surface and radiate to the Earth. What he saw there was a wonder and marvel of the natural world, and it left him wordless.

It was less surprising than the list of charges against Robinson. When the American Eagle busted someone, he did so for a good reason.

"I'm sorry, can you repeat that?"

"Get the fuck out of my way before I arrest *you*."

I'd like to see you try. He realized that right from the start that *was* what he wanted to see this guy try. The American Eagle had spent his whole life, centuries of it, daring bullies to "pick on someone your own size," which was always bullshit, since no *Homo sapiens* ever born was an even match for the American Eagle. But it was immensely satisfying to see the expression on a bully's face when he came to grips with the fact that they were in the presence of an immovable object that was also an unstoppable force.

Eventually, the authorities or the army would show up and take the bully away and the Eagle would leap into the sky and return to his hideout, safe in the knowledge that he'd done his bit for the human race he'd adopted as his own. This time, there'd be no authorities to take the bully away. He couldn't block Bianchi until the Internal Affairs squad showed up and stripped him of his badge, gun, and honor. That may never happen. The only way this standoff could end is with the American Eagle backing down.

So he did.

Bianchi scowled and pushed past him and the American Eagle leapt into the sky and returned to his hideout.

AT THE BAIL hearing, Bruce sought him out.

"Can I have a word with you?" the billionaire playboy said. The courtroom was nearly empty, of course, but everyone there stared at them. The judge had ordered the courtroom cleared and sealed a moment before, and so it was just the public defender, Wilbur Robinson, the prosecutor, Bianchi and a police union lawyer, the three other cops from the beating, the court clerk, the court reporter, and four bailiffs who'd taken up nervous stations around the Eagle, silently asking each other how the exact fuck they were going to remove the American *fer chrissakes* Eagle if he didn't want to go.

Everyone was pleased to see Bruce. Billionaire playboys made New York City go. There'd been a certain amount of palling around between he and the Eagle over the years, public ribbon-cuttings and the like. They didn't know about Bruce's secret identity (secret!) and couldn't know that he and the Eagle had fought alongside one another on several occasions, were veterans of the same long war on crime and super-villainry.

"Your Honor, do you suppose I could have a moment with my friend?" Bruce was smooth as a carbon nanotube smoothie. The judge—whose pet cause, an animal sanctuary on Long Island Sound, depended on Bruce's annual check to keep its lights burning—favored the billionaire with one of his most indulgent smiles and banged his gavel. The Eagle and

Bruce kept their eyes locked on one another as everyone filed out of the room.

Once the door closed, the American Eagle touched down and Bruce slouched into one of the lawyers' chairs behind the defendant's table.

"This has got to stop." Voice of command, a man used to having his orders obeyed. At least he didn't use his tough-guy gravel voice. That voice. So affected.

"I agree," the Eagle said. "This stops now, in fact."

Bruce rolled his eyes. "Come on, Eagle, complicated problems have complicated solutions. You can't punch racism until it sees the error of its ways."

"I'm not planning on ending racism in general. But I am dedicated to ensuring that Wilbur Robinson gets a fair trial."

Bruce got a shrewd look. "How does Robinson feel about this?"

The American Eagle squirmed. Bruce was good at getting to the heart of the matter. "I get the impression he thinks I'm a naïve idiot." Bruce snorted. "And maybe I am. But he's also pointed out that I'm no more of a white man than he is, but I get to be a pretend white guy, and that means I get to do things he can't do without being killed. Now I'm going to use that. It starts with Wilbur Robinson and I'm not sure where it ends."

Bruce opened his mouth, but the American Eagle was (naturally) faster, and he jumped in.

"You, Bruce, you have a lot of that privilege, too. You use that privilege to"—he dropped his voice, mindful of the court reporter's recorder, pitching his whisper for Bruce's ears alone—"dress up in a costume and beat up supervillains." He brought his voice back up to normal volume. "Have you ever considered that all the while, there are guys in uniforms who are, as a body, every bit as much of a supervillain as the evilest terrorist whose plans you've foiled? People who, as a group, cause as much misery as anyone on the public enemy list?"

Bruce looked exasperated. "Now we're back to punching racism into submission."

"I'm not going to punch anyone or anything, Bruce. I'm just going to make sure that one guy gets a fair trial. One innocent guy, Bruce."

"And then what?"

The American Eagle shrugged. "And then I'll do it again. Lather, rinse, repeat. I got a lot of time, Bruce. Hundreds of years. Think of me like a random audit. The IRS doesn't have to check everyone's tax returns, just pull enough at random that everyone else colors inside the lines."

"What if someone kills your 'innocent guy' because you got him off?" Bruce was getting angry, the American Eagle could tell by the infrared signature of the veins around his temples. "Are you listening to yourself? You think the IRS keeps people honest? Man, I'm a *billionaire*. You think the thing that keeps me filing my taxes is fear of the IRS? I can afford more lawyers than them. Better lawyers. More, better lawyers. I pay exactly as much in taxes as I deign to.

"The IRS doesn't have any power, Eagle, but I'll tell you who does: the NSA. You think you have a secret identity? You think your little countermeasures and opsec has kept them from tracing your identity? It hasn't." He leaned into the Eagle, pulled him down so he could whisper a name in his ear. If the Eagle had come from a species that paled when upset, he would have gone ashen.

"Yeah, Eagle, that's right. Think about that. Think about what else they know. *Who* else they know. You've been assuming you need to keep your identity secret to protect your loved ones from criminals and foreign spies. Once you have to keep that stuff secret from your own government, your threat model totally changes, and the right time to address that threat is about fifty years ago. Don't make me draw you a picture."

He didn't need a picture. The American Eagle could imagine Lois knocked on the floor of some jailhouse by some sadistic prick of a cop, subjected to the kind of search he'd stopped. He could guard her, sure—maybe even sneak her off to the high desert—but *a)* she wouldn't stand for it, and *b)* then he wouldn't be able to keep an eye on Wilbur Robinson.

He was briefly and powerfully furious: how could the most powerful being on Earth be so easy to outfox? But of course, he knew the answer: because he had allowed himself to care about humans. That was the source of *all* his problems. He could have spent 10,000 years in the heart of the sun, but no, he'd returned to Earth to interpose himself in the affairs of the intelligent life of that planet, which was not his own and never had been.

He mastered his emotions and thought. "You wouldn't let that happen, Bruce."

"You think I could stop the NSA?"

The American Eagle stared at him. Bruce was one of the richest men who'd ever lived, a contractor on both the white and black sides of the Pentagon's budget, with clearances to match the Joint Chiefs. He owned his own covert armory, and an *overt* armory, and corporations he had majority stakes in provided intelligence contracting to the entire roster of federal espionage and policing agencies, not to mention most major metros' police forces. He almost certainly got a paycheck every time the cops in Staten Island were advised by a machine-learning algorithm to go to the brown side of the Mason-Dixon line and start making Black people turn out their pockets and drop their pants.

Bruce looked away first. Something about staring into those alien eyes, it bested even the toughest terrestrial organisms. The American Eagle had once stared down a whale.

"I'll do what I can." He swallowed. "Listen, I love you. Your cause is a good one. But you can't win this. You have to understand that. You can't just stand between that poor bastard and what the system is going to do to him."

"I believe that's exactly what I'm doing."

"I'll hire him a lawyer. He's already lost his job with the city. Once he gets off, I'll hire him, give him a better job."

"I'm glad to hear it."

"You've got to stop this, before it goes too far." His face twisted up. "Look, you know that I know people. I've heard them talking about this. No one likes the idea of an extra-terrestrial declaring war on the U.S. government. That is not a good look, Eagle."

Right now, you are white, but that's a wholly contingent proposition.

It struck the American Eagle that Bruce had been calling him "Eagle" but hadn't mentioned the "American" part lately. Bruce used to jokingly call him things like "Yankee Doodle" and "U.S.A. Today," but today it was just "Eagle," which meant something, probably.

"I'm just fighting for the same things I always fought for."

Bruce grinned wryly. "Truth, justice, and the American way?"

"Equal protection under the law, the right of persons to be secure against unreasonable search and seizures, cruel and unusual punishments shall not be inflicted—"

"Okay, yeah, Con. Law 101. But Eagle, have you really *always* fought for this? I know it was before my time, but I never heard about you getting between Bull Connor's dogs and the NAACP."

Bruce had an uncanny knack for finding the places the American Eagle didn't want him to go. But the Eagle lifted his chin. "That's because I wasn't there. But I should have been. And now I'm here. What will you tell your grandkids when they ask you where you were today?"

"I'll tell them I tried to talk a friend out of destroying his life in a useless bid to assuage his white guilt."

The Eagle looked around the empty courtroom. *A wholly contingent proposition.*

"Then I guess we're done here."

Bruce looked at him long enough that the Eagle felt a rare urge to look away first. Then Bruce left the courtroom, and a moment later, everyone else filed back in. The judge and the bailiffs carried on as if he wasn't there. They had apparently decided to treat him as part of the furniture, like the elaborate eagle motif on some finial.

He listened to the reading of the charges and kept his face impassive through each absurdity. It seemed like the least he could do, given how stoic Wilbur Robinson was being. Bianchi was dressed in a suit that strained around his softball-sized biceps, and his tie knot was visibly digging into his bull neck. Clearly this was a guy who gave more thought to his weight training than his tailoring. The American Eagle caught Bianchi's eye, and Bianchi smirked at him.

"Bail is set at $500,000," the judge said. The American Eagle contained a gasp, and saw Wilbur Robinson's face tighten. The Eagle knew that this astronomical sum was the result of his own actions. He realized that he should have asked Bruce to post bail. He still could.

The public defender made a half-hearted objection, got gaveled back into his seat, and then the bailiffs started to lead Wilbur Robinson away. The Eagle followed them. They pretended they didn't see him for a while, then one of them turned around and drew himself up and said, "Sir, will you please step away? We have a job to do here."

"So do I," the Eagle said, but he let them go. Robinson, who had been acting as if he wasn't there, turned around and looked at him one last time.

THE EAGLE CALLED several of his State Department contacts that night, hoping one of them would find a channel to the prosecutors on Robinson's case. It pained him to do it, because he wanted the system to just be right, not to make an exception. It made him admit that rather than intervening during the beating, or at the hospital, or at the jail, or at the bail hearing, he could have pulled a string or two. He was the American fucking Eagle, and there were plenty of people who owed him a favor or two.

But as he quickly discovered, any debts the American people and their government officials owed him could be easily wiped clean. All that had to happen was for him to publicly declare himself to be a foe of the American system. He hadn't realized that that was what he'd been doing, but it was painfully clear that there was no way to separate the American system from whether a foursome of Staten Island cops should be allowed to beat the shit out of Wilbur Robinson, lie about it, and then send him to jail.

His phone rang: Lois.

"Hi, darling."

"Still up, I see. I saw you tweeting about your train set, and I said to myself, 'Lois, that fool of a man is up past his bed-time again and needs a talking to.'"

He laughed. He did indeed have a model train set, a really

elaborate one, and his secret identity was a member of all kinds of little forums and circles of other modelers, posting tilt-shift photos of their tables and the tiny, German-manufactured figurines. He genuinely enjoyed the hobby, and was able to paint his miniatures with an accuracy that was, of course, literally superhuman. Tweeting pictures of his minis was one of his pleasures, even if it did complicate his opsec (he had a randomizer that queued up tweets to go out during waking hours in New York, so that there were no suspicious gaps in the pattern that coincided with known American Eagle overseas missions). Lois had grown accustomed to his strange work-related absences and sometimes Twitter-stalked him to figure out when he was up and available, which sometimes meant that she tried to call him while he was defusing a rogue nuke or scooping a missile out of the sky before it could hit a refugee camp and flying it into the stratosphere to detonate harmlessly.

"How was your day, darling?"

"Ugh. Good, I guess. Another day of trying to second-source anonymous tips, another dollar."

"Poor baby." He crossed to his sofa and stretched out on his back, arm flung over his eyes, picturing Lois, remembering the smell of her hair and the feel of her skin. "I miss you."

"I miss you, too. Date night tomorrow!"

He'd forgotten. "I remembered!"

"Like hell. But that's okay, because *I* remembered and I got us a table at the Big Carrot." The American Eagle had trouble digesting most terrestrial food, but the lower on the foodchain, the easier it was for him to metabolize. The invention of veganism had been an enormous boon to him, and the raw food fad had been a godsend for his guts.

"You're a champ."

"I am. You pick the cocktail bar for drinks, first, somewhere around Flatbush or even Park Slope—anywhere with a hipster in a leather apron who makes their own bitters, please."

"Sold." Lois loved craft cocktails, and he loved being with Lois.

"Now, why the hell are you up so late, fella?"

"Work," he said, which should have ended the discussion. He and Lois had an understanding that he couldn't talk about his job. This ban drove her reporter's nosiness nuts, but she also had a reporter's circumspection, and understood that she couldn't be forced to disclose things she didn't know, and that two may keep a secret only if one of them is dead. It was an odd but enduringly sound basis for a lasting relationship between a professional nosy person and a professional haver-of-secrets, and the American Eagle suspected that she may have figured it out on her own, anyway. There were a few memorable celebratory joint press conferences with the governor in which he'd run into her while dressed in his Eagle suit and she'd been awfully familiar and knowing.

"You can't let it get to you, Clark. Let other people shoulder some of the load. It's not up to you to do everything." It was stuff like this that made him think she'd figured it out, but he wasn't going to admit anything. Especially not on an insecure phone line.

"You're right, of course, but it's easier said than done."

"Look, so long as you're up and farting around with your trains, why don't you come over here? I've got a filing deadline for oh-dark-hundred, so I'm likely to be up for hours yet, and I could use the company. You can make coffee and rub my shoulders."

He could be there in less than ten minutes, even figuring in his randomized sprints to get to a nonrepeating takeoff spot. "I'll see you in an hour."

"Good boy. Bring doughnuts."

HE FEIGNED SLEEP on her sofa until she was ready to go to bed, then let her "wake him up" and spent a few hours actually dozing with his arm around her shoulders, his face buried in her hair. He'd had other human mates, watched them grow old, become ancient, die. He'd revealed himself to some of them, but he'd just left the others behind, faking his death, sometimes with the help of a friend or two in government. The American Eagle got to call in a lot of favors. He always went to their funerals, which was a huge opsec lapse that could have connected his identities, but it was also the right thing to do.

Watching Lois filled him with indescribable emotions: the sadness of being the last of his kind; a different sadness in knowing that his connection with Lois would end with her withering away while he lived on; a fierce protective feeling about her that he thought of as "love" but which he knew might not match up with what Lois and others meant when they thought of that emotion.

He slipped out of the bedroom and tuned his hearing to the FM band, concentrating until he dialed in NPR. Increasingly this was how he got his news: analog radio reception didn't leave any digital trail that could be connected to him, unlike, say, a set-top cable box that might capture his interest whenever stories about the American Eagle were featured on a news channel. Someday the radio would go all-digital and he'd either have to learn to demodulate them in his head— like doing a million simple math puzzles, but all at once and every second—or he'd have to armor his news consumption with online anonymity tools.

The news was the usual mix of geopolitical chaos, domestic

strife, and promos for podcasts of artfully told personal memoirs. Lois always listened with a professional ear, providing back-of-house gossip about the other reporters, the personalities they interviewed. Despite his long life, the American Eagle didn't have her perspective, so what he heard just filled him with a kind of melancholy. Hadn't there been a time when things were better?

Now they were talking about him. A criminologist at NYU, a West Point war historian, and a national cop reporter, on a panel show.

"—the rule of law, not the rule of men. It's always the risk when you let someone operate outside of the normal legal framework, that he'll become a vigilante rather than a volunteer. In this case, he's not even human, so who can say what he's thinking, where his allegiances lie? We know he's got a much longer lifespan than we do, perhaps this is just a kind of teenage rebellion—"

The host broke in. "Leaving aside xenobiological speculation, can we return to the question: what should New York *do*? Should a Grand Jury be empaneled to indict a beloved national figure? Should the mayor ask him to come around to his office for a quiet one-on-one? Do we all sign a petition telling him to butt out?"

The war historian: "Long experience shows that there's always a no-appeasement crowd during these conflicts, but the peace is always attained through some kind of reconciliation. We don't have the facilities to imprison the American Eagle, notwithstanding rumors of rare metals that can debilitate him. We are going to have to make peace with him, eventually. Also, I remind you that he doesn't have to be the *American* Eagle: there's no law or force of nature that could prevent him from being the Saudi Eagle or the Chinese Eagle or the ISIS Eagle—"

The cop reporter made a rude noise. "Come on, the guy is taking a stand because he opposes police brutality. You think he's going to join ISIS?"

The host called time on the debate, saying they'd have to leave it there for now, and the American Eagle tuned out the radio energy. What he really wanted was news about Robinson, but no one was reporting on Robinson and everyone was reporting on him.

He heard Lois stir in the next room, put on a robe, pee, pad out to him. He held still, pretending he hadn't heard, so she could walk up behind him and tap his shoulder and he could pretend to be startled. This always pleased her and it let him keep up the human pretense.

She made them both coffees and gave him his black, with a kiss on the cheek. It smelled great. Lots of human food smelled better than it tasted. He sipped it though and made himself smile and smack his lips.

"Can't sleep, fella?" She blew on her coffee. He realized he probably should have done the same. By human standards, it was very hot coffee. Lois may have been testing him. He'd been married to a woman who did that, a century before. He liked 'em smart.

"Getting old, I guess. They say a good night's sleep is the first thing you lose—then your hair." He grabbed his own wavy hair and tugged at it, mugging.

"You've got a few good years left in you yet." She touched his hand, cupped his chin, looked into his eyes. "You want to talk about it?"

He looked away.

"Yeah, all right. But let me tell you about my troubles, then. Maybe that'll put your puny worries into perspective."

He chuckled. "Shoot."

"My editor has assigned me to write about Wilbur Robinson, but he really wants me to write about the American Eagle." The Eagle didn't bat an eyelash, though her eyes searched his face. "That's all anyone wants to hear about, of course. There are hundreds of Wilbur Robinsons in New York every year, but there's only one extraterrestrial super-man who's threatening cops and judges."

"But you really want to write about Robinson."

"I really do."

"So interview him."

"I can't. He's smart enough not to talk to me without a lawyer, and he can't afford a lawyer, so he's not talking to me."

"Ah. You can't blame him."

"No, I can't. So since he's not talking to me and since I don't want to write about the American Eagle, I've decided to write about predictive policing instead."

"What's that?"

She smiled. "Well, that's the thing: predictive policing is why those cops beat the shit out of Wilbur Robinson. Companies are selling police forces software, 'artificial intelligence' that crunches through all the arrest data to the beginning of time and makes predictions about where crime is going to be. The argument is that the math doesn't lie and math isn't racist. Its recommendations are supposed to be empirical, neutral."

"Sounds like you don't believe that."

"No one with half a brain should believe it. All you have to do is think about it for ten seconds. All the data they feed this system to predict crime comes from the cops, who are assumed to have some kind of bias, first because they're human and all humans have bias, and second because NYPD have a long history of getting caught in racial discrimination, which is why they're buying this stuff in the first place.

"Because cops only find crime where they look for it. If you make every Black person you see turn out their pockets, you will find every knife and every dime-baggie that any Black person carries, but that doesn't tell you anything about whether Black people are especially prone to carrying knives or drugs, especially when cops make quota by carrying around a little something to plant if need be.

"What's more, we know that Black people are more likely to be arrested for stuff that white people get a pass on, like 'blocking public sidewalks.' White guys who stop outside their buildings to have a smoke or just think about their workdays don't get told to move along, or get ticketed, or get searched. Black guys do. So any neighborhood with Black guys in it will look like it's got an epidemic of sidewalk-blocking, but it really has an epidemic of overpolicing.

"But now you take all those tickets and busts and you turn them into 'data,' which is treated as equivalent to 'crime statistics.' If the data says that an address in front of a housing project has an epidemic of 'blocking public sidewalks' and the same address has an epidemic of drug possession, these are proof that this is a crime hotspot, not proof that every Black guy who stops to wait for an Uber or chat with a neighbor gets stop-and-frisked, and then busted for petty weed possession because as soon as he is ordered to empty his pockets, his joint is in 'plain sight' and the cops can ticket him for it.

"Tell the computer to take all the data at face value and then ask it to predict where the crime is going to be and, no surprise, it will deduce with astounding machine insight that the cops will find weed if they ask everyone going in and out of that building to empty their pockets. Never mind that you'd find as much or more weed if you subjected everyone entering Trump Tower to the same treatment, because you don't have 'evidence' of the drug problem at Trump Tower—because heads would roll if chatting with your Fifth Avenue doorman about the ballgame got you ticketed and searched—and you have computer-verified proof that there's a drug problem south of the Mason-Dixon line.

"That's why Wilbur Robinson got six kinds of shit beaten out of him. When a New York cop pulls someone over, they have to fill in a form, a UF-250, with the reason for the stop. It's got checkboxes on it, like 'inappropriate attire' and 'furtive movement,' and so long as a cop ticks one of those boxes, he's made a solid stop.

"But it's bullshittier than that: cops have quotas, minimum numbers of these 250s they have to turn in, and guess what, if you are a not-too-bright cop looking for somewhere to go and make your quota and keep your sergeant off your back, the predictive policing model will tell you where to go and look for furtive movements and inappropriate attire.

"And the Patrolmen's Benevolent Association has rigged things so that these half-bright cops are impossible to fire— they get to review the footage from their body cams before they turn in their reports, they get to know the identities of whistleblowers who complain about them, they get to decide who can interrogate them and for how long—stuff no other perp gets. So psychos get to psycho, long after they've cost the city hundreds of thousands or even millions in settlements with the people they beat up, and they march out, armed with a computer prediction and a pad of 250s, and they start telling brown people to get out of their cars and put their hands up against the wall.

"That cop who led the beat-down, Bianchi? I found a dozen incidents like this in the news morgue. He's hiding in plain sight, a total psycho, but his disciplinary record is sealed and so are the settlements he racked up for the city. He never should have been out on the job to begin with, but 250s and predictive policing made him a trouble-seeking missile. He was going to put someone brown in the hospital, and Wilbur Robinson just lost the lottery."

"Lois—"

She smiled self-deprecatingly. "I know, I'm ranting. Thing is, if I write that, it lands on the editorial page as opinion. But it's fact. It's the true story of Gioffre Bianchi and Wilbur Robinson, and you can't understand them without understanding all that." She gave him a very significant look. "If I could explain one thing to the American Eagle, it would be that: he should be hanging city officials by their ankles out of their office windows until they explain how this fucked-up, ridiculous situation came to pass on their watch. Then he can move on to the police union. Then the software developers. I understand how a guy like that can end up feeling like he's just tinkering in the margins of the problem and wants to draw a line in the sand, but drawing it in front of Wilbur Robinson is a no-win situation."

The American Eagle considered her words carefully. "I guess the American Eagle would say that if it's hard to get people to take you seriously when you're standing between one of their fellow citizens and an unjust system, it's a lot harder when you're beating confessions out of police officials."

She gave him an even more pointed look. The American Eagle didn't squirm, but he wanted to.

"I guess the question is, does the American Eagle want to feel good about himself, or make a difference?"

THE JUDGE DENIED Wilbur Robinson's bail, and when people who'd read about his story—some thanks to Lois and her articles—raised money for a lawyer to appeal, he lost, too. Someone leaked a story about the prosecutor's fury at the American Eagle's intervention to Lois, but she couldn't get a second source to confirm it, so she didn't publish it. It ended up on the front page of the *Post* instead.

The American Eagle took the ferry to Rikers, smiling at people, taking selfies, signing autographs for kids. By the time he got to the guardhouse and asked to visit Wilbur Robinson, they were waiting for him: warden, deputies, a PR guy, a couple of nervous-looking screws in SWAT gear.

"Would you mind stepping into my office for a private conversation, sir?" The warden was young for the job, with a disarming smile and a couple of big scars showing under his brush-cut from the IED that had blown apart his helmet when he was patrolling Kandahar Province.

The Eagle considered it. "I think I would like to just go through the normal visitation procedure, if it's all the same to you, Warden." They had an audience: Black women and their kids, mostly, visiting loved ones, getting ready for the humiliation of pat-downs or even strip searches.

"Sir, I think it would be better if—"

The Eagle knew that once he was in the warden's office, away from those cameras, it would turn to a bureaucratic morass, him having to wait and wait and wait while the appropriate officials were summoned to their phones to discuss his visit with him, and that would leave plenty of time to think up excuses why he couldn't see Wilbur Robinson, or even to airlift Robinson to another facility.

"Warden," he said, leaning in. "Please let me see Mr. Robinson now. Let's not have a scene." The two guys in SWAT gear looked anxiously at one another. Everyone else in the room had gone silent, even the small children there to see their parents.

The warden eyeballed him for a long time. There was a famous video of the American Eagle bunker-busting an infamous dictator's redoubt, pulled from a cluster of armored point-of-view cameras that a DoD PR flak had convinced him to wear. He'd started the run with a dozen cameras and finished with only one, the rest destroyed by shrapnel, bullets, flamethrowers, and shockwaves as the Eagle had relentlessly pushed his way into the stronghold, batting aside guards, allowing the enemy fire to bounce off his alien skin, smashing down armored doors with his bare hands. Even though the cameras had been destroyed, they'd streamed to an armored hard drive on his belt, and that had uplinked to a nearby Army MRAP with a mobile video-support studio in it, and not one frame had been missed. The final product was edited to include the eleven camera-killing shots, with the final frames prior to each camera's destruction in extreme slo-mo, stretching out as the cameras' output fragmented and went dark. It was such a riveting piece of work that even the fiercest opponents of U.S. military adventurism had grudgingly admitted that making viewers flinch in empathy for a webcam was an impressive feat. The Eagle had borne the dictator out in a fireman's carry, the man's face turned away from the waiting exterior cameras except for one final shot of terror that the film had ended on, zooming out to show that the man had literally wet his pants on the journey from his private panic room to the surface. The American Eagle had been told that he could expect to testify at the dictator's war crimes trial, but eight years on, he was still waiting to be summoned.

At last, the warden spoke. "Someone please sign this person in on the visitor log."

The Eagle didn't set off the metal detector—he'd stashed

his keys and phone on the roof of a Jackson Heights office tower on his way to Rikers—but he submitted to a pat-down anyway. The C.O. who patted him down tried to stay calm, but his heart was racing and his hands trembled.

THEY LED HIM to a conference room with two bolted-down chairs on either side of a bolted-down steel table with a scratched surface. There were no cameras—not even the little pinhole kinds that humans couldn't see with their naked eyes. It was a room that was used for lawyer-client meetings. While the Eagle waited for Robinson to be brought out, he experimented with the table, tapping it, looking for its resonant points. By the time Robinson arrived, he had his spot picked.

Robinson was wheeled in by a deputy with a sour expression; the deputy said nothing as he wheeled Robinson to the table, locked down the chair's brakes from behind, and left, ostentatiously locking the door behind him.

The Eagle looked at Robinson. He was haggard and unshaven, and smelled of stale B.O. It wouldn't be easy to shower at Rikers while in a cast. Robinson stared back.

The Eagle found his spot on the table and started to drub his thumb on it softly and rapidly, setting up a beehive hum that rattled off the stone walls. "While I'm doing this, most mics will not be able to capture our speech," he said, projecting his voice so Robinson could hear it over the drone.

"That's a cute trick. You have a lot of those."

"For what it's worth, I'm sorry."

"You didn't hit me." Robinson shifted painfully in his seat.

"I admit that I didn't think this through before I acted. What I saw, it made me furious."

"How do you think I felt?"

The Eagle shut up. He knew that the person with a real problem here was Wilbur Robinson, not the alien being whom the humans had called the American Eagle for more than a century.

"Let me tell you a funny story. That cop that crippled me? Bianchi? First time I saw him, I was nineteen years old and he was on the S.C.U., the Street Crime Unit. That doesn't exist anymore, but they were pure hooligans. They had special t-shirts printed up, white on black, tight to show off all those muscles, with a quote from Mr. Ernest Hemingway: 'There is no hunting like the hunting of man, and those who have hunted armed men long enough and liked it, never care for anything else thereafter.' Those motherfuckers used to walk the actual streets of New York Actual City with those actual words on their actual t-shirts, and no one in authority said shit. No one believed the reports of their brutality. No one saw fit to ask why a peace officer sworn to uphold the law would be walking around wearing a shirt like that.

"Those gentlemen of the law, they invented a new kind of stop-and-frisk, called it 'social rape.' A social rape is when you're walking down the street, minding your own business, when along comes a squad of these S.C.U. types, maybe they're wearing their literary-type t-shirts, and they grab you, and they strip you mother-naked, right there on the sidewalk, balls swinging, cock out, and they bend you over and they grease up your asshole and stick a gloved finger up it, right there, right there on the street, in front of your friends, in front of your wife, in front of your *kids*. There has never been a group of heterosexual men more interested in the contents of the assholes of Black men than those fine police officers of the S.C.U. 'Social rape,' can you believe that?

"Your Sergeant Bianchi, he's had his fingers in a lot of

assholes. Not mine, but on the block, he was always the one who would make a show of snapping on that blue glove there, looking around, making sure everyone saw him do it, especially the fellow he was getting ready to search. Like the Spanish Inquisition, the old 'showing of the instruments,' making sure the victim knows what's about to happen to him, giving him a long moment to think about it, *anticipate* it.

"Your Sergeant Bianchi is a grade-A sadistic son-of-a-bitch, and I promise you NYPD knew about it. But that mother-fucker was still driving around with his gun and badge, with a *promotion*, and this week, he crippled me for life, and now I'm facing prison time, real time, if I don't drop my complaint against him.

"For that son-of-a-bitch to be doing what he's doing, there have to be a lot of people in on it: the D.A., the judge, his commanding officer, the other cops in the cruiser with him. Bianchi isn't any rotten apple, he's a prototype, Mr. Eagle, the very model of a modern major bushwhacker, and you can tell because every time he did it, he got promoted. He's how things are *supposed* to work, so you'll forgive me if I'm just not all that interested in how you feel about the injustice of seeing me lying out on the ground while Sergeant Bianchi and his pals beat me nearly to death for no reason at all."

Robinson's heart rate was elevated and his hands were trembling very slightly. The American Eagle kept on drubbing his thumb on the table, wondering whether there was anything he could say that wouldn't make things worse.

"I'm sorry," he ventured at last.

"Yeah, I can tell you are. But I'm not an act of contrition. I'm a human being, and this is my life you're playing with."

He thought about that, really thought. The American Eagle knew a lot of secrets and had seen a lot of things that no one had seen, and things that very, very few people had seen, but he rarely had cause to think about them, not this way.

"I'm really sorry. I have never asked you what you wanted me to do, and that was stupid and arrogant. Can I ask you now?"

Robinson grunted, and quirked his neat mustache in an embryonic smile. "You just figured that out, huh? Guess being a man of steel means that you get rusty around the brains."

The Eagle smiled back. "I suppose that's true. At least, I can't argue with it, given the way things are going now."

"Well, the thing is, the time to ask me what I wanted from you was *before* you created this situation. I would have told you to record it, put the video on YouTube, give it to my lawyer. Now…"

"Yeah."

Robinson had a beautiful smile, even with a broken tooth and a fat lip. "They're raising money for a lawyer, I hear. People who heard about me because of what you did. So there's that. Course, I might not need that money if you'd thought before jumping in. But money for a lawyer's always better than no money and no lawyer. Public defender, all they do is tell you to plea out, save their caseloads."

"That's about what I've heard." The American Eagle looked at his drubbing thumb. "Look, can I get you anything, something to make you comfortable while you wait on an appeal for your bail hearing? Food? Money? A pillow?"

Robinson shook his head, then thought a while. "Will you take a note to my daughter? I only get to see her alternate weekends and I'm going to miss our next one."

"Of course," the Eagle said. "I can get you some paper and a pencil, then pick it up tomorrow?"

"I'd like that," Robinson said. They stared awkwardly at one another.

"I'm really sorry."

"Yeah, I know you are. I'll see you tomorrow, Mr. Eagle."

"Tomorrow, Mr. Robinson."

THE AMERICAN EAGLE got word that the protesters were massing by tuning into a drive-time traffic report. He'd deliberately avoided them when he'd attended the bail hearing, staying too high to be seen with the naked eye until he could land on the roof of a skyscraper that overlooked the courthouse, then powering down to the courthouse roof in seconds, a streak in the sky that came to an abrupt halt with millimeters to spare, then he'd used the stairs to get to the courtroom.

But the protesters had never really gone away. The crowd at the courthouse was dwarfed by the crowd that marched from the Staten Island Borough Hall to the precinct house every night during rush hour, snarling traffic and raising a chorus of horns that the drive-time newscasters loved to get in the background as they aired call-ins from furious drivers who wanted to condemn the whole affair, from Wilbur Robinson ("The police don't do that if you're just minding your own business—when are we going to get the *whole* story about what happened that day?") to the protesters ("Those bums wanna help the Blacks, why don't they teach them some skills so they can get jobs?") and especially the Eagle ("Never liked the dude. Who knows who he really stands for, is all I'm saying? It sure ain't law and order, I can tell you that much.").

But the protests got bigger every day, not smaller ("They're busing in protesters from out of state now, agitators. Russians are getting those people all fired up with fake Facebook news.") and the longer the protests went on, the more of a coalition they became: undocumented immigrant solidarity groups, anarchists in ski masks, Occupy veterans carrying anti-capitalist slogans, Marxists with newspapers that no one wanted to read.

Traffic on Staten Island had turned into a running joke. The bike racks around the ferry docks were jammed as commuters stopped even trying to get a car to and from home. The hot dog vendors were doing a land-office business. The cops were *pissed,* and had arrested dozens of people on the bullshittiest of charges: littering, spitting, and, of course, stop-and-frisked "public displays of marijuana."

They were halfway to the precinct house by the time he touched down on a gas station roof to get a look at things. There were cops all over place. He spotted snipers on some of the other roofs (they didn't spot him). A portable guard tower on a cherry picker loomed over the intersection the protesters were filing through, ostentatiously studded with CCTVs and antennas that were doubtlessly hoovering up information from every working phone for a mile around.

"NO JUSTICE NO PEACE" was the chant, and there was a school marching band in the protest, white uniforms with silver piping and tall hats, drumming time for the chanters, brass bells of their horns raising in unison to blat out a golden note for each stanza; a kid with shoulders like a line-backer oomp-oomp-oomped on a sousaphone, walking up and down a major scale that gave the marchers a bounce in their steps.

The Eagle yearned to join them, but of course he didn't. When you're the American Eagle, everything you do Means Something, and he'd known that for the long years he'd spent among humans. Just once, he'd allowed himself to forget that and look where it had got him.

The protesters filed through the intersection, bouncing and

chanting, laughing and horsing around and unsuccessfully selling Marxist newspapers.

The Eagle could hear the high-pitched encrypted whine of the police radio, sense its volume even if he couldn't decrypt it and understand its message. He gradually became aware that it was growing, rising to a squeal that ratcheted through his skull like a dentist drill. He looked around him, varying his focus to peer down the long avenues, but he couldn't see anything out of the ordinary. Finally, he took to the sky, just to get a better vantage. He went up along the back of an apartment block, following the course of its ventilation shaft, where there were no windows, then crested the roof and saw the source of all the chatter: the NYPD had amassed an army.

Down the streets of Staten Island, there trundled columns of MRAPs, armored personnel carriers that were basically gunless tanks. These ones bore water cannons and the telltale dishes of Active Denial Systems—pain-rays that would make you feel like your face was being incinerated from the inside out. He'd seen them used on crowds in Afghanistan, watched crowds of protesters trample each other as they were overwhelmed by the unbearable sensation of being roasted alive. He hadn't been happy to be on the same team as the people wielding that machine, but they were there fighting the Taliban and that was a team he *definitely* didn't want to be on.

Watching these devices get wheeled into position for use on New Yorkers did something to the American Eagle. He'd seen striking New Yorkers beaten up by Pinkertons; watched the Stonewall uprising from a nearby vantage point, flown back from Syria in time to help dig survivors and bodies out of the rubble of the Twin Towers. He'd rescued trapped secretaries and C.E.O.s from stuck elevators in blackouts and plucked people out of the waves during Sandy. He'd seen New Yorkers scared, brave, defiant, beaten, noble, and cowardly, and he'd never once wondered which side he was on. Now he had to choose a side between New York and New Yorkers.

"Shit," he whispered. The American Eagle didn't swear.

He watched as a column swung around a corner to block Stuyvesant Place, a block ahead of the protesters. Another column swung into place behind the protesters, hemming them in. NYPD cops in full battle dress—armor, visors, shields, helmets, conspicuous gas-masks—marched in military ranks between the MRAPs and the police buses behind them, banging their batons on their shields, chanting, "WHOSE STREETS? OUR STREETS," which was a pretty tasteless sort of joke, in the Eagle's view. Hardly "Serve and Protect."

The protesters pulled up short and looked around. The music died. They started to hold up their phones, aiming their lenses at the cops, recording and streaming, sending up a squeal of electromagnetic noise that made the Eagle wince until he damped it.

A baby cried. Another, and then some of the younger kids. The cops thumped their shields, "WHOSE STREETS? OUR STREETS!"

The kid with the bass drum gave it an experimental thump, then another, then set up a booming rhythm, BOOM BOOM BOOM and the snare kicked in and then the cymbals crashed and—"WHOSE STREETS? OUR STREETS!" and the protesters started marching in place, adding the tromp of their feet to the defiant music.

The column ahead of them lurched forward, the MRAPs with their huge, squared-off dishes revving their engines and slow-rolling, the ranks of masked and helmeted cops pacing them from behind and between.

From a bullhorn on the cherry picker guard tower. "CLEAR

THE AREA." It was tooth-rattlingly loud, and obviously farci-
cal, because the protesters were fully boxed, with no way to
go forward or back. The sound made the babies start crying
again.

The band picked up the tempo, and the chant split—"NO
JUSTICE NO PEACE" and "WHOSE STREETS? OUR
STREETS" in counterpoint, coming together on the "eace" in
"peace" and "eets" in "streets," getting funkier.

"CLEAR THE AREA IMMEDIATELY."

The column behind the protesters started to roll, too. The
chant wasn't just defiance, it was courage, too, a way to keep
the group together, to stop it from becoming a terrified mob.
The drumming got faster. Phone cameras all around, trained
on the faceless visors, the remorseless rolling armor.

Parents scooped up their children. Some sought refuge deep
in the crowd. Others stayed at the edge, where it would be
easier to run.

The columns halted again. The American Eagle could see the
buses rolling into position behind the officers. Enough buses,
he thought, to take every one of these people off to jail.

He'd let them take Wilbur Robinson off to jail, trusted that
his moral authority would hold the system to account, force it
to reckon fairly with the kind of person it was accustomed to
treating with utmost unfairness. Should he let the NYPD take
the rest of these people, hundreds of them, off to jail, too?

His body answered before his mind was able to consciously
formulate its response, taking flight and interposing itself
between the protesters and the forward column. The active
denial system wouldn't be able to hurt him; that he was sure of.

Everyone stopped what they were doing and stared at him:
chanters and musicians, protesters and cops. The guy in the
sniper nest had the presence (or absence?) of mind to point

his rifle at the American Eagle. The Eagle didn't like that, no one should be pointing firearms in a crowded city. Not an American city. Not New York City.

"Put it down," he barked. He could do drill sergeant better than any U.S.M.C. top-kick, and when he projected, he could raise his voice to a volume that would leave a human's ears ringing. He was that loud now.

The sniper twitched involuntarily and the Eagle saw his finger tighten on the trigger, but he was able to check the reflex before he fired. Good.

The Eagle glowered at the cops on the line. Their tilted, visored faces looked blankly back at him. "These people have my safe passage for their peaceful protest. You will disperse your column and stand down. If there is any outbreak of civil unrest, you will be permitted to deal with it in a measured, proportionate way. You will not use those less-lethal weapons."

The silence was broken by the whupping of an overhead news chopper, then another, then three NYPD choppers. The phone cameras on the ground tracked the cameras beneath the helicopters overhead. The world was watching. The American Eagle was doing something he'd done often, when Taliban irregulars tried to stop girls from going to school, or Thai troops rushed an uprising of democracy activists. Americans had cheered the footage of these intercessions. Would they cheer when he checked the rush of New York's Finest? He had a strong suspicion they wouldn't.

Some of the kids in the crowd were cheering, though, and among the grownups, some of the tension had dissipated. Even a few of the cops seemed to be relieved, judging from their armor-obscured body language. Only a psycho would have been looking forward to what had seemed inevitable a moment before.

The cops were all looking up at him through their visors. He looked back, and one of the cops gave him The Nod, a respectful gesture of thanks. He was the American Eagle again, hero of a nation, defender of all that was right and good.

THE NEWS NETWORKS *slaughtered* him. No one had footage of the crowd before the cops showed up, so instead they used B-roll of protests that had turned violent, then long-lens shots of the cops' armor columns moving in on the protesters, then the American Eagle intimidating the NYPD with his superhuman powers, letting these apparent lawbreakers go free.

Activist Twitter was a little kinder, but even the people who praised him for intervening to uphold Americans' rights against one of their own police forces always had an implied or explicit "*finally*" in their tweets.

"This is a declaration of *war*," said a talk-radio blowhard. "This monster from the stars styles himself *The American Eagle* but he is no American. He isn't even a human. He has no allegiance to our planet, nor our species, let alone this *country*. We got in bed with an extraterrestrial creature and now we've got to figure out how to divorce him. This isn't a comic book: we don't have any handy kryptonite lying around. This has *got* to be our top priority now: our nation cannot be said to be secure while it is in conflict with an unstoppable, inhuman super-being."

Conspiracy Twitter was a dumpster fire. There had always been low-key conspiracy theories about the Eagle, going back centuries: he was a demon summoned by Freemasons to subjugate America; he was a secret laboratory experiment gone horribly wrong (or, sometimes, exactly right); he was a special effect created by hologram projectors or AI-based video-doctoring algorithms, and the people who claimed to have seen him were hypnotized, or crisis actors, or special effects themselves.

Then Bruce asked to see him and brought along a small, air-gapped tablet on which he'd stored PDFs of the Intellipedia entries about the Eagle, along with their edit histories, as NSA analysts and private-sector contractors from Booz Allen and Palantir and S.A.I.C. debated their own conspiracy theories about his use as a secret Chinese (or European, or Russian, or private-sector crime syndicate) asset, and what someone might have offered him or threatened him with in order to turn him.

"This is insane," the Eagle said. Bruce had arranged the rendezvous for one of his safe houses, the penthouse of a willowy, ninety-story building that was almost entirely empty, consisting of unoccupied condos that served as safe-deposit boxes in the sky for offshore criminals. It was Bruce's place, so the generic designer-showroom furniture slid aside to allow access to arms caches, a small operating theater, and a B.D.S.M. dungeon that was meant to be discovered by anyone who went looking for the dark secret of the billionaire playboy's playpen.

"Not insane, just professionally paranoid. You know these people. You've spent decades around them. What the fuck did you think was going to happen?"

Bruce didn't swear often. It made the Eagle anxious.

"Bruce—"

He held up his hands. "Just stop." He turned to stare out the window—silvered on the other side for privacy—and looked into infinity, over the rooftops of midtown Manhattan. "They know about Lois." He whispered it and a normal human wouldn't have heard it. The Eagle heard it just fine.

"Lois who?"

He turned back and glared. "Don't fuck around, Eagle.

They know where you live. They know who you are, when you aren't the American Eagle. They know who you spend time with. They *know* about *Lois*." He muttered a number. Ten digits. The American Eagle's Social Security Number, the latest one, the one that was supposed to be ironclad. "They're the NSA, asshole. You think that your opsec is up to defeating them? They figured all this shit out *years* ago. It's their *job*. Your little games can't beat their facial recognition, their pattern analysis."

"How do you know all this, Bruce?" The Eagle was angry, something he wasn't used to, but that had become more familiar just lately. "Don't answer that, I know: it's because *you sold them the tools,* right?"

Bruce didn't have to answer.

Part of him knew this, of course, the same way that he knew that the NRO could reconstruct his flight paths and that there were government labs where generations of scientists had studied his hair follicles and shed skin cells. But it's one thing to be known, and another to be *scrutinized*.

Another thing altogether to be the subject of a plan of attack.

"Look, Eagle, all I'm trying to say is that you have set yourself on a path that cannot possibly end well. The best-case scenario right now is pretty terrible, and it only gets worse from here. I told you I'd hire a good lawyer for Robinson, and I have. The best."

"What about all those protesters who were about to have their faces roasted by an active denial ray? Do they get lawyers, too?"

Bruce made a pained face. "You know that's not how it works—"

"I imagine *you* know, so I'll take your word for it. You make them, don't you? Just another service your family business provides to the municipal, state, and national governments of the world?"

Bruce shook his head. "America has a legitimate interest in defending itself. Would you rather that the troops in Afghanistan use AR-15s? Should the NYPD be firing rubber bullets? Or live ammo?"

"Maybe they just shouldn't shoot at anyone."

"Are you volunteering to fight every one of America's wars and police all of its streets? I know you're superhuman, Eagle, but you're not omnipotent. So long as American cops and soldiers are going to be warfighting and crimefighting, they're going to need tools to support them. I'm not going to let you make me feel like a supervillain for supplying them with those tools."

The American Eagle knew what was supposed to happen next. He was supposed to acknowledge that no one could be held responsible if someone else misused the things they made or distributed—it was the argument about the Taliban fighters that the CIA had armed in Afghanistan and it was the argument about Sergeant Bianchi's buddies on the line with their face-roasting rays.

He'd heard this argument so many times. Only a very unreasonable person could possibly object to it.

He wasn't in a mood to be reasonable.

"It doesn't really matter to me whether you feel like a supervillain or not. All that matters to me is that there were armed cops about to torture peaceful protesters, including children, with a weapon you sold them."

"If I hadn't sold them, someone else—"

He held up his hands. "I'm not going to even dignify that with a response, Bruce, no more than you would if it were some pimp explaining why he'd turned out a teenager to peddle her ass on the street."

They glared at each other. Finally Bruce sighed and looked away.

"We're on the same side. Literally: we have stood side by side, fighting together. I'm not telling you this because I want to be an asshole. I understand where you're coming from. It's a big, messy, imperfect world, and we're a messy, imperfect species. I know there's plenty of times when I want to start knocking heads together, and I'm a human being. I can't imagine how frustrating this must be for you."

The American Eagle had been living among humans when Bruce's grandfather was in diapers. He'd loved humans, saved humans, fought for them. When supervillains taunted him for being an alien, he'd laughed at their clumsy speciesism, their unfounded belief that he was insecure about his status as an honorary *H. sap*. Why should he have any anxiety on that score?

"I'm pretty good at coping with it, Bruce. I've had a lot of experience."

Bruce's expression made it clear that "experience" was no substitute for twenty-three chromosomal pairs in a leftward-twisting corkscrew.

"Look, Eagle, all I'm trying to say is that if your goal is to make sure that Wilbur Robinson gets a fair trial, you're not achieving that goal. If your job is to muster public sentiment for police accountability, you're *really* not achieving that goal. I will stipulate that you're right about everything, but this isn't about right and wrong. You can be right, or you can be effective. Being effective means not reminding the entire human race that you are an unstoppable spaceman who only follows the rules when it suits you. As soon as you start reminding them of that fact, it will become the focus."

"So what do you think I should do?"

Bruce looked away again. "You need to back off. Just disappear. For a while. Years. Decades, maybe. You have no *idea* how panicked they are out there in spookland. There's plenty of people who never trusted you. I don't think you understand how much your champions have stuck their necks out for you over the years. That's over now. Maybe forever, Eagle. You have really fucked this up."

"Back off, huh?"

"Look, if it's about Lois, I can fix that. I'll talk to them. She's a noncombatant, and she's press. There's plenty of ugly possibilities if they move on her. I'll protect her. I'll also keep paying for Wilbur Robinson's lawyers. We're appealing the bail decision; filed today, and we've leaned on a clerk to get a hearing this afternoon. We're asking for permission to get him to the Mayo Clinic to see an orthopedic surgeon about his leg."

"That's how you think this should all be taken care of, huh?"

Bruce nodded solemnly. "Running headfirst into the system doesn't change the system, it just gives you a headache. If you want justice for Wilbur Robinson, this is the most expedient and reliable approach."

"And what about Sergeant Bianchi?" He knew the answer.

Bruce made a sour face. "That guy is a piece of shit, sure. I've talked to the Commissioner; they're going to offer him a buyout, enough to make it worth his while to take early retirement. Going to call it partial disability for his P.T.S.D. from, you know—" He looked pointedly at the Eagle.

"So he gets rich and walks away a free man?"

"Without a badge, without a gun, without his police union behind him."

"Without a criminal record. Without any problems getting a job as a cop somewhere else, or in private security. Without any recognition that he'd done anything wrong."

Bruce shook his head. "Be realistic. This is the best we can hope for right now. Don't let the perfect be the enemy of the good."

"I'll take it under consideration."

Bruce grabbed him by the shoulders and stared into his eyes. "Don't fuck this up, Eagle. I know you've been doing this for a long time, but things are different now. No one cares about what you did a century ago, but they'll remember what you did last week for a long time. Don't make it worse."

The Eagle didn't say anything. He'd never kept a scrapbook of all his accomplishments—it would be a hell of a clue if anyone ever found it—but other people had, and he'd seen them go for top dollar on eBay in fierce bidding among collectors who would pay thousands for albums of yellowing newspaper clippings and autographed headshots, generations' worth of lives saved, wrongs righted, villains vanquished.

"Think about this story, Eagle: 'Once he was our hero, but then something went wrong with him, and he became our greatest threat.' You are stronger than any of us, and you can fly and see through walls—but you don't have superpowers of persuasion. The people who are pissed off at you? That's *their* superpower. They can convince people of anything. And you have got them scared. You don't want to pit your superpowers against theirs. They have the kinds of powers you can't just punch out."

The Eagle had met propagandists over the years, letting them talk him into posing for photo ops, delaying missions until the cameras could be rolled into position. They'd always struck him as unrealistically confident about their own abilities, but on the other hand, it was hard to argue with results.

"Why would the NSA want to stick up for dirty NYPD cops?"

Bruce smiled. "It's not so much that they'll stick up for them—but imagine the kinds of countermeasures you're fielding against New York's finest being used against the same weapons systems in Kandahar province. If you can neutralize those systems, then you have to be neutralized."

That made perfect, terrible sense. The Eagle had an untethered feeling of dread and remorse, and the carefully suppressed fear that he'd burned the wrong bridge bubbled up.

"You can make sure Lois is safe?"

"Please don't do anything stupid, Eagle."

"You can keep her safe, though?"

"Eagle—"

"Bruce, I need to know if you can keep her safe."

He sighed. "I can keep her safe."

The American Eagle nodded his thanks and launched himself off the balcony.

THE DEMONSTRATION IN support of Sergeant Bianchi was the whitest, raggedest gathering he'd ever seen in New York: angry guys, older guys, a smattering of alt-right kids with hipster haircuts, a few glowering skinheads, some open-carry nutjobs, and veterans in uniform. At the front, ranks of cops in dress uniforms, seemingly okay with being part of the same crowd as people carrying placards with openly racist slogans. Not to mention the arts-and-crafts squad who'd whipped up an effigy of the American Eagle out of wheat paste and tempura paints.

He watched them from a rooftop, forty storeys above them—too far for any human eye to discern him, close enough that he could read their lips as they chanted: "HEY HEY IT'S THE U.S.A. BUG EYED MONSTERS GO AWAY." He hadn't heard the phrase "bug-eyed monster" since the 1980s, and even then it had been an anachronism, but these guys (all guys) were the anachronism squad.

They marched from City Hall to DHS headquarters on Varick Street, and the cops lined the steps, facing out, an honor guard behind the speakers, while the crowd stood on the plaza, facing back and listening as they were harangued by megaphone. Onlookers looked on from around the edges, some jeering and others cheering.

The American Eagle had been marched against before. Al-Shabaab had organized mass street protests—mandatory protests—against his presence in Somalia, filling town squares with thousands of halfhearted chanters, firing their weapons into the sky as punctuation for their denunciations.

He'd flown into some of these, catching the bullets in his bare hands and letting them trickle down over the stage, turning aerial cartwheels that made the kids (and even some of the grownups) giggle, driving the militants into furies that would have been terrifying for the crowd if not for the American Eagle's imperviousness to their rages and bullets, and his ability to protect the crowd from reprisals.

Could he do that again here? Would the NYPD open fire on him right there in Greenwich Village? He doubted it. Even Bianchi had more common sense than that. Sergeant Bianchi liked to do his dirty work when the cameras were off. When the cameras were rolling, he was performatively aggrieved, a spat-upon soldier who had tried to do his duty and been punished for it.

He was saying as much now, from his perch on top of the stairs, into the megaphone he'd been given, and while he wasn't the most articulate orator the Eagle had ever heard, he knew his crowd.

The Eagle spotted the counter-demonstrators when they

were still two blocks away. They were a lot browner than the Bianchi crowd, but by no means entirely brown—a New York mix: multiracial, well-dressed, funky, with signs that were much funnier than BUG-EYED MONSTERS GO AWAY.

At their front, walking with a cane, was Wilbur Robinson, his expression fixed in a mask that might have been fear and might have been determination.

He set their pace, so they went slow, and soon there were cruisers pacing them, and the news of their impending arrival reached the police demonstrators as one after another they checked their text messages or put their heads together to talk.

The people on the street recognized Wilbur Robinson, took pictures—a few trickled in to join the march. The mass worked its way slowly towards the cops, and when they turned the corner so that both camps could see each other, they all stiffened noticeably. Bianchi stopped talking into his megaphone and squinted at them, made a face like he'd just smelled a fart. He tried to pick up his speech from where he'd left off, fumbled with his notes. No one was paying attention anyway.

Wilbur Robinson led his column of marchers towards the mass of white cops and Nazis and closeted racists and authoritarians. The Nazis—there were only a dozen of them—chanted a slogan that contained the N-word, drawing attention from news cameras and people's phones. Everyone around them edged away, not wanting to be captured in the same shot as someone openly using a slur that they more commonly reserved for private company. From the Eagle's vantage point, the little clot of white-polo-shirt-wearing Nazis with their red armbands looked like the pupil of a great, seething eye of pro-cop demonstrators.

The two camps were now close enough that they looked like they might merge. The on-duty cops—who had only a moment before been raptly listening to Sergeant Bianchi's fumble-tongued speech about "protecting decent people" and "social justice warriors who'd let animals run wild" and "telling it like it is"—started to move between them, to serve as a buffer. Wilbur Robinson continued to walk forward slowly, relentlessly, until he ran up against the uniformed police lines.

"Excuse me, sir, may I get past, please?" The American Eagle could read his lips from his vantage point, but even if he hadn't been able to, Robinson's body language was plain to see.

The uniform cop didn't budge. The counterprotesters started to chant, "LET HIM PASS LET HIM PASS." Bianchi, megaphone in hand, standing on the steps, looked confused and angry. He'd lost control over the scene, and now he looked foolish and cowardly, a pumped-up gym-jockey backed by a rank of dress-uniform cops, protected by another rank of regular uniform cops, all to keep him from being confronted by a slender Black man with a cane.

Like a sleepwalker, he drifted down the stairs, walking slowly through the crowd, which parted for him, all eyes on him, until he was standing on the other side of the cops who blocked Robinson's way.

"You got something to say to me?" His back was to the Eagle, but his body language spoke volumes, and the words were picked up on the open mic of his bullhorn. He fumbled with it, but before he could click it off, Robinson spoke.

"I want you to know that I'm not going to give up." The cop between Robinson and Bianchi shifted uneasily.

"Are you threatening me?"

Robinson considered this for a long moment. "I expect I am, Sergeant Bianchi. You are a disgrace to your uniform. When you dragged me out of my car and crippled me, you committed a crime. When you lied about it, you committed another one.

When your friends covered up for you, they committed a crime. The fact that you're standing here whining, and I'm out on bail and facing thirty-five years in prison, means that there's no justice at all in this city.

"Someday, people are going to realize that. Someday, enough white folks, enough *rich* white folks are going to realize that living in a lawless city where hooligans like you can administer beatings and then get your victims locked up for the crime of complaining about it is no good for them.

"But long before then, everyone else is going to wake up to that fact. Brown people. White people. Chinese people and Puerto Ricans and everyone else. They're going to see that you are proof that the system is broken beyond repair, that you and all your friends can't be 'reformed' into something that New York can tolerate. When that day comes, it's going to be you and your hooligan friends against all of New York City, and you will lose that fight, Sergeant Bianchi.

"So yes, I expect I am a threat to you. And nothing you do will change that. Lock me up, I'll be a threat to you. Set me free, I'll be a threat to you. It's not over, Sergeant Bianchi, but this is the beginning of the end for you, if not for the hooliganism you represent. I don't give up. I always get my man."

Incredibly, Bianchi hadn't had the good sense to turn off his megaphone during this exchange and the sound ricocheted off the building and into the hungry mics of the phones aimed at the pair.

Bianchi was good at being a tough guy, but he was no good at being a calm guy. He bulged: veins in his forehead and throat, the point of his jawbone as he flexed and ground it, his neck red and straining at his collar. He clicked his megaphone off with a hand that visibly shook.

Wilbur Robinson smiled serenely at the rage-filled cop,

knowing that there was a decent chance he was about to get hit, knowing that if such a thing were to come to pass, there would be chaos. Wilbur Robinson had run out of fucks to give about chaos.

So had the American Eagle. He silently cheered on Wilbur Robinson, joining in with the loud cheers from the counter-demonstrators who'd been held behind the police lines.

After the mic was off, Bianchi called Wilbur Robinson a name that included the N-word. He was in profile to the American Eagle, but the mouth shapes were unmistakable, as was the reaction of the counter-demonstrators who saw it and perhaps heard it. Bianchi wasn't a quiet man.

Robinson's smile didn't waver. He said only one word, or perhaps he only mouthed it: *Coward.*

That's when Sergeant Bianchi slugged him.

THE AMERICAN EAGLE didn't intervene in the ensuing riot. There were cops on the scene and they at least were conscious of the cameras on them, even if Bianchi wasn't.

He watched as the police pulled apart the struggling bodies, separating them into two camps, forcing them behind hastily installed sawhorses. A skinhead threw a bottle over the police line into the midst of the counter-demonstrators, who dodged it. When it shattered, some of the glass cut a small child—she was no more than five or six—and her wails made everyone look at her. While their attention was elsewhere, the skinhead flipped the bird with both hands and then melted into the crowd. The Eagle tracked him and considered swooping down to grab him.

Wilbur Robinson was sitting on the ground, being attended by an EMT who was shining lights into his eyes and carefully feeling him from toes to skull for fractures and sprains. Reading his lips, the Eagle saw that he was repeating, "I'm okay, I'm okay," though Bianchi had given him a black eye that was swelling up despite the EMT's ice pack.

Robinson eventually pushed the EMT away and struggled to his feet. A younger man, one of the counter-demonstrators, dressed in a narrow-lapeled black suit, neat hair and wire-rims, like a latter-day Malcolm X, rushed to help him. They conferred briefly and he called out to a friend who brought him another megaphone.

Robinson lifted it to his lips.

"Officers, I would like to swear out an assault complaint against Gioffre Bianchi. I would like you to arrest him and charge him. I have many witnesses here who saw him attack me, including each and every one of you." He stared at them, mildly, unblinkingly. "Please, do your duty."

Not one cop moved.

He brought the bullhorn back to his lips. "Sergeant Gioffre Bianchi, I place you under citizen's arrest." He walked toward the cop, who planted his feet and stuck his chin out. "Please, come with me."

Bianchi shoved him, and his cane flew out into the crowd as he windmilled his arms.

Slowly, he got back to his feet. The younger man brought him his cane. He walked toward Bianchi again. Again, Bianchi shoved him. This time, he cracked his head on the pavement and sat up slowly, obviously dizzy, rubbing his head gingerly. The young man helped him back to his feet. People around— not just the counter-demonstrators, but the spectators, too, and there were more of those every minute—shouted at him, cheering him, telling him not to get hurt, calling Bianchi a coward, exhorting the cops around them to do something.

The cops exchanged nervous looks. An officer arrived in a cruiser with its siren and lights going and made his way to Bianchi. He spoke too quietly to be heard, even by the American Eagle. Bianchi shook his head once and started walking toward Robinson. He bunched his fists together and got ready to swing. The Eagle could see it would be a hell of a blow, with all the muscle Bianchi had put on pumping iron, the kind of thing that could break Robinson's jaw. The Eagle was about to leap off the building and arrow down to intercept the blow, when a hand in an armored glove caught Bianchi's wrist and held it. Bianchi tried to swing and just succeeded in knocking himself off balance, dangling from Bruce's iron grip as Bruce stared down at him from within his cowl. He shook his head slowly, keeping eye contact with Bianchi.

Bianchi had gone pale, from surprise or from the pain of his wrist bones grinding together, the Eagle couldn't say which. Bruce spoke, lips visible beneath the peaked nose guard of his cowl.

"Don't. Do. That."

He released Bianchi's wrist with a snarl and let him fall to the ground, and before he hit, Bruce was already stalking toward the captain, his cape billowing behind him. "Do your goddamned job," he said, his face inches from the officer's, and then he was off, leaping onto his motorcycle and roaring off down an alley. From his vantage, the Eagle could see Bruce emerge from another alley in civvies, the bike transformed to a rusty beater that he chained to a lamppost. The Eagle supposed Bruce would send the boy out later to retrieve it.

The officer led Bianchi into a cruiser, letting him sit in the front. He quietly Mirandized Bianchi while he sat, wooden faced and fuming.

The two sides looked at one another; then, as a mass, they dissipated. The show was over for today.

LOIS WOULDN'T ANSWER her phone. After two days of unreturned messages, the American Eagle put on civvies and took the subway to her apartment. She didn't answer the buzzer. He started to feel a slow roil of fear, and walked around back and climbed a dumpster and leaped onto the fire escape, then climbed it with convincingly human awkwardness, found Lois's window and peered in, using x-ray vision to look through the whole place, though even a quick glance showed him that the place was empty, cleaned out.

Forcing himself to be calm, he called the newspaper and asked to be put through to her extension, and got voicemail saying she was "on an overseas assignment" and referring him to another reporter if he had any juicy tips.

He had barely hung up the phone when it rang again.

"Hi, Bruce."

"She's safe. But she wanted out, so I helped her get out."

"Bruce—"

"It was her idea. She had figured it out. Had heard from her intelligence community sources that things were happening, things that could involve her. She's fine. I found her a source in a major Russian defense contractor who's willing to reveal how they spy on the oligarchs for the Kremlin. She's happy as a pig in shit over there, believe me."

"She's in Russia?"

"Safer than here, right now. You've made enemies, you understand?"

"And she didn't want to talk to me about it?"

"She was very adamant on the subject." There was an

awkward pause. "Give it time. You have lots of that, right?" Another pause. "Or don't. Find someone else. Or take a sabbatical. You've earned it and God knows you're not gonna get much done the way things stand. You really fucked things up."

The American Eagle groped for words that wouldn't come.

"Come on, don't you have a fortress of solitude in the Arctic or something?"

"That was a promotional stunt." It had been decades since he'd relocated the remains of his landing craft to the dark side of the moon.

"Well, let me know if you need a place to hide out. I've got places besides Russia where you could cool off."

"That's okay. I can take care of myself."

"I know you can, brother. I just wish you would."

Stung, the Eagle hung up.

WILBUR ROBINSON LIVED in a low-rise apartment building on the wrong side of Staten Island's Mason-Dixon line, with a basketball court out front and community gardens out back. His apartment was on the third floor, and he was alone in it when the American Eagle rang his bell, timing it so that there was no one on that floor anywhere near their doors and the elevators were empty.

He opened the door on the chain, took a long look at the American Eagle, then closed the door and slipped the chain and let him in.

"You drink or eat?"

"Not really."

"I do." Robinson's dinner was on the dining room table, a plate with a hamburger and some peas and carrots, a glass of beer next to it. He sat down at the table and took a bite of the burger and chewed it thoughtfully, staring at the Eagle.

"You ever hear of Emmett Till?"

The Eagle nodded slowly.

Robinson set his burger down and rose painfully to his feet, went to a bookcase next to his TV, and got down a thick hardcover book, bristling with Post-it notes with neat lettering on their protruding tongues. He peered at these, then opened the book. The American Eagle looked at the photo there reflexively, though he knew what he'd see, then looked away.

"I imagine you've seen this picture."

"I have."

Emmett Till lay in a casket in his parents' living room, a fourteen-year-old boy in a Sunday suit, the only recognizably human parts of him beneath the suit. The head that emerged from the white starched collar was a pulped mess, only hinting at facial features. He'd been beaten, mutilated, and dumped in a river by two white men who thought he had whistled at a white woman. The Eagle remembered that moment.

"I imagine you may have seen it when it was published."

"I did." It felt like an admission. Certainly, he thought he understood Robinson's point: where were you when this happened? The two men who'd admitted to the killing had been acquitted by an all-white jury.

"He was a boy, but the testimony was all about his terrifying Black body and its amazing strength. It's always about terrifying Black bodies, our superhuman strength, our incredible endurance. They have to keep hitting us, because when you hit us just once, we get back up again. I'm told that the first anti-cocaine laws were passed after a white sheriff testified that he'd had to switch to higher-caliber sidearms because

Black men weren't going down with just one shot once they'd done a line or two." Robinson gave him a long look.

He squirmed. Finally: "Superhuman strength isn't everything it's cracked up to be."

"I wouldn't have minded it. Bet Emmett Till wouldn't have minded, either."

He'd covered the trial for the paper, in a small way, doing man-on-the-streets in Times Square with New Yorkers looking on in horror at the travesty in Mississippi. He'd interview these white, upstanding northerners and they'd say all the right words, then his superhuman hearing would pick up what they *really* thought when they walked off, whispering to their friends. *Let one of them try it on my sister, they'll think that Till kid got off easy—*

"Bet he wouldn't have."

"Mr. Eagle, I can't help but notice that you had plenty of chances to fly down to the Jim Crow south and sit at a lunch counter. I can't help but notice that you didn't do any of that, but you were moved to intervene when I was getting a beating from Sergeant Bianchi and his little gang of sadists."

The Eagle nodded.

"Care to explain that discrepancy?"

The Eagle heaved a sigh. "That's a question I've asked myself more than once. I guess..." He trailed off. Robinson's apartment was homey, lived in, a poker mat and chips under the glass coffee table and folding chairs peeking out of the closet, ready to be brought out and set up when there was more company than the dining-room set could seat. The Eagle never had company, not even Lois. "I guess I just hit my limit."

Robinson looked at the photo for a long time, then closed the book. "Took you long enough."

The Eagle didn't know what to say to that. Robinson was right.

He let himself out. From behind the closed door, he heard Robinson limp across the room to put the book away.

BIANCHI WAS TAKING a nap in his cruiser when the Eagle found him. His Tempe P.D. uniform was sweaty and rumpled, his face tanned from the Arizona sun, except for the bridge of his nose, which was sunburned.

The Eagle let his shadow fall across Bianchi's face, watched him stir, then open one eye, then sit upright, reaching instinctively for his sidearm.

As Bianchi woke more fully, he took his hand away, then lowered the window.

"You enjoying yourself?"

"Not really." The Eagle hadn't worn his cape and cowl in months, not since he'd left New York. Not since the third time he'd been taunted by a human telling him to go back to where he came from. Since then, he'd been mostly walking, taking old roads that were made obsolete seventy-five years ago, when the interstates had gone in. He'd walked those roads before, in another time, another America. Or at least, an America whose story he selectively told himself. It felt weird to be wearing it now.

"We're within a hundred miles of a border. What if I asked you for proof of citizenship?" Bianchi's smile was shitty and small.

"Then I imagine we'd have a problem. I would have thought you'd have lost your appetite for problems."

"I don't back down, not from any fight where I'm in the right. Maybe you'd get me kicked off the Tempe P.D.? So what?

All that would mean is that I'd get *two* early retirements and another pension. I hear they're hiring in Florida."

"Maybe you'd go to jail this time."

"Be serious, you jamoke."

The Eagle had killed hundreds of humans. What was one more? They'd never catch him. Though of course, Bianchi's body cam was rolling. He'd have to take it with him, crush it into powder. He wouldn't leave fingerprints. He didn't *have* fingerprints.

"I don't want trouble. I just wanted to see what you'd made of yourself. Whether you'd learned anything."

"Un. Fucking. Believable." Bianchi rolled up his window, blasted the AC, put the cruiser into gear. The Eagle put a hand on the hood before it could lurch into motion, held it still while the engine ground and the wheels spun. Bianchi was about to grab for his gun again—the Eagle could almost see the nerve impulse running down his arm—when the Eagle let go and the car lurched forward, throwing Bianchi against his shoulder belt. By the time Bianchi looked back, the Eagle was long, long gone.

THE NEXT TIME he saw Wilbur Robinson, it was on YouTube. Robinson was looking better fed, and his mustache was perfectly groomed as he led a crowd that held their cameras on a cop while he frisked a young Black man. The cop looked like he wanted to punch all of them out, but he didn't.

It was an ugly scene, and the kid on the other end of the frisk wasn't enjoying any part of it. But the cop didn't find anything, and walked away looking furious.

The Eagle thought about phoning Lois. He missed her. She hadn't returned any of his calls, though, and he knew how to take a hint.

Bruce answered on the second ring. "I don't think it's a good idea for us to talk anymore."

"Really?"

"I have certain obligations, thanks to my relationship with the U.S. government, and they include helping them locate potential enemy combatants."

"Oh."

"There's some things America is willing to tolerate. Some things, though—"

"I get it."

He hung up. He wondered why he wasn't more upset. After thinking it through, watching the thunderheads roil beneath him as he hovered in the troposphere, he realized that what Bruce had said, he'd known all along. It was why he hadn't been there when Bull Connor released the dogs. Why he'd ignored all the other Wilbur Robinsons along the way. Some things, America would tolerate, but other things, it would never, ever forgive.

radicalized

ON JOE GORMAN'S thirty-sixth birthday, his wife Lacey called him three times in a row on his cell phone. He was in a meeting with his manager, a vice-president who had rescheduled twice. It had taken ten days and a latte to the VP's PA to get face time with this guy, so Joe bumped his wife to voicemail three times. She was probably calling to wish him a happy birthday or confirm something about the big dinner they were having at his favorite steak house that night.

"Do you need to get that?" The VP didn't really bother to hide his irritation.

"Sorry," Joe said and made a show of switching his phone off and pocketing it. He went back to his proposal: he'd found a logistics outsourcer who could manage all their returns, which was the most stubbornly expensive line on his division's balance sheet. He'd worked really hard on the proposal and this VP could make or break it. Within a couple minutes, though, the VP's PA knocked on the door and Joe's heart sank. Someone more important than him must have clobbered his long-sought time slot. But the PA—Gloria, a stylish middle-aged Black woman who had been with the company for longer than either Joe or the VP—spoke to Joe, not her boss.

"It's your wife, Joe."

His guts roiled. He had never been more angry at Lacey in

their eight years of marriage. She *knew* that he had this meeting. It was all he'd talked about, when he'd talked at all, when he wasn't sitting at the kitchen table with his laptop working on his proposal. Jesus fucking Christ, couldn't she handle the stupid restaurant reservation or guest list or whatever on her own? She was a grown woman. It was his *birthday*. Some birthday present.

"Sounds like you need to get that," the VP said. He sounded jocular but there was also a sardonic eye roll in there that Joe couldn't miss. "Have Gloria set up another time, OK?"

Gloria gave him a sympathetic look as he hustled out of the office, out into the parking lot, where it was blazing hot and blindingly sunny. He took out his cell phone and unlocked it and called Lacey.

"Lacey, honey—" He only called her *honey* when he was furious with her.

"Joe—" was all she got out, and then she was sobbing.

His emotions whipsawed. Lacey was *not* a crier. His mother had been a crier, and he'd dated some girls who felt everything so keenly that tears were never far beneath the surface, but Lacey wasn't like that at all. He was suddenly scared, the anger roiling around, too, but unattached.

"What is it?"

More sobbing. Then a deep breath. "I saw the doctor." A long pause. Joe wanted to hang up. More than anything. Because he knew that he was about to go through a door that led out of his life as it was and into a new, worse life. It was a door that only swung one way and once you went through it, you could never go back. There was a split second when he actually almost hung up on Lacey, but of course he didn't.

*

IT WAS STAGE-FOUR breast cancer, metastatic, nodules in her liver, pancreas, and one lung. Lacey had three months to live. Six, if they tried for the most extreme interventions. Lacey had stopped crying after the first two days and had become a laser-focused, stoic self-advocate who had read everything and even found a Dying with Dignity Facebook group that she had become the queen bee of. She'd had all these picture books about kids whose parents were dying, and she read them regularly to Madison, snugging Maddie up on her lap and reading in the same quiet, sing-song storytime cadence she'd always used at storytime, as though she wasn't preparing their six-year-old for a life without a mother.

The doctor laid out all the ways that her three months could be lengthened to six, and Lacey looked her straight in the eye and said, "If you had what I had, would you try any of those therapies?"

The doctor pursed her lips. "Honestly? No, I don't think any doctor would."

"Thank you for your honesty," is what Lacey said, and Joe knew then she wouldn't be doing anything else.

Just because you've decided to die of cancer, that doesn't stop everyone you know from consuming your last months on this Earth by sending you links to miracle cures. They deleted these and politely told everyone—even their parents—to cut that shit out, but people can't help themselves.

Lacey's mom found the link to adoptive cell transfer therapy. It wasn't woo: the US National Cancer Institute was part of the NIH, and they had gotten multiple papers on the therapy published in *Nature,* with huge numbers of citations. Joe and Lacey read the papers as best as they could, and Lacey talked about them with her dying Facebook friends, and they all decided that maybe this was worth a shot.

The way it worked was, they sequenced the genome of your tumor and looked for traits that your own white blood cells could target, then they sorted out your own white blood cells until they found some that targeted those traits, and grew 100 billion or so of those little soldiers in a lab and injected them into you. It was just a way of speeding up the slow and inefficient process by which your own body tuned its own white blood cell population, giving it a computational boost that could outrace even the fastest-mutating tumor.

Joe and Lacey even found a private doc, right there in Phoenix, who'd do the procedure. He had an appointment at Arizona State University, had published some good papers on the procedure himself, and all he needed was $1.5 million from their health insurer.

YOU KNOW WHAT happened next. Their insurer told Lacey that it was time for her to die now. If she wanted chemo and radiation and whatever, they'd pay it (reluctantly, and with great bureaucratic intransigence), but "experimental" therapies were not covered. Which, you know, OK, who wants to spend $1.5 mil on some charlatan's miracle-cure juice cleanse or crystal therapy? But adaptive cell transfer wasn't crystal healing and the NIH wasn't the local shaman.

They underwent—*Joe* underwent—a weird transformation after her last call with the supervisor's supervisor's supervisor at their health insurer. Lacey had been so good about it all, finding peace and calm and determining to make her death a good death. She'd dragged Joe out of his anger at cancer and back into his love of her and a mutual understanding that they'd make their last days together good ones, for them and for Madison.

But after the insurer turned them down, the rage came back. Maybe the therapy wouldn't have worked, but it was a *chance*, and a realistic one, not a desperate one, a real possibility that his daughter would have a mother and that he would have a wife and best friend to grow old with.

He wanted to sell the house and borrow more money from friends and family and do a GoFundMe, but Lacey wouldn't hear it. She pointed out that everything they—and all their immediate families—could spare wouldn't touch that $1.5-mil ticket, and the only thing worse than a family losing its wife and mother was that same family losing its house and savings, too. She was much smarter and much calmer than Joe.

Joe was *furious*. Joe couldn't be angry at cancer, but he could be coldly, murderously enraged at an insurance company and the people who worked there. He worked for a blue-chip, *Fortune* 100 company, and he'd bought the top tier of insurance, and they took more than $1,500 out of his paycheck every month for that coverage, and some faceless, evil fucker had just decided that they wouldn't even *try* to save his wife from a painful, grotesque death.

The anger consumed Joe. He never rescheduled that meeting with the VP. He spent all his time writing to the HR department and the CFO, and when he wasn't doing that, he was literally crying in the toilet.

And all the time, Lacey was getting sicker.

Madison grew scared of Joe, shying away when he got home. They tried switching so he was in charge of tucking her in, telling her a story and singing the requisite three songs. She endured it but it did nothing to reduce her obvious fear around him.

"Babe," Lacey said, her equivalent to his "Honey," and Joe knew he was in trouble. "You can't keep up like this. You're going to drop dead before I am. Or shoot someone. You need to get help." Refusing chemo and radiation meant that Lacey hadn't gotten thin, but the pain had been keeping her up nights and she had a hollow, otherworldly, one-foot-in-the-grave look that he could barely stand.

She took his face in her hands. "I'm *not* fooling, Joe. You get help. Because if you don't get help, our baby girl is going to have zero parents, because you are headed for a mental institution, jail, or a courtroom defending your fitness to be a father." Her eyes burned into his. "I don't have a lot of strength or time to work on this with you, Joe. I know that normally finding a shrink or whatever would be my job in our division of labor but you are going to have to step up. Am I making myself clear?"

The words made Joe furious, and the fury made Joe sad. He cried some, then said, "You're right. I will." She gave him a long, long hug, and he went to the guest room and sat on the bed with his laptop and started googling.

HE HAD EIGHT tabs' worth of Yelp reviews for local shrinks open when he found the forum. Ostensibly, it was for fathers whose wives were dying of breast cancer (there are enough people dying of enough cancer that the forums had become that specialized) but actually it was for fathers whose wives were dying of *treatable* breast cancer who had been denied coverage by their insurers.

Joe read for hours, long past the point when his butt went numb and he got a crick in his neck. The words on his screen seemed to come straight out of his own head. They were secret things, things he'd never dared say to any other human, because Lacey was right, they were the kinds of things that you couldn't say aloud without risking incarceration or involuntary commitment.

Here were men saying those things. And other men who heard them and told them that they understood, that they had felt the same unspeakable feelings and they understood those feelings. Even before he posted his first message to the forum, it had soothed something raw inside him, and maybe someday it could even heal the wounds that had been widening since his thirty-sixth birthday.

He never bothered to find a shrink. He didn't need one. The fathers of the Fuck Cancer Right In Its Fucking Face forum were all the therapist he needed. The weeks went by and everyone in their house came to understand that Joe's time in the guest room with his laptop were the reason that he had changed, and no one resented the moments he stole there.

ONLY AN IDIOT really believes in spontaneous remission, which is doctor for "Your cancer went away and we don't know why." Oh, it happens, but so do lightning strikes and lottery jackpots. Spontaneous remission isn't a plan, it's an unrealistic daydream.

Some people do get hit by lightning, though. And some people win the lottery.

And Lacey got spontaneous remission.

Three months to live became four, then five, and her doctor started to make the most cautious, preliminary noises about the nodules shrinking, and new tests, and then, one day, the doc summoned Lacey to her office, and Joe went along, because when your doctor wants to discuss test results in person, it's better not to face that on your own.

The doctor was running late, and that made Lacey and Joe

run nervous, the tension stretching. It was an oncology practice, so the waiting room was full of bald, sunk-eyed, dying people and their haunted loved ones, and they were actually in better shape than the people who still looked well, because those people had just been diagnosed and were coming to the doctor to find out what happened next. Those people were wrecks.

The nurse didn't bother taking Lacey's vitals, so she and Joe just waited in the exam room on a pair of orange waiting-room chairs, holding hands tightly.

The doctor came in and closed the door and apologized for making them wait and made a joke about it being one of those days and sat in her padded roller chair and squared up some papers on her desk. Then she looked at them both for a long moment, and, unexpectedly, *beamed* at them.

"Lacey, Joe, I've been in practice for fourteen years and I've given out a lot of bad news. I don't mind; it comes with the job. But it gets to you. Even when I have good news, it's still not happy news: we took out half your organs, removed your breasts, poisoned you, irradiated you, and now, we think, you are better. Sorry.

"But once in a very, very long while—a *very* long while—a doctor in my job gets to give out *good* news. This is one of those days."

She let that sink in. Lacey and Joe stared at each other. There were two words on the tips of their tongues, words they had never dared to utter without a sarcastic eye roll. They said the words now, Lacey starting, Joe joining in, both of them tentative and questioning: "Spontaneous. Remission?"

The doctor *beamed* at them.

Joe cried before Lacey did. He always was the emotional one. But then Lacey cried. And then the doctor cried, and after Joe and Lacey had hugged for a long, long time, the doctor hugged Lacey, and then Joe, and then all three of them hugged, and Joe had nothing to say except *thank you thank you thank you* and everyone knew he wasn't exactly thanking the doctor, but no one was sure who he was thanking. Not even the doctor.

JOE NEVER DID stop visiting Fuck Cancer Right In Its Fucking Face, which surprised him. That night, he and Lacey made the slowest, tenderest love in their entire relationship, fucking so slowly that they barely moved. Joe handled Lacey like she was made out of brittle china, and Lacey clung to Joe like he was the only thing keeping her from falling off the world's tallest building. Afterwards, they clung to each other, then moved apart, fingers twined. Before long, Lacey was sleeping, softly snoring, hogging the blankets, and Joe slipped out of bed and went back to the forum.

THERE ARE LOTS of support forums online and the best ones perform an incredible, nearly magical service for their participants, proving the aphorism that "shared pain is lessened, shared joy is increased," and making the lives of everyone who contributes to them better.

Fuck Cancer Right In Its Fucking Face was not one of those forums.

Fuck Cancer Right In Its Fucking Face was a forum for very angry people whose loved ones were dying or dead. Some of the denizens of FCRIIFF got better, maybe even partially due to the chance to vent in the forums, but also because they were surrounded by people who loved them and brought them back from the brink, people who shared their grief but had better coping skills.

In a forum for ex-drunks, there's a big group of elder states-people who've been sober for years and years. They're a wise, moderating voice, and they are the existence of proof of life after addiction. Whenever someone on the forums went on a bender and was recriminating with themselves, there was a dried-out elder who could tell a story to top theirs, about being put out on the street, losing their kids, losing their limbs, even, and coming back from it.

Fuck Cancer Right In Its Fucking Face did not have those peo-ple. The people who got over their furious grief left FCRIIFF, chased away by its rage culture. The people who stayed were really *into* their anger, clinging to it like a drunk refusing to let go of a bottle.

If your anger took you to a place you couldn't handle, a place that scared you, the elders of FCRIIFF would help you all right: they'd explain to you that this was the right reaction, the only reaction, and it was never, ever going to get better. This was your life from here on in.

When Lacey was pronounced well, Joe's anger drained out in an instant. The insurance flunkies who'd sentenced Lacey to die could stew in their juices and look themselves in the mirror every morning, and Joe would have his beautiful, brilliant wife and his amazing, sweet daughter, and that was all that mattered.

But FCRIIFF called to Joe. That first time he logged back in, he understood in a flash that for all that it had helped him—saved him—to see the thoughts from his own endless men-tal loops on the screen, coming from other people, it would also have destroyed him. If Lacey had died—oh God, just the thought made his guts churn—this would have been his sup-port system, and he would have taken the anchor they threw him and let it pull him right to the bottom of the ocean.

Joe decided he had a duty to FCRIIFF.

*

HE MADE THE decision early on not to talk about his forum time with Lacey. She would probably understand, but she had enough to worry about.

He mostly lurked, anyway. He never picked fights with the Great Old Ones who counseled despair and rage. But he'd private-message the new ones who showed up all twisted in knots and do his best to untwist them. He kept a list of suicide-prevention numbers handy, and he gave a measured, routine twenty dollars to each GoFundMe that was posted to the forum. Even at that modest contribution level, there was one month when the family GoFundMe bill crossed the $500 mark, and Lacey demanded to know what he was doing, and he told a half truth, saying it was for a friend's cancer fund (but not how many friends').

Lacey couldn't be angry over that, but she gave him a stern talking-to about their finances, and he agreed to cap the GoFundMe to $250/month, and she agreed to let him donate $300 in each election cycle to candidates who were pro-universal health care.

He stayed on the forum.

HE WAS READY to quit FCRIFF—which old-timers like him called Fuckriff, or Ruck Fiff when they wanted to sound polite—when LisasDad1990 joined. His first message:

Lisa is six years old. This is what she looks like. I have put her to bed every night since she stopped breast feeding. I used to read her Hand, Hand, Fingers, Thumb *and then we graduated to* Green Eggs *and now we're reading Harry Potter. That's right, a six-year-old. She's SMART.*

Last year, Lisa started falling down a lot, bumping into things. Her teachers said she wasn't concentrating in school and I saw it too. Her mom's not in the picture. I took her to the doc's and they said she had a brain tumor. I can go into details later, but it's not a good brain tumor. It's not little or cute. It's an aggressive little fucker, and it's growing.

Lisa can only see out of one eye now, and she walks with a walker, or I wheel her in her chair.

But the good news is that it's treatable. Not like 100% but the oncologist says he can whack that bastard straight out of there and blast her with some rads and give her some poison and she'll live. She'll always have some problems, but she's young and she's full of life and she'll figure that shit out.

But our insurance? Not so much. I was working for a customs broker when it hit, my first real full time job, with insurance and everything. Paid so much into that insurance. SO MUCH. But they say that the kind of surgery the doc wants to do, it's experimental. They say it's not covered.

Guys, I'm 28 years old, a single dad. My parents haven't given me a dime since I told them to go fuck themselves and moved out at 17. If my ex had a dollar to spare, it'd go to oxys, before the student-debt collectors could get it.

I have a GoFundMe, but that only works if you know a million people or one millionaire. My kid is the greatest thing in the world, but everyone thinks that about their kid, and from all the evidence so far, I'm the only one who can see it.

The thing is, my daughter Lisa is going to die.

I mean, I can kid myself about it, but that's what it's about. My six-year-old kid is going to die even though she doesn't have to (or at least she has a chance she won't get to take).

It's because some random asshole earning half a million dollars in an office at the top of a tower full of random assholes

earning less than me decided she should die. He doesn't know
her and he won't ever know her but he knows that there are
so many kids like Lisa that are going to die because of his
choices.

I've been sad, I've been angry, I've been worried. I hold Lisa
so much that she tells me, dad stop it, but some day I'm going
to hold her and she won't say anything because she'll be dead.
That's my truth and my life and I live that truth every day.

When Lisa goes, I'm going to go too. I never said that out
loud but I'll write it here because you guys know what I'm
going through. I'm dead fucking serious. With Lisa I had
everything to live for. Now I got nothing. Can't even afford to
bury her, not after all the out of pockets. Red bills every day,
every credit card wants to send a guy around with a bat to
break my knees. Maybe I'll buy a gun and shoot the first one
that comes to the door, then stick it in my mouth...

JOE COULDN'T STOP reading, but he wanted to. It was so
raw, and it brought him back to a dark place he thought he'd
left behind.

Trembling, he picked out a message with the National Suicide Prevention Lifeline, a number he'd memorized by now,
1-800-273-8255, and some numb words of comfort. It was the
closest he'd ever come to talking about Lacey's spontaneous
remission on Fuckriff, because he couldn't think of anything
else to say and that poor bastard needed some hope.

But he deleted the sentences and hit SEND.

> ONE MESSAGE WAS PUBLISHED AHEAD OF YOURS

★

DO IT [wrote one of the Great Old Ones]. *Seriously do it. I'm going to do it, some day, when I'm all used up. Why shouldn't you? Why should those evil corporate fucks live when my wife is dead? When your kid is going to die?*

I was going to buy an AR-15 and do it but fuck that. AR-15s are for people who want to shoot their way out, or people who need to shoot their way in. I don't need to do that. I'm an old, middle-class white guy. I could walk right in, go right up to the top floor with a nice little fertilizer bomb and take out the whole fucking C-suite. Some "innocents" will die but they're not all that innocent, are they?

I grew up on a farm in Wyoming and my dad had a book called the Blasters' Handbook *that told you everything you needed to know about blowing shit up on an as-needed basis, like if a horse dropped dead and froze solid and you needed to blast it into manageable chunks.*

The Blasters' Handbook *has gone digital and to save you the trouble of searching for it and getting on some kind of watchlist, I'm attaching a copy of it here. You'd be amazed at how easy it is to make something that'll go boom. Hell, my old man was simple as fuck and he managed it.*

All I'm saying is, if you're going to do something drastic, don't let it go to waste.

HE SIGNED IT with his screen name, DeathEater, which Joe had been staring at for years but never really had thought about until just then. Jesus, *DeathEater.*

Joe hit reply, then stopped himself. What did you say to something like that? Should he call the cops? The guy who started the message board, BigTed, barely ever logged in anymore, but Joe had his email address somewhere from when he'd locked himself out of his account once. He decided that was probably his first port of call, so he pasted DeathEater's message into an email. Just as he sent it, he had a moment's twizzle as he thought about what kind of bot might scan that email between him and BigTed, what kind of watchlist he might be putting himself on.

He stayed off the thread, but other Fuckriffers jumped in. Some of them were scolding and moralizing, calling DeathEater a monster or pretending he'd been kidding and telling him off for a making a joke in such poor taste. Others ran with the "joke," spinning more and more elaborate scenarios of mass mayhem. Lots of them posted screenshots from the *Blasters' Handbook* and talked about ways to improve on the design— wrapping the package in duct-tape, adding washer nuts and ball-bearings for shrapnel.

A very few users talked to LisasDad1990 about his daughter, offering him the kind of comfort Joe had tried for. LisasDad1990 didn't reply to any of them.

BIGTED CLOSED THE thread the next day and gave DeathEater a three-day time-out. LisasDad1990 went silent. Joe private-messaged him a couple of times, but mostly he forgot about it.

Madison turned seven. They had ice-cream cake, played games, and finished with a sleepover with her best friend from across the street, Rose, who wet the bed at 12:00 A.M. and woke them both up in floods of humiliated tears. Lacey got Rose cleaned up and Joe sorted out the mattress, putting a trash bag over the wet spot, then putting fresh sheets over that.

Lacey went right back to sleep and so did Rose. Joe couldn't sleep. He padded to the guest room with his laptop and started Fuckriffing.

＊

SHE DIED TODAY [LisasDad1990 wrote].

I'm sorry about all the mess my last message made. I was in a low place. But I want to thank you all for weighing in, even the ones who joked and whatnot. I even laughed at some of that. It kept me going, all of it.

We're burying her next week.

THE TIMESTAMP WAS only six minutes gone. Joe private-messaged him.

> If you need to talk I'm up

He stared at the screen for a long time, waiting for a pop-up, hitting refresh, hoping LisasDad1990 would reply.

Minutes dragged by. He tabbed over to Facebook and skimmed, tabbed back. He looked up the estimated arrival of an Amazon box he'd just remembered he was expecting. He took a quick glance over his Gmail spam folder, which he tried to do every month, before flushing it.

He was about to close his laptop (or possibly about to start doing all this all over again) when a reply popped up.

> Thanks. It's not a good night. Funeral's next week. Put it on my last credit card. Gonna be a real sendoff

> That sounds like a worthy thing to use that card for. But how are you holding up

> Put it this way: I don't plan on paying that credit card bill

Joe's stomach sank.

> I know I sent you the suicide crisis number before but here
it is again. 1-800-273-8255. Or you just text HOME to 741741
and someone will be there. Both are 24/7

> I called that number. It was nice of you to send it to me.
I can tell you're the kind of person who wants everyone to
have hope. That's a nice kind of person to be. Lisa was that
kind of person.

A long pause. Joe was about to type something. Then
LisasDad1990 started typing again.

> That was all she could talk about. Kid just turned seven
and all she could say was Daddy you got to have hope, you
are going to be OK. She wanted me to watch *Annie*, if you
can believe it. Stupid Netflix.

That actually made Joe laugh involuntarily. Chuckle, really.
He got the feeling that he and LisasDad1990 would probably
enjoy each other's company.

> She was right.

He took a deep breath.

> Look, where are you? Maybe you and I could get together.
I'm in Phoenix.

> Not me. I live in Cow's Asshole, South Carolina. But that's
nice of you.

> How about a phone call? I could crack a beer, you could
crack a beer, and we could have a beer together.

> You're a nice guy, I can tell. Thank you for that. I'll take a
rain check.

Then he did log off.

Joe didn't think he'd be able to sleep that night, but he was
a man, a human being approaching middle age, and human
beings need sleep, and so he slept.

THE NEXT DAY was Sunday, his day to cook breakfast. He
managed to get all the way through it with Madison and her
friend (whose nocturnal embarrassment had been dissipated
by a few more hours' sleep and a set of laundered PJs) without
thinking to check the news out of South Carolina or the posts
on Fuckriff.

But once Rose's slightly mortified parents had picked her
up and Madison was in her room making slime and watching
YouTube, he got out his phone and Google News-searched
"south carolina suicide."

The search results were empty. Of course. LisasDad1990
wouldn't do it until the funeral was over. Joe had all week to
talk him down.

WORK WAS NEVER the same for Joe after Lacey got sick. He
never rescheduled that meeting with the VP. He just couldn't
muster the fucks needed to give it his all for on-demand whole-
sale distribution. People he'd started with left to work for
experimental divisions doing partnerships with self-driving

forklift companies, or diving into cloud-based self-serve platforms for ecommerce dropshippers, or all that other stuff that
helped people get their Squatty Pottys and strobing LED USB
chargers delivered to their doors with five nines of reliability.

Joe settled into his cubicle and did exactly the things in his
job description and clocked out at 5:00 P.M. every single day.
He had a work phone and a personal phone, and he'd had lots
of training about the fact that the work phone's traffic was all
logged, even the "secure" traffic, because the company had done
something to its operating system so that everything he did with
it would be visible to the compliance team. They had to do it,
they said, for their insurance. It was important, therefore, that
he strictly segregate his personal activities and work-related
activities. No one wanted to read his sexts or eavesdrop on his
search history when he was coping with an embarrassing itch.

This had been a real struggle with Joe at first, because he was
the kind of guy who liked to pull the handle on his work-email
slot machine, checking to see whether his boss wanted him to
do stuff after hours. That meant that the phone he was most
likely to have in his hand at any given moment was that work
phone. Sometimes he even forgot to charge his personal phone.

But then, after his company's HR department told him it
wasn't their job to stop his wife from being murdered by their
health insurer, he got demotivated. Now it was his work phone
that was usually out of battery.

So at the office, he used his personal phone to check in
with LisasDad1990. He'd read FAQs about what to say to
suicidal people and he was working his way through the list.
LisasDad1990 didn't always respond, but he responded sometimes, and that meant he was listening and that meant that Joe
wasn't going to give up.

The days ticked by until Lisa's funeral. LisasDad1990 posted photos from the funeral—sad photos of weeping relatives, his snaggletoothed, ravaged addict ex included. Pics of the tiny casket, the urn of ashes.

The men of Fuckriff were respectful and solemn about these pictures. They had a thing they did when they wanted to perform their solemnity, posting a message with just a single space character, so it looked blank, like *words fail me*. The photos had a massive trail of these.

But DeathEater's had another copy of the *Blasters' Handbook* attached to it.

LISASDAD1990 DIDN'T ANSWER any more of Joe's private messages. Joe told himself that he was just wisely taking some time away from Fuckriff's seductive, toxic environment and taking comfort from real-world friends who were less violence obsessed.

But Joe found himself pulling out his personal phone and searching for "bombing" and "south carolina" almost automatically, any time he let his thoughts wander.

It was the end of May and Madison was graduating from second grade, and the school was making a big deal out of it. Joe had missed the kindergarten and first-grade versions of this ceremony, but he no longer had the burning ambition that made it so hard to ask for half days off for personal time. So he got in his car at lunchtime and drove to the school, stopping to buy a lei and a mylar balloon from a Mexican guy who was walking the line of parents waiting outside the auditorium with a pushcart, admonishing them to "show your kids how proud you are of them and how important their education is to you." The pitch was pretty naked, but it still skewered Joe in some deep, guilty parenting instinct.

Lacey beat him there and saved him a seat and they held hands while the kids gave speeches about their dreams for the future and sang songs and made tributes to their teachers. The kids were plenty cute in their little dresses and suits, but it got pretty repetitive, and Joe twitched his phone out of his pocket and discreetly ran his search.

Normally, "south carolina bombing" returned a bunch of pages on the Mars Bluff B-47 nuclear incident, when the USAF accidentally nuked the town of Mars Bluff in 1958. Today, the top of the listing was a series of Google News links to a story about an explosion at the Columbia headquarters of BlueCross BlueShield of South Carolina.

The singing onstage and the bored whispering and shifting of the parents around him vanished instantly and totally and his vision tunneled down to his screen. He tapped a link for an AP story, and Lacey hissed at him to put his phone away, and he startled guiltily and looked up, but he couldn't focus his eyes.

"Going to the bathroom," he whispered, and made his way down to the aisle, threading between parents' knees and the seat backs in front of them, stumbling, then into the school hall hung with art and poetry, into the boys' bathroom with its miniature urinals and the scarred stalls. He stepped into one and read the AP story.

It was light on details, just a breaking news piece, but the facts were devastating: an explosion had gone off at the BlueCross BlueShield headquarters. Police suspected terrorism. There were ten confirmed dead already and the strong presumption that that number would go way up as the rescue teams sorted through the rubble. The pictures of the building were sickening; like a rotten tooth, a huge hole had been blasted through the upper-story walls, spanning three floors.

The jerkycam images ganked from Twitter were all smoke and fire, and stumbling, bleeding people in office clothes.

He stood there in the stall for god knew how long, staring at his phone, wishing he had never pulled it out, wishing that this was a senseless mystery for him instead of an event that was not mysterious in the slightest. He should call the cops. He really should just go call the cops.

There was noise from outside the bathroom, crowd sounds, then the door to the boys' room banged open and kids' voices filled the room. He pocketed his phone and ran out of the bathroom, barely hearing a smart-alecky kid calling after him to wash his hands.

LACEY WALKED HIM to his car after they'd had their pictures taken with Madison and given her her balloons and lei and seen her off with a friend's mom to go back to their place for a movie and popcorn party.

"What is it?"

He wasn't going to tell her, of course. Jesus, bad enough he was in this.

"You know that message board—"

She rolled her eyes. She didn't approve of Fuckriff.

"I know, I know. But there's a guy there who's having a really hard time. His daughter. Same age as Maddy, and I just want to be there for him. They were there for me when I needed it. I'm paying that forward."

She rolled her eyes again, but pulled him into a long hug. "You are a good man, Joseph Gorman. Just remember, you can't carry the world on your shoulders, and you have a family who need you, too—don't spend everything you've got on strangers."

"Thank you, Lacey. I know, it's good advice. I try to keep it all in perspective, but, you know…"

"I know. Of course I know. That's why I'm reminding you. You've got a big heart, and you need help caring for it. I married into that job."

"I love you."

She gave him a longer hug this time, squeezing him fiercely with all the strength that had returned to her body since their miracle. Even as he was noticing this, he was thinking of the phone in his pocket and wondering where he could pull over and get online and read the news reports and log into Fuckriff.

LISASDAD1990 POSTED A video explaining what he was doing, but thankfully he didn't mention Fuckriff. Even so, everyone on Fuckriff was tense as hell and there was a lot of going back and deleting stuff until the cops announced that LisasDad1990 had used Tor Browser extensively and had left behind no browser breadcrumbs, nor any records at AT&T's data centers. Inevitably, this set off a whole witch hunt over the "dark web" and everyone wondering where the mystery man from the video had been "radicalized."

LisasDad1990 was a soft-spoken, slightly heavyset man with sad eyes and a three-day beard. In the video, he spoke in a monotone, staring straight into the camera with red-rimmed eyes. His hair was limp and greasy and the kitchen behind him was in chaos, with empty pharmacy packaging and pizza boxes. In a quiet, calm, gentlemanly Southern voice, he talked about the decision that BlueCross BlueShield had made to deny his daughter's coverage, and what that had meant. He held up a photo of a smiling little girl, brown pixie-cut, missing tooth, a dusting of freckles on a little upturned nose. He talked about

Lisa's stories, the drawings she'd do to accompany them, the kitten she'd rescued and nursed to health, her inconsolable grief when the cat was hit by a car. He talked about her illness and her bravery, and her pain, and her promise.

He spoke extemporaneously, no notes in evidence, and when he was done, he stopped for a long time, then wiped his eyes with his thumbs, opened and shut his mouth a few times without being able to speak, drew in a deep, shuddering breath, and composed himself.

"So that's why I'm doing this. It's not vengeance. I don't have a vengeful bone in my body. Nothing I do will bring Lisa back, so why would I want revenge?

"This is a public service. There's another dad just like me and another little girl just like—" Another moment to compose himself. "Just like Lisa. And right now, that dad is talking to someone at Cigna, or Humana, or BlueCross BlueShield, and the person on the phone is telling that dad that his little girl has. To. Die.

"Someone in that building made the decision to kill my little girl, and everyone else in that building went along with it. Not one of them is innocent, and not one of them is afraid. They're going to be afraid, after this. After today, every one of those people is going to spend the rest of their lives looking over their shoulders for a man like me. Ordinary looking. Harmless. A little sad, maybe.

"Because they must know in their hearts. Them, their lobbyists, the men in Congress who enabled them. They're parents. They know. Anyone who hurt their precious children, they'd hunt that person down like a dog. The only amazing thing about any of this is that no one has done it yet.

"I'm going to make a prediction right now, that even though I'm the first, I sure as hell will not be the last. There's more to come. To those fathers and husbands, mothers and wives, grandparents and lovers, the ones who'll come after me, I want to salute you. We are going to scare them, we're going to make them *so scared* that they will never get a night's sleep again. They will right this wrong, this stain on our country, not because they love your kids as much as you love your kids, but because we will *scare* them into it."

He stared into the camera for a while longer, his eyes burning and glittering. Then he nodded to himself, stood up, and walked out of the frame. When he came back a moment later, he had a duct-taped package the size of a pot roast that he carefully lifted and placed into a backpack. He nodded once more, shrugged into the backpack, and clicked the video off.

IT OCCURRED TO Joe that even though LisasDad1990—his name was Saul, but Joe thought of him as LisasDad1990 still—talked so much about "fear," no one on TV or in the news mentioned "terrorism." There were some Twittery types who pointed out that LisasDad1990 had the wrong color skin to be a terrorist and instead he was "not right in his head" or "mentally ill" or even "traumatized." Not even the families of the people killed in the Columbia explosion used the T-word, though plenty called him a murderer and a monster and worse.

Certainly, none of the Fuckriffers wanted to whisper the T-word.

There was a furious debate that danced around the T-word, about when it was OK to "spout off" and "fantasize" about violence and when that crossed the line. BigTed might have had a view on this, but twenty-four hours after LisasDad1990 killed all those people and himself, BigTed announced that he was going to stop administering Fuckriff and that he had passed the torch to DeathEater, who had the "time and energy" to "give it the attention it deserved."

Once DeathEater was the lord and master of Fuckriff, the debate ended. DeathEater declared that there was only one way to be a Fuckriffer, and that was to meet grief in all of its guises, including rage, to be authentic and true to yourself.

DeathEater also announced that the majority of the boards on Fuckriff were moving to a Tor Hidden Service that they'd need Tor Browser to read, and set up a complicated protocol to let them claim their existing IDs on the Fuckriff in the Dark, which is what the new service was called.

Joe ignored this for a while. He was even secretly relieved. If all the worst of the worst of the broken Fuckriffers disappeared into the Dark, then he could hang around on the nub that was still visible on the open web, and play fairy godfather and Jiminy Cricket to the people who weren't beyond help.

But DeathEater was determined to suck as many souls into the dark as he could. Anytime a thread really got going on Fuckriff, he'd close it and announce that it had moved to the Dark. The newbies would follow him there. The third time this happened, Joe realized that DeathEater maintained Fuckriff as a gateway drug to the Dark. The Dark *was* Fuckriff.

Once he figured that out, Joe was done with Fuckriff. He parked his account and walked away from it.

THE SECOND BOMBER went after a Tennessee Republican state senator who'd voted down the Medicare expansion, despite his campaign promise to make sure that "every Tennessean who wants insurance will get insurance."

The bomber was named Logan Lents, and his people had been in Tennessee since it became a state in 1796. Though his background was wealthy, he was broke—his parents had lost the family fortune when he was a boy and he'd been a scholarship case at TSU, where six generations of his ancestors had matriculated, and he'd been the president of Phi Beta Sigma, like his father, grandfather, and great-grandfather had been.

Logan Lents was the widower of Patricia Lents, another Tennessean of long and fallen lineage, whose uterine cancer was treatable (according to her OB/GYN) or not (according to Cigna's insurance underwriters). Patricia lost a baby early in the cancer, which everyone secretly counted as a blessing, what with her illness and all, and when she died a year later, at the age of twenty-six, Logan had been shattered.

Logan bombed Senator William Blount's office on a fine Saturday, after a day's worth of constituency meetings during the spring recess. Logan was considerate enough to wait for all the voters and staffers who'd been there for the day's business to clear out and only killed himself, the senator, and a Tennessee state trooper. Another trooper and a cleaner were maimed, but they survived.

The men of Dark Fuckriff declared it a "surgical" mission and praised its "clean" execution.

Logan's video was really well done, eloquent in the way of someone from a fine old family who'd once talked his way into the presidency of an exclusive frat. He had that American Brahmin thing, like a southern Kennedy, and it was easy to forget that he was about to blow himself up along with anyone standing nearby to make his point, which was that health care was a human right and that evil men had conspired to take it away from many Americans, which meant that they would die.

*

THE THIRD BOMBER was DeathEater.

Joe and DeathEater had gotten into much more open hostilities in the weeks after Logan's death. DeathEater had access to Fuckriff's logs, so he could see how Joe was sending private messages to everyone DeathEater egged on, and, being the admin and all, he was able to read these messages and see that Joe had turned himself into a shoulder-angel to whisper antidotes to all of DeathEater's poison.

DeathEater confronted him in a private chat that started out hot but cooled down quickly as DeathEater told his story —adult son dead of a metabolic disorder whose pharmaceutical therapy was deemed "experimental," wife dead "of heartbreak" within a year, seventy-four years old and conned into switching from Medicare to an HMO that told him that the dialysis he'd been doing for twenty years was "out-of-network" and had referred him to an alternate therapy that left him in constant agony.

> Old white guy in a wheelchair, no one searches that guy

Joe had had versions of this conversation so many times, and usually they came out all right. After all, there had only been two bombs so far, and Joe didn't think he'd ever talked to Logan.

> All you're going to do is make a whole bunch of men and women miserable for all their lives, leave a bunch of kids without a mom or dad

> Yup, that's what I aim to do all right. Seems only fitting considering.

Now what? *Two wrongs don't make a right?* This was Dark Fuckriff, not Pinocchio.

> Call me first? If you can't talk to a real live person and
tell them what you're doing, how can you say you're sure
enough of yourself

> I'll think about it

> Call me

> I'll call you

And then Joe's phone rang, at 6:00 A.M., and he said, "Hello, hello?" until he worked out that the noises in the background were a wheelchair and someone setting up a laptop to record a video straight to camera. The voice was wheezy but strong with emotion.

"I'm going to make a bunch of men and women miserable today, make them grieve for the rest of their lives for the husbands and wives they're going to lose. A lot of kids will never see their moms and dads again.

"I'm not proud of that. I truly grieve for you. But I have to do this. Enough is enough. The people I'm going to kill today are part of a machine that every day, every year, cost so many of us our wives, husbands, parents, and children. We watch them die bad, slow, painful deaths, and why? Because it's always someone's job to watch the money, and no one's job to keep those people alive, who don't have to die yet.

"Somewhere along the way, there have to be consequences. There's plenty of good people working for meth dealers, just trying to scrape by. I expect there are good people who just need to earn a living, who work for human traffickers, too. We arrest those people, send them to jail for the rest of their lives, even though they're just trying to get by like the rest of us. Why should working for a legal murderer mean you're innocent? That you get off scot-free?

"If you work for a health insurance company, or their lobbyists, or a senator or congressman who votes against health care for everyone, I want you to be afraid. Scared to leave home. Too scared to sleep. I want you lying awake at night, feeling a rush of fear every time you hear a creak. I want you to have a concealed carry permit, a shotgun by the bed, and still find yourself wondering every morning whether today's going to be the day.

"If you can't take that, quit your job. Tell your boss you didn't sign up to get blown to pieces by some grief-crazed suicide bomber. Eventually, those insurance executives and lobbyists and politicians will have to move on to Plan B. Which is health care for everyone.

"They say violence never solves anything, but to quote *The Onion*: 'that's only true so long as you ignore all of human history.' Violence is the only way to get some people's attention. You know which ones I mean.

"Brady, I'm sorry, son. You deserve a better legacy than this. Marla, you too. You both deserve better, but this is all I got. I love you. I'll see you soon."

DeathEater clicked on something and the video ended, but he kept talking to Joe, monologuing as he rolled his chair around his cramped home, getting ready to blow himself up.

"Hope you heard all that, Joe. Sorry about leaving a trail pointing at you, but you did ask me to call you. I printed out our chat logs so they'll see that you were trying to stop me all along." A scuffle as he picked the phone up, his voice getting louder and clearer. "Thanks for trying, Joe. Tikitiki6538 is going to run things from now on."

Joe tried to say something to him, but he wasn't sure if the video was still being recorded, and he knew that someday—soon—he'd have to explain this call to some very serious men from federal law enforcement, and whatever he told them would have to be reconcilable with whatever fragment of his voice was on the recording.

And anyway, DeathEater hung up on him.

JOE DIALED 91-, and his finger hovered over the 1. It was 3:00 A.M. in Phoenix, 6:00 A.M. on whatever East Coast city DeathEater lived in (Clearwater, Joe learned later). Lacey and Maddy were fast asleep, the breath of the AC drowning out their soft little snores. He tried to imagine what would happen if he pressed 1, and spoke to a Phoenix 911 operator, explained that someone whose name he didn't know in a city he couldn't name was planning a bombing. Another bombing. Tried to imagine the Tempe PD cops who'd come to his door, the conversation they'd have, the conversation he'd have to have with Lacey.

He couldn't do it.

He looked in on Maddy and adjusted her covers, smoothed her hair, kissed her forehead. Then he climbed in next to Lacey, the smell of her wafting out from under the covers as he crawled between them, and he stared at the ceiling for a long time. He must have fallen asleep eventually because the next thing he knew, the room was filled with sunlight, Lacey and Maddy were arguing about whether Maddy was allowed YouTube before breakfast (she wasn't) and Joe had his phone in his hand, scrolling through headlines.

DeathEater had wheeled himself into a health insurance conference at a Sheraton, a big trade show that had put on extra security because the people who went were already a little afraid. But DeathEater had booked a room weeks before, and he paid for valet parking and had a bellman help lift him into his chair and hang his pack on the chair back, then wheeled himself in, checked in, and wheeled toward the elevator bank, flashing his room key at the private security guards who were stopping everyone who tried to go past the ballrooms. No one wanted to pat down an old white man with a room key, wearing a gaily colored aloha shirt and a battered straw hat, pale skinny legs sticking out of baggy shorts.He had timed his arrival for ten minutes before the morning plenary, when all the conference-goers were milling around out front of the big ballroom, drinking coffee and eating muffins and chattering. He wheeled himself dead center of the crowd and—

The death toll was spectacular.

LACEY DIDN'T KNOW what was wrong with Joe, but she knew *something* was up.

"No more of that message board, Joseph," she said sternly.

"Too much screen-time, Daddy," Maddy said, a perfect impression of her mother, made all the more uncanny by their increasing resemblance and a recent matching mommy-daughter haircut with blue highlights.

He picked up Maddy and gave her a hard squeeze while she squealed and kicked and laughed. "OK, kiddo," he said, and caught Lacey's eye. Lacey looked worried.

Joe had the school run that morning. Lacey had gone back to work, landing a job at a call center that handled reservation problems for a big hotel chain, and Joe had shifted his hours around so that he could do the drop-off in the morning and Lacey could do the pickup at night. It wasn't a good career move—there was a direct correlation between being at your desk at 8:00 A.M. and getting a promotion—but since the day of Lacey's diagnosis, all his passion for a career had leaked out of him and been replaced by an equally urgent sense that his time with his family was a fleeting thing to be savored.

On the drive to school, Maddy wanted to talk about when mommy got sick, which was a topic that came up a lot. Neither Joe nor Lacey were religious, but inevitably, Maddy had a friend at school who wanted her to know that God had saved her mommy and that she should be giving thanks to God. She kept bringing this up and was obviously, visibly anxious that they weren't doing enough on that score and maybe God would change His mind.

"So you know that I don't believe in God, right, kiddo?"

He snuck a glance away from the slow-moving traffic and looked at her. She was nodding solemnly.

"I think that Mommy just got really, really, super lucky. Like rolling two sixes in Monopoly, ten times in a row. But that doesn't mean we shouldn't be grateful and thankful that we get to have her with us. I wake up every day and I'm thankful. Aren't you?"

"Yeah." Her voice was tiny.

"Yeah. So if there is a God, then She or He"—*She or He* was a phrase Lacey insisted on when they talked about God with Maddy—"knows how you feel."

He heard her crying in the back seat and pulled the car over. "What is it, baby? Why are you crying?"

She snuffled and he gave her a tissue. "Sometimes I'm not grateful. Sometimes I get mad at her because she won't let me wear what I want or she says I didn't brush my teeth right. What if God sees that I'm not grateful and takes her away?"

For the ten millionth time, Joe cursed the little evangelical kid in Maddy's class who'd put all this crapola inside her innocent, traumatized head.

"Well, kiddo, I'm the wrong guy to answer that one, because

you know I don't believe there is a God. But I don't expect you
not to get upset with Mommy. I get upset with her sometimes,
too. That happens even when people love each other. Especially
when people love each other! It's hard work, loving someone.
All that matters is that you talk about things when you're upset
and work them out. You know that even when we get really
angry with each other it always works out and we always end
up loving each other again, right? So what we need to do is just
concentrate on getting past the mad part and getting back to
the happy part. I'm sure if there is a God, that's all She or He
expects from you."

Maddy seemed satisfied with that answer, so Joe put the
car back into gear and pulled out into traffic. By the time they
reached the next set of lights, she was singing the chorus to
"Yellow Submarine" over and over and over again, which was
always a good sign. He dropped her off in front of the school,
and she blew him a kiss and then came back for her forgotten
lunch and blew him another one.

Joe drove to work. He tried to focus on thoughts of his
daughter and what he could say to her the next time she had
questions like this. He tried not to think of the FBI pulling
DeathEater's phone records and conducting forensics on
his computer. He tried not to think of fathers in Clearwater,
Florida, who'd be explaining to their kids for years to come
why a strange, angry old white man in a wheelchair murdered
their mother. He failed.

"ARE YOU GOING to tell me what's wrong, Joseph, or am I
going to have to drag you to couples' therapy?"

The week since DeathEater's attack had gone from bad to
worse. Every ringing phone, every strange face made him jump

and sweat and think about some DHS type, a federal marshal or an FBI agent. He did not log in to Fuckriff, which was hard because it was his customary 2:00 A.M. no-sleep therapy and he was having a lot of 2:00 A.M. no-sleep nights.

Lacey asked him several times what was going on, and he made vague noises about work stress, which was laughable, given how little he cared about work. Finally, it had come to this. They were in bed, Maddy was down for the night, and he was lying on his side, trying not to grind his teeth, his mind circling around and around from DeathEater to the FBI to the dead people of Clearwater, and now Lacey.

He rolled over. "I'm sorry, Lace. It's just some shit in my life that I'm not able to shake off and that I don't want to dwell on. The last thing I want to do is go over it with you." *And make you an accessory to a crime.* "I just want to put it out of my mind."

She gave him a look of pure skepticism. "You're really doing a shitty job of it, if you don't mind my saying so. Doing the same thing over and over and expecting a different result is the definition of insanity. I love you very much, my husband, but if you can't figure out how to deal with this on your own and you won't let me help you and you won't get help from anyone else, then you and I are going to have a serious fucking problem." Lacey didn't swear often.

"I hear you," he said. "Give me forty-eight hours? I probably just need to download that meditation app or go for a run or something."

"Forty-eight hours, and then you either spill everything to me or I frog-march you to a shrink."

Joe put on his bravest face.

"Deal."

*

MEDITATION PROVED IMPOSSIBLE. There was no way
he could get his thoughts away from the DeathEater video,
the words they'd exchanged, the thought of all those families
torn apart. But he did go for a run, strapping his phone to his
bicep and putting in his earbuds.

It was late fall and hot, but not blazing hot, and he lost
himself in the rhythm of his footfalls and the Creedence Clearwater Revival in his earbuds.

The effect of losing himself was near miraculous, weight
lifted from his chest and shoulders. Sounds were sharper, smells
better. He picked up the pace.

Inevitably, he overdid it. Too much running after too long
a hiatus. He stumbled and nearly went down, and when he
straightened up his head was whirling and he nearly lost his
balance again. He was in a cute pedestrianized shopping area
and he found a bench and sat down on it, his legs trembling
and his balance whirling.

He put his head in his hands until the whirling stopped,
then sat back, sweat coursing down his face and back. His
playlist ended and he got his phone out and started prodding
for another round of music for a slower jog home, and autopiloted his way to the headlines.

A shooter had targeted Senator Graham—Joe's own senator—on the steps of the Capital dome. Graham had won an
insurgent seat with promises to "consider all options" and
"fix the mess" in health care, and had joined the obstructionist
block in the Senate, voting the straight ticket with the party
leadership as they blocked every proposal, no matter how
modest. After his first year in office, he'd canceled all town
halls and *Politico* had done some data journalism showing
that he was the hardest senator for a constituent to sit down
with either at home or in D.C.

The shooter had winged two D.C. cops and a federal marshal, injured nine bystanders, got a center-mass shot in on the senator's chief of staff, and took a piece out of the senator's earlobe with a modified full-auto AR-15. That was all in eighteen seconds, which is how long it took for the horde of cops present from six agencies to shoot him forty-seven times. The senator was initially reported to be badly injured, but it turned out that he was merely covered in gallons of other people's blood and in hysterics.

The shooter had uploaded a suicide video to YouTube before leaving his hotel room in Adams-Morgan, and though Google had taken it down within minutes of it hitting Twitter and Facebook, it had already been mirrored to a bunch of overseas servers on smaller platforms and was getting a lot of play on the #YouShouldBeAfraid hashtag, which had started with the second bombing.

Joe read and read, and his trembling wasn't going away. Did this shooter have a Fuckrift account? Did he live near Joe? When would the Feds show up at his door? The senator's bloody, terrified face was perfect viral content, and it raced around the net even faster than the suicide video.

The sweat he'd worked up running had turned icy.

The talking heads had spent weeks wondering where the president was amid all these killings. Apart from a few tepid statements of sympathy for the families of the victims, he'd been playing it very low-key. His proxies had praised him for his restraint and his canny refusal to glorify the "sad, sick people" who had committed these atrocities, lest he inspire more people to follow in their footsteps.

But with a shooting on his doorstep, the president could no longer afford silence. He'd been en route home from his Capetown summit on Air Force One when the news broke, and after huddling with his communications team, he'd sat down with the press corps and delivered an unhinged, rambling statement that ranged over America's "best health-care in the world," the evils of "something for nothing culture," and the ongoing project to "clean up the Obamacare disaster" before getting onto the main attraction: calling the shooter a "terrorist."

The word rang in Joe's ears. His earbuds felt sweaty and itchy. He'd been a teenager on 9/11 and his strongest memory from then was this new word, "terrorist," and its weird resonances, like it described an orc, ravening and remorseless, superhuman and subhuman at once. It was a word to shrivel the balls. He'd heard white people called terrorists before, but only weirdo kids from Berkeley who ran away from home to join jihadi guerrillas in the Middle East.

This was the dropped shoe he'd been waiting for, a moment he could never come back from. He knew that once "terrorist" stuck to you, you couldn't unstick it. It spread from the person it landed on to the people around them. It even traveled back in time and stuck to people the terrorist used to know. For example, if you happened to spend a lot of time in a message board where terrorism was planned, then you were very likely a terrorist, too. And if that message board was on the dark web? Forget it.

HIS JOG HOME was curiously lighthearted. He'd been cringing, waiting for this to happen. Now it had happened. The bell had rung and he couldn't unring it. Nothing he did on Fuckriff, no amount of patient arguing or conspicuous calls for reason would change it. He was, in some weird sense, free. What's more, it might be his last freedom, because now there would certainly be Feds.

Lacey was doing yoga in front of the TV when he got home. She asked him skeptically if he was OK, and he must have been convincing because she sentenced him to a shower and announced they'd be going to the farmer's market for Saturday brunch.

It was a sweet Saturday. Even Maddy—who hated the market—had a good time, thanks to Joe's relaxation of family policy on cakes and cookies. He took enormous pleasure watching her stuff her face on baked goodies and then sprang for a face-painting. Lacey grumbled a little about the indulgences, but she was clearly very happy to see the old Joe coming back.

When Joe woke up at 2:00 A.M. to pee, he autopiloted into the spare room and fired up Tor Browser, heading straight for Fuckriff. All his anxiety about logging in was gone. Here on the other side of the point of no return, there was no reason not to visit his old friends. Things were what they were and nothing he did from now on would make them worse or better.

But Fuckriff was gone: both the light and dark versions were 404, page not found.

And that set him off again.

Because—he realized—the Fuckriffers were his people. They were his community. Some of them scared the shit out of him and some of them made him want to punch a wall, but it was his place in the digital world, a place where a truth he'd come to feel deep in his bones was universally acknowledged. Most Americans knew that the health-care system was fucked up, and they even knew that health industry execs and the politicians they purchased on the cheap were behind it. But the Fuckriffers alone understood how *central* those two facts were, and how *evil* they were. Joe didn't want to kill anyone, but deep inside, he knew that there were plenty of people who warranted killing.

*

THERE WERE TWO bombings and another shooting the next week. Nice, middle-class white dudes who'd watched their wives and kids die, or who were living under death sentences themselves.

The news was full of stories about the checkpoints being set up outside hospitals and insurance company buildings and politicians' offices, and then three guys in three cities with no obvious connection to one another went and blew themselves up at three of those checkpoints, blowing up the huge crowds of nice people with good jobs who'd been waiting to clear the scanners so they could earn a living for their families. The bombs went off within minutes of each other and killed more people than all the other attacks combined.

It was clear that there were other Fuckriffs out there. They were in the press, too, and then the president mentioned them—"the dark caves where good people are made evil"— and still the Feds did not come for Joe. It occurred to him that they might have more leads for this epidemic of nice, respectable white dudes blowing shit up than they could follow up, and they might be a long time indeed in coming for him.

"Why are those men killing those people?" Maddy asked over breakfast. Another classmate had been telling her that she shouldn't go to the doctor because crazy men were killing anyone near a hospital.

"They're crazy," Lacey said, shoving a bowl of berries and yogurt under her nose. "Sick in the head."

"But why?"

"Because some people just go crazy, honey."

"But *why*?"

"Joe?" Lacey threw a dishwasher tablet into the machine

and headed to the bathroom, scooping up the laundry as she went.

"Daddy?"

"How come I get the hard ones?"

"Because you're so good at them," Lacey called down from the bathroom.

Joe smiled and that made Maddy smile, but she hadn't forgotten. "How come, Daddy?"

"Because," he said, and shook his head. "There are some very bad men who decided that they could be rich if they made it so going to the doctor was very expensive. They made it so expensive that people are dying because they can't afford it. That's what nearly happened to Mommy." Madison's face clouded over, the way it always did when this subject came up. "So there are other men who've had to see their babies and their wives and their friends die, and it makes them go crazy, and so they go and kill people who work for the bad guys who made the doctor so expensive."

Maddy looked frustrated. "But why?"

He broke it down into smaller pieces, hearing himself use terms like "bad guys" and "good guys" and thinking about how Lacey would not approve of this framing, but that the Fuckriffers surely would.

"I don't think killing people is good."

"It's not, sweetie."

"You said that the bad guys killed people by not letting them see the doctor, though."

"Yes, that's right."

"So they're killing people."

"Yes."

"So they're the same as the people who are shooting people."

"Not really."

It was time to get dressed and get into the car. Maddy wouldn't let him put music on during the drive. She wanted to shout more morally fraught questions from the back seat. This was a "teachable moment," Joe knew, and his responsibility as an adult was to follow Maddy where she wanted to lead.

"Why do the bad guys want to kill people?"

"They don't want to—" He stopped himself. Keep it simple, stupid. "Because they get rich and they can buy nice houses and cars and vacations if doctors are expensive."

"Why do the guys with the bombs want to kill people?"

"Because they're angry at the bad guys."

A long pause from the back seat. He swung into the school drop-off horseshoe. "All right, kiddo, we'll pick this up tonight after school."

Standing on the sidewalk with her lunch and her schoolbag, she tapped on the passenger window and he rolled it down. "I think the bad guys are worse than the guys with the bombs. The guys with the bombs are just punishing the bad guys for killing their kids."

And a future Fuckriffer is born. Joe tried to imagine the conversations that Maddy's friends would have with their parents that night, after Maddy got through with them.

THE FBI STAGED coordinated raids on four private homes and two data centers, claiming that they had seized three different message boards where the "deranged killers" had planned their attacks and arrested the owners of those boards.

Joe watched the perp-walks on social media, four white guys in middle age in their pajamas, cuffed hands behind their backs, terrified looks and curious neighbors. The cops had served no-knock warrants on all four, gone in with guns drawn and

SWAT backup—but had somehow managed to fail to shoot any of them in the process. Joe took some comfort in that.

Social media exploded with the personal lives of these four guys, who were, to put it mildly, basic as fuck. They had bullshit jobs: jobs that no one, not even them, thought worth doing. One was a management consultant. One was a customer service manager for a call center. One was an ad-tech programmer. One was a marketing specialist for cryptocurrency startups. All shared one trait: they'd watched the slow death of an insured loved one who'd been denied coverage. In an earlier age, they'd have stewed in private misery, become alcoholics, shot themselves. Instead, they'd followed simple online instructions for starting a message board and hosting it on a bulletproof server accessible only via the Tor network. They hadn't detonated bombs or gone on a shooting spree—they hadn't even egged on the people who had. But they'd provided a place for it all to happen, had watched it all happen, and hadn't shut it down. That was enough.

One of them—the management consultant—was a Canadian expat, and his Twitter was full of comparisons between US health care and the Canadian system, and that kicked off a whole other social media storm about Canada and what America could learn from it, and also whether Canadians were secretly terrorists, which was jokey but not entirely. The *South Park* memes were epic and late-night comedy had a ball with it.

The Canadian Prime Minister weighed in on the subject and said that even though she was a conservative, she understood that there were some places where markets couldn't do the job, and health care was one of them. It won her a lot of points with her base, and it also played really well with the undecided Canadian voters who generally held the Tories in bad odor, but who were swayed enough by this demonstration of compassionate conservatism that they elected Quebec's first-ever Conservative provincial government later that month. If there was one thing that would motivate Canadians, it was the sense that American politics were so screwed up that they made Canada shine by comparison.

None of the four got bail.

MADDY HAD A cold and it took forever to get her to cough herself to sleep. Joe found Lacey sitting up in bed with her bedside light on, reading her phone.

"You remember that message board you used, when I was sick?"

He tried to stay casual as he hung up his robe and slid into bed next to her. "Yeah."

"It was one of these, right?" She showed him her phone. There'd been a failed bombing, a guy who'd been shot as he approached the armed checkpoint at the end of a Kaiser hospital driveway. He'd blown himself up, and the shrapnel had injured some other people, but none seriously, and at least they'd been close to a hospital. Kaiser had even waived their copays.

"Not exactly," he lied.

"How do you mean, 'not exactly,' exactly?" She sounded pre-pissed, like she wasn't in a mood to be screwed around with.

"Lace—"

"Don't, Joe. Just tell me. Those guys who you spent all those hours talking to, are they the ones running around committing mass murder?"

"Honestly?"

She just stared.

"I don't know." Which was a lie. "I mean, they could be.

They were pissed enough about it. And I don't know any of their real names—everyone used a screen name. I stopped logging in, and then it shut down, anyway."

"How'd you know it shut down, if you weren't logging in anymore?"

Shit. "After some of the killings, I decided to have a look. I was curious, too. But it was gone."

"Do you think it was one of the ones the FBI shut down?"

"No, it was before that."

"Good. Because if it was, that would mean that there was a server in an FBI evidence locker with details that pointed back to our home and our family."

"Yeah. That's something I've been thinking about, too."

When Lacey finally fell asleep, Joe slipped out of the bedroom and looked up the Arizona ACLU phone number and did his best to memorize it. Just in case.

THE FBI ARRESTED forty-two people the following week, acting on leads from the seized servers. Every one of them was planning an act of mass murder, supposedly.

Joe tried not to watch the news reports of the arrests, clicked away from social media doxxings of the guys in custody. He caught Lacey staring worriedly at her phone more and more.

A bipartisan group of senators introduced a Medicare-for-All bill with a lot of fanfare, and half of America cheered them on, while the other half followed Fox News in condemning them as appeasers who had caved in to terrorism.

The next day, a guy took a shot at the senator from the Great State of Maine. He was killed by the Secret Service, and immediately doxxed online. The guy had run for Congress eleven times as the only Republican seeking the nomination in a hardcore Democratic-machine seat in suburban Chicago. Each of his campaigns had featured rants about cartels of Jewish bankers and George Soros. In between The Blues Brothers "I hate Illinois Nazis" memes, there were posts from people who said that this was inevitable and would only get worse and blamed "health-care extremists" for starting it.

Joe stopped sleeping at night. He'd lie in bed, earbuds in, listening to old comedy podcasts, until Lacey dropped off, then he'd go into the basement and jog on the treadmill and lift his old weights, trying to obliterate the whirl of thoughts going around and around his brain. He drank coffee all day at his desk until his guts burned, and nearly killed himself falling asleep at the wheel one night.

Lacey made a doctor's appointment for him and told him he was calling in sick to work the next day and wouldn't hear any argument.

THE DOC LISTENED attentively, if impersonally, then shook his head.

"Sounds like you're having a hard time, Joe."

Joe felt tears well up. "Yeah," he said, barely a whisper.

"How is everyone else in your family?" The doctor looked at his screen. "How's Lacey?"

Joe had talked extensively with the doc about Lacey's health, back when everything had been so scary. He remembered the doc commiserating about the bastards at the insurance company who'd turned down her therapy. From the doc's expression—startlement, mistrust—he'd just remembered it, too.

"Lacey's great." He felt the tears slipping down his cheeks, but he didn't know what they were for. "Full recovery. Her hair's down to here now." He touched his shoulders.

The doc handed him a Kleenex box. "That's great news, really great." He shifted in his chair. "A miracle, really."

Joe was really crying now.

The doc tapped at his computer for a while. "Look, I want to refer you for psychiatric care but it looks like you only get twenty-five percent coverage. There's a woman I really like, she used to be an ER doc and then became a psychiatrist. You'll really like her, I think. She's not afraid to prescribe mood-stabilizers but they're not her first choice, either. But she's not cheap. I know this is a hard question, but do you think you can afford it?"

Joe started to laugh, still crying, then sobbing. The doc looked uncomfortable, then alarmed. Joe didn't know exactly how much time they had for the appointment, but he was pretty sure he'd run over and there would be other patients waiting. He pulled himself together, blew his nose, and wiped his eyes.

"I'm sorry," he said. "It's just..." He waved his hands and dropped some snotty Kleenexes. He picked them up. "My insurance won't pay for me to go to a shrink to talk about how screwed up my insurance is."

"Yeah," the doc said. "Look, we doctors hate this even more than you do. You only have to deal with them when you're sick. We have to deal with them every damned day. I have two admin people out there whose only job is chasing payment from them."

"I'd heard about that."

"You haven't heard half of it, believe me." The doc pushed the cart with the computer away, started to rub his eyes, then took his hands away from his face and reached for a pump of hand sanitizer from the wall-mounted receptacle. He looked at Joe. "You've been through a lot, Joe. Nearly losing your wife, it's hard stuff. It's a miracle that she survived, but it also means that you didn't get any counseling or care, the kind of thing that would have kicked in automatically if she hadn't made it. So you're just hanging out there. I had an insurance rep on the phone yesterday, telling me that I could refer for unlimited psych care for anyone who's lost someone—they've figured out that the cheapest way to keep from having their heads blown off is to remove barriers to psych treatment." He smiled mirthlessly.

"I'm not a psychiatric professional, Joe, but I've seen enough PTSD cases to know one when I see one. You need treatment. For the sake of your family, and for your own sake. I know you want to be the dad your daughter needs.

"There's a reason there's so much medical debt in this country: your health is just that important. More important than your credit-card balance or your credit rating or even your mortgage. If I write you a referral to Dr. Haddid, will you find a way to see her? You can try discussing all-cash payments. A lot of doctors offer discounts for cash up front."

Joe blew his nose. "Yeah," he said, "thanks."

DR. HADDID'S CASH rate was $125/hour, plus $75 for the initial consultation. $200 later, Joe knew he'd never be going back to her. He'd frozen in the office, unable to talk, terrified of what might come out. Terrified he might start spouting off like a Fuckriffer of the worst kind, inspire her to call the cops.

Instead, he stopped at a CVS and bought four different kinds of over-the-counter sleeping pills, and drew up a chart on some scrap printer paper from the guest room and kept track, looking for a pill that gave him the most sleep with the least hangover.

What he really wanted was some Ambien, which he'd tried a couple times in college when he was too wound up to sleep and a buddy had helped him out. There were lots of places to get Ambien cheap and prescription-free, using darkweb markets. He even had some cryptocurrency he'd speculated on when it seemed like it wouldn't ever stop rising. Might as well spend it now before it was completely worthless.

But of course, he couldn't remember the obscure .onion addresses for the marketplaces, and the only one he knew by heart was Fuckriff's, and before he could stop himself or even remember that the site had gone down, he was logging in.

The log-in banner informed him that the site was back up, with all the accounts intact but all the archives securely deleted. It asked him to delete any screengrabs or saved messages he might have stashed away himself, and welcomed him back on behalf of the new manager, someone called Deadzone874755, who he couldn't ever recall working with.

For the first time in more than a month, he felt relaxed. All the tension drained out of him as he skimmed the boards, laughing at the bullshit sessions and bon mots, reading updates from old friends. Like it or not, these were his people, this was his place. His spiritual home. And if there were fringe elements in his community who did bad things, unconscionable things, well, what of it? No one faulted soldiers for staying in the army just because someone wearing the same uniform shot up a village or waterboarded a prisoner. The camaraderie and understanding he got from the Fuckriffers, the bond of shared experience—it was irreplaceable. He had a right to that, and no one had the right to make him stop. He never egged anyone on to an act of violence. In fact, he'd done everything he could to stop violence.

Not to mention: the cause was just. The most just one. Letting people die because saving their lives would erode profits was a wicked act, and people who endorsed that act were wicked people. Blowing them up or shooting them wasn't right, but a world in which the wicked went about their days frightened of retribution was a more just one than a world where the wicked held their heads high.

THE DEPARTMENT OF Justice sent sternly worded memos to five large internet companies asking them to seriously contemplate suppressing the #YouShouldBeAfraid hashtag. They stopped short of demanding this. Later that day, someone dumped a set of leaked emails between the general counsels of the internet companies and a senior DoJ lawyer, who had made this request in private and got told to go pound sand. The consensus was that the DoJ didn't think they could make a court order stick, but having failed to secure quiet, voluntary cooperation, they were trying to get the public on-side, getting people to blame the platforms for abetting the killings.

It worked, sort of. Joe's friends were evenly split between people who thought that banning the tag was ridiculous and people who thought that the internet companies were total assholes for not falling into line. People used that tag to talk about the issue and the tactics, to share safety tips and discuss motivations. On the other hand, people used the tag to glorify and publicize mass killings. On the other hand, making a new tag wasn't exactly rocket surgery: #AfraidShouldBeYes, #YShldBFrd. Of course, the Fuckriffers didn't care, they got all the #YouShouldBeAfraid talk they needed on their private boards.

BlueCross BlueShield of Minneapolis broke ground on a new building in an industrial park at the end of its own gated cul-de-sac, with high guard towers, automated license plate recognition systems in a one-mile radius, panic rooms on every floor, and a large staff of 24/7 armed guards. Their shareholder disclosures costed this out and amortized the capital over five years, explaining how the running costs would be covered by a combination of a "security surcharge" on all premiums and a tiny per-share dividend hit. After a short bobble when the shorts moved into the market, the share price closed up and some shorts took a big hit.

> They want to prove they're not afraid

DamFool was the newest Fuckriffer. Fuckriff was a lot harder to find than it used to be, and new recruits were brought in by old hands, vouched for. His son, Tommy, was fourteen years old, track star, accelerated math, Eagle Scout.

Non-Hodgkin's lymphoma.

Tommy's cancer had not responded to two rounds of chemo. He was strong and young and vital, and the same youth that gave him the strength to withstand all that terrible medicine also caused his cells to divide with terrible, regular rapidity, even the cancerous ones.

His doc thought that Tommy was a good candidate for chimeric antigen receptor T-cell therapy, a therapy that was experimental by anyone's lights. But if anyone could survive it, it was Tommy. People who survived that therapy had a good chance of making it three years cancer free, and then the sky was the limit. Tommy was up for it. He even wanted to freeze some sperm in case he decided to have kids later in life. That was the kind of life choice that people who were planning on surviving made.

The insurer—Cigna—had other ideas.

The bottom line: they would not spend three-quarters of a million (table stakes, the total could be much higher) to kill Tommy with an experimental therapy. Not even if Tommy was a fighter and an optimist and young and healthy (except for dying of cancer) and wanted to freeze his sperm.

DamFool's wife was inconsolable. His older son, Rhett, had died of an opioid overdose in his senior year, five years ago, and the two of them had put everything they had into Tommy, throwing themselves into his life and upbringing with a vigor that Tommy seemed to embrace. They'd all been hurt by what happened to Rhett.

For his part, DamFool was barely holding it together. He spent as much time away from Tommy as he could bear to, not wanting to overshadow the boy, and when he wasn't with Tommy, he was trying to console his wife, who was in no mood for consolation, or trying not to drink all the beer in the fridge. Tommy was in a lot of pain, partly because he resisted the painkillers because they were the same ones that Rhett had been addicted to. It was a bad situation.

The Great Old Ones of Fuckriff were grooming DamFool. There were these hit lists that people had made, doxxing health care execs, analysts, investors, lobbyists, as well as lawmakers at the state and national level who'd carried their water. The dumps had home addresses, known travel routes, even architectural drawings from public records departments showing the floor plans of their homes and offices. These lists weren't hard to come by—they were circulated with glee on the #YouShouldBeAfraid hashtag. The first time Joe saw one of these files, he thought of how chilling it must be to see your home, your family, your picture, your license plate on a list like this. It gave him a lot of satisfaction that he tried not to think about too much.

DamFool lived in Montana and, for such a sparsely populated state, Montana sure had a hell of a lot of high-value
targets. Small populations had big old-boy networks, and they
made it easy for corruption to spread, favor to favor, friend to
friend. You could see the diffusion pattern in the hit list, which
was extensive.

The Great Old Ones were good at this pitch. They were just
hinting now, not giving DamFool the hard sell. That would
come after Tommy's demise. Right now, they were just getting
him in position. Joe had seen the playbook before. It was his
cue to dive in with a highly symbolic and largely ornamental
bid to save his soul.

Joe just couldn't. He'd been reading these op-eds by Black
Lives Matter activists about the official neglect that people
with sickle cell anemia endured, stories about agonized teenagers being tied to hospital beds and told to stop shouting
if they wanted to get untied. The general tenor was that the
whites who'd suddenly decided that the health-care system
was too sick to live were late to the party, and by the way, let
me tell you a little story about the Tuskegee airmen.

Joe found himself imagining what his life would have been
like if Lacey had died. If he'd been alone with Maddy, a huge
hole in both their hearts. He imagined what life must be like
for a parent going through that themselves, watching their
kids go through it, watching their nieces and nephews and
their friends go through it. He couldn't imagine it. Couldn't
imagine tolerating it. How could they tolerate it? He wasn't
stupid. He'd heard of white privilege. It was a thing. He got it.

The more he thought about this, though—what if Lacey
died, what about all those people who've tolerated that and
worse, what about everything he could get away with that all
those people couldn't?

When you thought about it that way, he practically had a duty to kill a health-care executive or two.

TOMMY DIED ON July seventeenth.

Maddy was in Wisconsin with Lacey, visiting Lacey's cousins, whom she had started talking to again after she came back from the cancer, making a conscious choice to put the old rifts with her family behind her.

Without family to give him focus, Joe found himself actually paying attention at work again, answering emails until late at night, then smoothly transitioning into a long session with Fuckriff. Even though Lacey wasn't around, he still took his laptop into the guest room when it was time for Fuckriff.

DamFool was incoherent with grief at first, then coldly violent, writing the most detailed fantasies of murder and mayhem. Then he disappeared.

Joe had not engaged with him at all, letting the Old Ones egg DamFool on while Joe watched from the sidelines. But once he went quiet, Joe had a crisis of conscience and sent him a string of private messages begging him to call before he did anything stupid.

DamFool didn't answer Joe's messages, but the next morning, he was walking fuzzy-headed to the toilet in a pair of boxers, holding his phone and thinking about his first cup of coffee, when he saw something out the window. He stopped and peered at the shape, trying to make sense of what appeared to be a futuristic robot, at least in the brief instant it took him to realize that it was a man in SWAT armor with a visor and a very large gun, which he was swinging around to point at Joe.

Joe opened his mouth to say something—"no" or maybe

"what the fuck?"—when he discovered that he was lying on the floor and he couldn't breathe. He tried to get up, because something was on his chest and he had to get out from under it, but it wasn't just his lungs that weren't working—he couldn't make his legs or arms move, either. It was very noisy all of a sudden, too, and eventually, as he was surrounded by more robot-men in body armor with very, very large guns, he realized that he had been shot in the chest.

THE OFFICER WHO shot Joe was a SWAT veteran with twenty-two years on the Tempe PD, during which time he had shot a total of nineteen suspects, but Joe was the first white person Officer Connor had shot. Joe was also the first one who survived, and there were social media pundits who hypothesized that Connor's latent white supremacy—the same force that had animated his trigger finger all those times before—had spoiled his aim, sparing Joe's life. He had been hit "center mass" but had only suffered a collapsed lung and no damage to his heart.

The officer said he'd mistaken Joe's phone for a gun.

Joe learned this last detail from the FBI agent who questioned him once he was clear of the anesthesia, handcuffed to his recovery bed and coming to his senses. (He learned about the other eighteen shootings later).

The FBI agent had read Joe's entire series of messages with DamFool and wanted Joe to know that in his, Agent Sebold's, opinion, Joe had tried to do the right thing. Agent Sebold could tell that he and Joe were on the same team here, both of them trying to help these poor, confused, heartbroken men channel their grief into a less pathological course of action.

Which was why Agent Sebold had come up with the

singularly great idea of helping Joe escape any potential criminal liability in exchange for Joe's cooperation in infiltrating Fuckriff and catching the Great Old Ones. Agent Sebold strongly implied that there were other collaborators already working with him on Fuckriff, but that the Great Old Ones' wiliness had foiled their efforts. By working with the Bureau, Joe wouldn't be pioneering the idea of undercovers on the system, but he would be using his unique skills and long-standing access to further his joint mission with the Bureau to save these poor, impressionable men, to say nothing of their victims.

Joe was very groggy. The anesthetic was still in his blood and then there was the fantastic calamity of sensations from his chest cavity, bones, and swollen, stitched skin.

A muffled voice in the back of his mind was chattering intensely at him, telling him he needed to talk to Lacey ASAP because she'd be out of her mind, telling him he should *not* talk to this cop without a lawyer present.

Joe listened to the cop talking. Agent Sebold was good: calm, reassuring, friendly. He only wanted the same things Joe wanted. He wanted to help Joe. He knew Joe wanted to help, too.

Joe tried to speak but couldn't. His mouth was gummed shut with thick, dried saliva, his tongue was as thick as his fist. Agent Sebold clearly knew his business: gently, he dipped a large cotton swab in water and swabbed at Joe's lips, then the front of his teeth. A trickle of the flat, room-temperature water moistened Joe's tongue. It felt incredible.

"Lawyer," Joe said. The agent looked angry for a second, then he mastered himself and switched to disappointed. "Sorry," Joe added. Then, "Lawyer." It was all he managed before his tongue dried out again. The FBI agent left.

*

IT WAS TEN days before Joe saw a lawyer. In the interim, he was kept in restraints except during doctor visits and physio. These were under guard—stone-faced Phoenix PD cops—and each time one of these officers entered his room, he asked to see a lawyer. It got to be kind of a game. Not a good game.

He didn't see Lacey. When he asked the cops, the doctors, the nurses, the PT, about her, they acted like they hadn't heard him. He was pretty sure he could see Lacey whenever he wanted, provided he asked to speak to Agent Sebold first.

He almost broke down every day. But he didn't.

You know what kept him going? The visit from the guy from hospital billing.

His insurance wasn't covering his stay. There was an exemption in his policy for "acts of terrorism" and they were invoking it. The hospital's accounting department wanted to know about his assets. They were the only ones who would talk to him about Lacey, and what they wanted to know was whether she had separate finances from his.

The billing guy seemed like a decent fellow stuck with a shitty job. Joe knew, somehow, that he made less money than Joe. It was the cheap shoes, and the seven-dollar haircut. He was embarrassed and apologetic, but he had a job to do. It wasn't his fault the system was so totally fucked up. There was nothing that one guy could do about it.

When the billing guy visited for the third time, Joe decided that he'd go to jail for a hundred years before he betrayed Fuckriff and all who sailed in her.

Agent Sebold visited just ahead of the lawyer, looking pissed and harried. The last time, he'd gently persuaded, but this time he wheedled and it tipped Joe off that things weren't going the way he'd hoped.

THE LAWYER WAS an old Chinese American guy who'd been doing pro-bono work with the Arizona ACLU since his college days. He showed up an hour after Agent Sebold left the bedside and introduced himself.

"Your wife is fine. She wanted me to make sure you got that first. She was very adamant. I wouldn't be here if it wasn't for her. She did a lot of legwork, convinced the ACLU that this was something we should be paying attention to. There are a hell of a lot of potential clients who fit your profile, and we've had to prioritize the cases that could make good law or prevent bad law from being made. You're in the latter case. No one alleges that you abbeted anyone, even the FBI says you did what you could to stop things. But you knew about serious crimes that were going to happen and you didn't go to the cops. They say that makes you an accessory to terrorism. There's an Arizona congressman who called you an 'enemy combatant.'"

Joe suppressed a groan.

Leonard, his lawyer, patted his hand, frowned at the restraints. "Look, there's a long process ahead of us. I want to start with some basics: get you out of these cuffs, get your family in to see you, get you released on bail. *Then* we can talk about how we're going to keep you out of prison."

"At least you didn't mention the death penalty." Joe was joking. Leonard didn't smile.

"Was saving that for when you got your strength back," Leonard said. "It's not something I'm unduly concerned with, but whenever there's even a small chance that a court will order an execution, it's something we have to factor into our planning." He gave Joe a moment to soak that in. "Now, I want to know everything." He got out a yellow pad. "Start at the beginning."

THE LAST VERIFIED #YouShouldBeAfraid killing took place a year and a half later, while Joe was in solitary in the Tucson supermax pen, having been transferred after he caught a beating at the Maricopa County pen while waiting for a hearing on Leonard's appeal on his bail. The Tucson warden took one look at Joe's beat-up face and taped ribs and ordered him into "protective solitary." It had been a week.

The killer had been a Jacksonville, Missouri fireman whose BlueCross BlueShield refused to cover treatment for dialysis after an acute kidney injury he experienced on the job when a ceiling joist fell on him. They disagreed with the doctor's analysis of his condition. His doctor privately told him that he had better scrape together the cash for the dialysis or he could expect a short and unhappy life ahead of him.

The fireman had no wife and no child, which made him different from the others. He'd had elderly parents and he'd gone into deep debt paying for their home care in the years before. Now that they were gone, all he had was his job and his health, neither of which he had anymore.

The insurer reported the fireman to the sheriff, as was standard procedure now when denying a claim like this one, but the sheriff had a lot to do and not many deputies to do it with, and the deputy who was supposed to look in on the fireman had pushed it to a later date twice while he got caught up in more urgent matters.

Firemen know a fair bit about explosives, as it turns out.

*

JOE GOT WORD of the passage of Americare during a rare visit from Lacey. Leonard had advised him against pleading out, saying that the ACLU was hopeful that they could get a good precedent out of his case. But then they met with the prosecutor, who discussed in eye-watering detail what thirty-five years in prison does to a man. Leonard insisted that the thirty-five-year number was total bullshit, that it would require the judge violating the United States Sentencing Commission's guidelines to such an egregious extent that the appeal would be practically automatic.

But thirty-five years rests heavy on a man's mind. Joe imagined himself separated from Lacey and Maddy while Maddy grew up and Lacey grew old, stepping out of the prison gates to meet a fifteen-year-old grandchild for the first time.

Joe and Lacey cried a lot, and Maddy got scared, but in the end, the prosecutor was offering five years, paroled in two. He'd already been held for most of a year while the trial dragged and dragged, while other Fuckriffers were arrested, while witnesses turned state's evidence.

So Joe agreed to another year, maybe four more years, and a felony rap, and a chance to grow old with his family. The warden decided that he'd been the kind of prisoner who tolerated protective solitary well, and so that became a permanent condition, with the effect that visits were all but impossible to arrange. There was one right at the start, then three months, then another.

"They passed Americare," Lacey said. She looked terrible, exhausted and emotionally wrung out, her rosacea hectic, the way it got when she got stressed. Joe was acutely aware of the paunch he'd watched develop around his waistline, the six days that had passed since his weekly shower.

He wanted to say something like, "It's been three months and all you want to talk about is *Americare,*" but he also recognized that safe subjects were few and far between for them, and Maddy's eyes were red and big as saucers and everyone was just doing their best.

"That's good news."

"It didn't have everything we wanted, but it's still pretty amazing. No one believed it would pass. No one believed the president would sign it. The lawsuit was dead on arrival, too, even though they got to choose their venue. The Federal Circuit appeals judges took about ten seconds to tell 'em to go fuck themselves. No one seriously believes the Supremes will take the case, and the share prices are—"

"I've missed you, Lacey."

She stopped. Her eyes were bright with tears.

"Are you OK?"

He looked at Maddy. "Yes," he said. When Maddy looked away, he mouthed "no." Lacey put her hand on the glass and he did the same, conscious that it was such a cliché, but also feeling the psychosomatic ghost of the warmth of her skin through the thick plexi like a space heater radiating directly into his own palm.

Lacey was crying now. So was he.

"They really passed it, huh?" he said through the snot.

"Who says violence doesn't solve anything?" she said.

Joe's laugh was so unexpected that he sprayed the glass with a Jackson Pollock of snot, and that set Maddy laughing, and that set Lacey laughing, a dam broken between them.

Only nine more months, assuming good behavior.

the masque
of the red death

BEFORE THE EVENT, Martin Mars spent a lot of time trying to game it out. Would the collapse be sudden, catching him off guard and unprepared, having to fight his way to his fortress as he escaped from Paradise Valley and into the desert hills? Or would there be some kind of sign, a steady uptick in civil disorder and failures from the official powers that counted down to the day, giving him a chance to plan an orderly withdrawal to Fort Doom?

This was important. If Martin spooked and ran for Fort Doom too early, he'd have to slink back to the city and his job after however many days he'd spent bunkered up. Not only would it be humiliating, but it would cost him credibility with The Thirty, the people he'd invited to survive the apocalypse with him. Once Fort Doom was buttoned up for the duration, he'd need to be a credible leader or he could lose control. Who the fuck knew what would happen next? He had visions of some distant descendant cracking the big doors and finding their mummified corpses sprawled in the postures they'd crumpled into when the ravening mob had turned on itself.

Every time he sounded the alarm and brought The Thirty out, he increased the chance that one or more of them would leak the existence of Fort Doom. They were all under strict pledges of secrecy, but when shit's going down, someone's

gonna leak to that cute girl they were trying to get with, and/
or leave a trail that some curious rando would follow. There
would come a day when The Thirty would have to defend
what was theirs from the people who'd lacked the foresight
to build their own fortresses, but Martin's preference was for
that day to be a long way off, after they'd had a chance to
cohere into the mutual-survival unit they'd need to be to wait
out The Event.

So there were so many reasons not to send up a flare and
summon everyone to the Fort prematurely, but what about
the costs of waiting too long? Paradise Valley was all right,
sure, but Phoenix was right there on their doorsteps, and there
were so many people with so little to lose out there, people
who were already killing and raping each other. What would
they do once the cops were all too busy struggling for their
own survival to defend the stolid burghers of Paradise Valley?
Wait too long and it might be *Mad Max* time, fighting his way
through god knew how many bad guys to get out to the hills.
What if they followed him? He could get the Fort buttoned
up even if he was fighting a rearguard action—the Fort's
defenses were explicitly designed for that—but any of The
Thirty who showed up would be torn apart by the besieging
army before they could get to the Fort's door, or worse, they'd
make it to the door but it would be too dangerous to let them
in. That would be a real confidence-booster when it came to
his leadership, watching helplessly from inside the Fort while
the CHUDs and zombies ripped a work colleague to shreds
on the doorstep.

It was a hard problem; it was never far from Martin's mind
as he sat at his Bloomberg Terminal and watched the markets
move, the currencies rise and fall, the assets bubble up and
tank.

*

MARTIN KNEW THAT The Event was coming. The fact was the world just didn't *need* all those people anymore, and the market had revealed that fact, squeezing them into tinier, more uncomfortable places. He wouldn't tolerate it if he was in their shoes. He'd be the first one to build a guillotine, and because he was Martin, it would be an *awesome* guillotine, so absolutely badass and overengineered, with a turbocharger and a self-sharpening blade. Because that was Martin, all the way. It's why Fort Doom was the incredible place it was.

It was all about information asymmetries. Markets corrected them. If knowing a secret could make a stupid, unworthy person rich, then sooner or later, smart, superior people would find that secret out and clear out the misallocated wealth of all those dimbulbs. Markets were awesome at this.

Back when everyone lived in shithole mud-street villages, the superior people had no choice but to breed with whoever was in the vicinity. Even a one-in-ten-million, six-sigma genius would end up hitched for life to some cow-eyed milkmaid, diluting the incredible genes he'd been handed by nature's Powerball lotto.

But little by little, humans got smarter, as the geniuses found smarter milkmaids, until they could build markets and then the information systems that markets thrived on, and then the information asymmetry started to collapse, slowly at first, then all at once, like a cliff that had been undermined by the inexorable tide of millions of human actions harnessed to the common goal of improving the species and its dominion over the earth.

Once the information about where the best people were hanging out became public knowledge, then anyone who fluked into good genes and a high sigma knew exactly where they belonged. Little by little the world's cities filled up with powerful, self-governing people whose discipline, hard work, and brilliance meant that they got richer and richer.

Give the socialists credit, they had this figured out. They knew that the world was heading to a state when the number of betas and gammas the alphas needed to keep the systems running would far exceed the demand, and that those unnecessary people would be squeezed out, little by little, and then, all at once. They wouldn't go without a fight, of course. Of course! Who would?

It was just like "gentrifying," but on a grand scale. Fuzzy-headed crybaby lefties thought that gentrifying was some kind of conspiracy to screw poor people, but it was just the market again. Location is an asset: if you happened to luck into a house that was a short drive from some place really important, a financial center, say, or a beautiful view, and all you did with that location was build a shitty little house you couldn't afford to maintain on that plot of land, then the market would solve the problem, and it would hook you up with someone smarter and better than you with the capital to pay you more for the house than you thought it was worth, and then they'd do something with it that made it worth even more. Lots more. That's what markets did: they moved fallow, underutilized assets out of the hands of the incompetent and moved them into the hands of their betters, who put those assets to work. Like a Monopoly player who couldn't figure out how to corner suited properties and build houses and hotels, the semi-employed, semi-employable dimbulbs who lucked into a prime piece of location would soon find themselves gently ushered to a place that was better matched with their worth to society and the human race.

Lather, rinse, repeat: the smartest and best had figured out how to improve even the most marginal assets, well beyond the capacity of the 99 percent, and now the 99 percent had found themselves relieved of all their worldly goods and lacking the sums to rent anywhere to perch while they waited to die.

This was an adjustment period, two words that sounded bloodless and bureaucratic, but which described the chaos that would reign while the unnecessariat were eased out of existence and humanity realigned itself around the strongest and brightest that evolution could select.

(Martin wasn't a racist: any couple could win the genetic lottery, and that's why there were a couple of Black guys and all those Indian women working at the fund with him, smart as hell—but at the same time, he couldn't help but notice just how many of the smartest people he knew had the same color skin as him.)

Economists called it an "adjustment period" but people like Martin called it The Event.

MARTIN HAD WRESTLED with numbers and personalities before settling on The Thirty. First, why thirty? The Fort had been built with fifteen bedrooms and he'd done the math on per-person food, water, and other consumable reserves, and every person you added multiplied all those numbers, adding linear feet of shelving to hold toilet paper and MREs and bottled water. Each one translated into more solar panels, more batteries, more gas for the gennies.

But each one was also another strong set of hands to carry and build and fight. Half of them would be women, half of them would be men. Half single, half coupled. Martin was single and he had obviously kept that thought in mind when he picked the single women to invite. He'd made it clear to all the singles that there would be no plus-ones on the day—this was an invitation for them and them alone. If their circumstances changed, if they got into a serious thing with someone, then they could tell Martin and he'd pick someone to replace them. It wasn't like they were paying. One of the decisions Martin made early on is that this would all be on his dime. It was a baller move, an alpha move, the kind of thing that would give him leadership credibility when it mattered. And there was a pretty good chance that cash would be worthless after The Event. He'd built a hidden vault into Fort Doom with some gold ingots, some encrypted thumb drives with BtC, some dollars, some sapphires, and a few neat packets of renminbi, which felt right. You never knew. He could afford it.

He could afford all of it. Martin and the market understood each other. He was a star at the firm, personally managing a portfolio with $11 billion in it, which he had personally grown from $9 billion. There was talk of giving him his own fund, giving the most ultra-high-net-worth types the chance to subscribe directly, and giving him tons of freedom to do as he saw fit with it. When he thought about this, his brain kind of split into two different, mutually exclusive thought processes: the first one started adding up bonuses and commissions and new base pay; the second one wondered how much of that would arrive before The Event.

Maybe The Event would never happen. He was a Bayesian reasoner, not a fortune-teller. He gave odds, not certainty, like a good poker player. When he started planning Fort Doom, he was like 40–60; and it wasn't until he hit 50–50 that he broke ground on it, using the kind of discreet contractors that specialized in panic rooms. The firm he'd picked had a long waiting list, but when he described the size of the job he was planning, they brought in trusted subs they'd worked with on other big projects and started right away. Now it was done, he was more like 75–25 on The Event, and of course, it was possible that he was feeling that way because Fort Doom was so fucking *cool*, it would be *awesome* to hole up there and wait out the chaotic months or years until stability was restored.

HE CALLED IT too early. When the markets opened on January second, there was a flash-crash, seemingly precipitated by wild-fires in the Canadian prairies, which were supposed to be under too much ice for anything to burn at that time of year. A bone-dry autumn, a failed harvest, then an unseasonably hot winter that screwed up things in the big oil sands pipeline, touching off a spill in a wooded area that turned into a forest fire that turned into a wildfire. It had been rumbling along all through the Christmas week, a constant background beat to the news reports: *Here's how fucked up things are in Saskatchewan; and now, a story about a soldier who made it home in time for Christmas.* Martin moved some assets around, bought some swaps, and hedged up like a pro, even getting called in to facilitate a firm-wide meeting on the systemic risks the Canada Situation presented.

But other firms weren't nearly as well-managed as Martin's. Nevertheless, they had a lot of money under management, which started to vanish like faerie gold as the sell-off touched off more sell-offs and it all began to blaze.

More panic-selling, more contagion, and Martin was still keeping his head cool, moving stuff around one trade ahead of the flames, even scooping up some bargains when frightened fools sold the assets they should have been holding. Not just financial instruments, either: he took possession of a shipping container full of early Picassos, in a climate-controlled facility outside of Amsterdam, and even used his personal account to buy some legendary Château Mouton Rothschild, which he had shipped by bonded courier straight to the office. They came in their own lithium-cell-powered piezoelectric coolers that kept them at optimal temperature and humidity, and he plugged them in next to his go-bag. Four bottles, each worth as much as a new Mercedes; and one more bottle, worth as much as a decent two-bedroom house in a nice part of Phoenix. It made him giddy to leave it there, by the door, instead of downstairs in his cellar with its special locking vault.

Maybe it was the thought of toasting the apocalypse in Fort Doom with his investment-grade wine, but he found himself on a hair trigger, almost ready to call The Event and head to the Fort six times a day.

The Second Arab Spring was a lot uglier than the first one. It was winter, for one thing, and the food riots were as out of control as the Canadian wildfires. Every shitty-ass dictator in the region had learned the lesson of Bashar al-Assad: when the people hit the streets, you hit the people. Hard. The blood was incredible.

Then the bombs went off in Houston, *pop, pop, pop,* targeting a police station, the highway patrol headquarters, and the FBI building at 1 Justice Park Drive. The president vowed revenge, Feds swarmed Houston, and Atlanta went off, *boom, boom, boom,* and then there was a prison uprising at Rikers Island that no one could shut down.

The Thirty were all in a private Signal group, and there was a lot of chatter about when and if they should grab their bags. Thing was, no one could go to Fort Doom until and unless Martin was there. The Fort had serious defenses, and only he knew how to disable them, and he wasn't going to tell anyone else how to do it, not until he was safely inside. He trusted The Thirty enough to spend a long time in a lockdown with them, but he didn't want to tempt any of them with the power to lock him out and change up the guest list. Fort Doom was *his*.

The house next to Martin's got burgled. Each of the houses on his road had their own gates and security, as well as the complex's overall security, manifested by rent-a-cops, mostly ex-military, zipping around in golf carts and watching giant banks of monitors fed by infrared CCTVs all around and outside the fence line.

So naturally, it was an inside job. Frank Patel had not been subtle about the liquidation of the majority of his assets to convertible, portable wealth in the form of precious metals and gemstones. He'd talk your ear off about the clever ways he'd found to hide the loot: in hidden pouches in clothes for him and his family, in hidden panels in his car, in a hidden floor safe in his basement, behind the firebrick in the walk-in fireplace in his great room.

Word got around, and two of the guards fritzed the cameras on his door, knocked at it like it was a routine callout, and then bulled their way in, tied him and his kids up, and got all of it. More than ten million dollars in anonymous, convertible wealth. The guards disappeared off the face of the earth, and G4S, who supplied them, brought in heavy lawyers and insurance underwriters and PIs who started hinting heavily that Patel was in on the robbery. It was ugly. It got worse when Patel blew his brains out. He was heavily leveraged and had just lost his life's savings. To be honest, Martin was surprised he didn't take his wife and kids with him. It was the sight of them, the next day, their faces blank masks as they drove into Patel's gate toward his house and garage, that spooked Martin so that he made the call, firing off a mass text to The Thirty and then autopiloting through the routine to get his go-bags and other gear (including the Rothschilds in their portable life-support machines) into his armored Toyota Tacoma with its overcab cargo pod, camouflaged to look like a camping accessory, but actually as armored-up as the Tacoma's body and windshields, with spare gas, tires, guns, ammo, food—even a chainsaw.

He'd rehearsed this once a week, using the interior door connecting the house to the garage. He also had a randomizer that ordered him to drive the Tacoma periodically, so it wouldn't be unusual to see him leaving with it. He generally made a point of stopping at a lumberyard on the way home and driving back with some fifteen-foot two-by-fours or plastic pipe sticking out of the back of the overcab, just in case anyone was looking.

So he hit the road at 5:30 the next morning, which was within the parameters for his normal work schedule (there were days when market-moving events were predicted for London or Frankfurt when he'd go even earlier). He had the house in lockdown, and he waved to the security guard on the gate as he cruised through, then he slipped his gate and toll-transponders into a Faraday pouch and stuck them into the glove compartment. At a deserted red light he peeled off his top layer of business clothes to reveal well-worn, high-quality fishing gear. He ostentatiously placed a tackle box on his passenger seat, so anyone who took a close look would see a middle-aged, fit guy heading out of town for a weekend of fly fishing—not a multi-millionaire with interesting quantities of easily convertible wealth and the kind of vehicle that you could live out of for a week, without a resupply, over rough terrain, in the face of hostile belligerents.

Thus camouflaged, he switched his phone into airplane

mode and drove at one mile under the speed limit for the next four hours.

ONLY SIXTEEN OUT of The Thirty showed up in the first forty-eight hours. He took pains to disguise how furious that made him, because The Sixteen needed to see him as a cool-headed, forward-looking leader, not a child who was upset that half the guests hadn't come to his birthday party. The no-shows included four singles, all women, including the hottest two, roommates who were definitely not lesbians based on their dating history (though he'd sometimes pondered the possibility that they weren't exclusively hetero). (He had the only king-sized bed in Fort Doom.) The Sixteen trickled in, maintaining radio silence the whole way. He had a satellite internet link at the Fort and he personally vetted every device for location-data leakage before he let it connect to the Wi-Fi downlink from the disguised dish.

He greeted the new arrivals with ice-cold perfect Manhattans that he'd premixed and sealed in plastic sous-vide pouches, complete with cherries. As they cycled through the airlock into the Fort, he'd pull a pouch out of the freezer, snip it open, and pour it over ice, adding a twist of lemon rind and putting it on a little antique silver serving tray he'd picked up on a trip to Versailles.

He relished those moments, when someone tense and tired stepped into Fort Doom's hospitality suite—the first room past the airlock—with its thick Persian rugs and soothing water-colors, seeing him, the leader, in his comfortable, broken-in tactical pants and shirt, smiling his wide smile, eyes twinkling, offering a cocktail. The semiotics of it were: *Welcome to the apocalypse! This is going to be fun!*

The hospitality suite was as grand as it was in part to offset the inevitable disappointment in the spartan "staterooms," singles and doubles, with shared chem-toilets and a communal shower at the end of a hall. There was plenty of fresh water in the Fort, assuming they were able to resupply within the first month, but until things shook out, most "showering" would be accomplished via the Fort's ample supply of unscented baby wipes.

There were other communal areas: a game room, a dining room, a kitchen, a panic room hidden beneath the garage. He drew up a rota: cooking, cleaning, inventorying, anything to keep everyone busy. He "proposed"—that is, mandated—a daily hour of news consumption in the hospitality suite, when they'd all tune in at once, crowdsourcing a scour through all their channels and recommendations, finding the noteworthy stories that seemed to encapsulate and summarize the chaos outside, and then discussing them in a round-robin circle with Martin moderating. It was hard to tell whether things were deteriorating or whether it was just the usual baseline of craziness, made more vivid by the fact that they'd all hunkered down in a fortress to await the collapse of civilization.

Getting worse or not, stuff was happening hard outside in the world. A bombing in New York. Riots in a suburb of Atlanta. A conspiracy theory about the oil pipeline fire in Canada that blamed the fires on a cover-up, though what the cover-up was, no one could understand. Everyone joked that it was a cover-up of pedophiles, because the theories were always about covering up for pedophiles.

A refugee ship had arrived in Miami, a flotilla from a dozen drowning Caribbean islands, sailboats and scows and dinghies lashed together and coming ashore on a trash-strewn beach, rushing the CBP lines in the teeth of rubber bullets and drifting clouds of gas.

But Phoenix? Not so much. Calm. The mayor and the governor attended a reception together for the library system and then led the attendees on an "evening constitutional" to celebrate the end of the heat wave and by the time they'd gotten three blocks word had got out and thousands of people had joined them. Traffic jammed as people read about it on social and got in their cars and streamed in, and when the traffic got too bad, people just pulled off the road and threw block parties, buying out grocery stores and handing around beers and snacks. No fights. The hashtag filled up with great pictures, bands playing on front lawns while kids danced in the streetlight glow.

The next day, The Sixteen became fourteen when one of the couples went home. Privately, Martin was enraged, but he didn't want to show it. He made a performance of giving them soulful hugs and long hand-clasps and assuring them they could come back if and when it was time.

He wondered how long before The Fourteen became The Ten, The Nine, The Eight, until it was just Martin, waiting for the apocalypse in his private fortress?

IT WASN'T LONG.

Despite his official one-hour-of-news-a-day policy, he (of course) had a bunch of bots that checked the headlines for him and messaged him when certain keywords started to cluster.

The Phoenix street party pumped a lot of good vibes into the city, but it wasn't enough. A livestreamed traffic stop ended with a Phoenix cop spooking at what he said was a gun (it may have been a phone) and shooting into a car. The family in it were as respectable as you could ask for, literally on their way home from church on Sunday, and the little boy who died in his mother's arms was wearing a tiny suit and bowtie and white shirt that showed the blood.

The streets erupted. Protests, counterprotests with white nationalists carrying sticks and flagpoles. Fights. Riots. Arson.

Martin noticed one of the single girls quietly unpacking a suitcase he'd earlier noticed her quietly packing. The Fourteen alternated between looking smug and looking worried. He got notice that seven more were on their way out to the Fort and then one of the two really hot single women emailed him to ask if she could bring her equally hot coworker. Martin looked up the coworker on Facebook and made an exception to his policy and told her to go ahead. He instantly regretted it. It wasn't good leadership. But what was done was done. And hell, maybe it would blow over.

THE FIRST CRISIS came two weeks later. The internet had been coming in and out and had finally gone down the day before. There were eight ground stations that the satellite he subscribed to could use, and six of them had been sporadic, but then they went dark, and then the other two—in mountain strongholds, far from the madding crowds—had disappeared.

He'd put the perimeter on full alert and buttoned down the Fort. The Fort had high ground over it, and cameras on the peak watched every road for the approach of anything bigger than a jackrabbit and put it up on screens all over the Fort, and they'd had plenty of false alarms. They made jokes about how much unexpected big game there was in this part of Arizona and asked how many steers would fit in the freezers. They pointedly didn't discuss why steers were wandering around, untethered and unaccompanied by ranchers.

But then there was a Jeep, driving straight for Fort Doom, in a beeline that made it clear the driver knew where he was going. A few of The Thirty had trickled in after they'd gone on high alert, but this wasn't any of the vehicles he'd collected profiles on. Grimly, he unlocked the guns. Of the twenty-two in the Fort, eight were really good with rifles, and four were merely competent. The Fort had sniper points, with firing slits, and a foreign currency specialist and a mergers and acquisitions lawyer climbed the ladders up to them with guns strapped to their backs.

The vestibule was a killing zone. Once you were inside it, you were dead, assuming Martin wanted you dead. Even full body armor wouldn't protect you from a modified AR-15 on full auto firing into the room. Even if you hit the deck. The firing slit was well designed.

The Jeep pulled up in the designated waiting zone, and five people got out. One of them waved towards the front door. Martin zoomed in the feed and swore. It was Albert, who he knew from the gym. They'd gotten to be buddies outside of the gym, went hunting together once and Martin had been impressed by what a great shot Albert was. He was ten years younger than Martin, too, and ran a marathon every year. Martin had thought about how useful it would be to have someone who could chop wood for eight hours straight and then blow out a deer's brains from two hundred yards, and then he'd invited Albert to join The Thirty, making a little ceremony out of it at a nice whiskey bar they both liked, in a back booth. They'd toasted each other at the end of the night, and Martin let Albert pick up the tab.

Albert had brought friends.

He waved again and then made a sweeping gesture to take in his friends—three dudes, all about his age, all Hispanic like

Albert; one girl, no, a woman, in her forties—and shrugged broadly and apologetically. He gestured at the others to stay and then jogged up to the vestibule, stepping into it, into the killing zone.

"Martin, you there?" he said into the mic grille.

"What is going on, Albert?" Martin kept his voice cold and businesslike. Everyone else in the Fort was watching them.

"You made it!" He smiled into the camera. "Thank god. Can you let me in?"

"Albert, you know the rules."

Albert's smile faltered. He dropped his voice. "I'm sorry, man. My cousins and my aunt. My uncle—" His voice dropped more. "He got shot. It was just in the arm, but he went to the hospital and never came back. There's a militia controlling it now. I couldn't leave my aunt and cousins. She's an amazing cook, and the boys will work like mules. Strong, you know?"

"You know the rules." Martin wondered if he had it in him to murder Albert, his cousins, his aunt. What if they went away and came back with friends? The Fort could withstand most small arms, but a siege could outlast their water and food. He swallowed and quietly cursed Albert. What an asshole. What a fucking idiot. He was going to turn Martin into a murderer.

Albert was wheedling now. "Come on, don't be like that. I'll pay you back for whatever they eat and that, just as soon as it's all over. With interest. Come *on*, Martin."

Martin pressed the intercom button combo that played a bowel-loosening gun-cocking sound with lots of extra bass. "Go, Albert. Go and don't come back."

Albert jumped at the sound of the gun cocking, took an involuntary step. "I can't believe you, Martin. Jesus fucking Christ, do the people you've got locked up in there know what they've gotten themselves in for?"

He very nearly shot Albert right then. Martin could withstand many things, but challenges to his leadership were an existential risk to the whole Fort Doom project. An internal rebellion could leave them all dead or weakened to the point where they'd be easy pickings, once the marauders started coming out.

He did not pull the trigger. But he did detonate one of his precious roadside charges, blowing out a chunk of the trail leading up to the Fort. He chose a lower one, to keep the antipersonnel shrapnel from hitting any of Albert's asshole relatives, because he wanted them to leave, not linger and die on his doorstep. What a fucking mess.

Albert stared into the camera for a wild moment, then reached around to the small of his back, right where you'd keep a pistol, and Martin nearly blew him away, but then Albert put his hands back in front of him.

"Fuck you, Martin. Jesus Christ, you psychopath, you asshole, I can't believe this shit. I hope the people you got in there know they've locked themselves in with a psycho!" He leaned into the grille to shout the last few words, making them distort in the speakers on the other side. Martin winced.

"I'm going, Martin. You have a real good life." He trudged back to his car and held a short conference with his relations, replete with violent hand gestures. They all piled back into the Jeep, and then Albert got in, giving Martin a long look at his middle finger before gunning it and driving away.

That night, Martin recriminated with himself for long hours, struggling to fall asleep. He had recurring visions of Albert showing up in the days or weeks to come, still furious, heavily armed, with friends. Or cousins. Albert came from one of those big Catholic Hispanic families. He'd have lots of cousins. Martin's buried roadside bombs included a pretty big one, right at the trailhead. He could have taken them all out at the press of a button. He finally drifted off after midnight, still uncertain whether he doomed them all.

As it turned out, he never saw Albert again. But he did see the aunt.

IT WAS A month later, and there'd been a little bit of news on the shortwave, a mix of BBC World Service, RT, and apocalyptic apostate Mormon preachers with high-wattage transmitters on the Arizona Strip, shouting about the "White Horse prophecy." They'd been drinking well water to conserve the bottled supplies, boiling it just in case, and their diet was half MRE, half elk and deer sniped from the towers.

There were twenty-three of them now, and they had a good little routine of divvying up the cleaning and cooking and hunting and such. There wasn't all that much to do, so they played epic chess matches and had movie marathons and some of them paired off and snuck away for outdoor sex, or commandeered one of the bedrooms and hung a handkerchief on the doorknob.

There was always at least one person staffing the CCTV feeds looking for intruders, and a few times they'd all rushed back and buttoned up when convoys or lone cars had gone by. It was lonely territory and there wasn't much of that. A few times Martin had caught members of The Twenty-three going outside without their mandatory walkie-talkies and he'd torn strips out of them, impressing on them that while things were calm and peaceful out at Fort Doom, there was still plenty of mayhem and murder out there in the world and they were putting everyone at risk by getting out of contact. If intruders came down the road and Martin had no way to call everybody in, someone might get spotted and that might bring back a full force of bad guys. Blood and death would follow.

The Jeep came back up the trail and rang every bell in the Fort as it climbed closer and closer. It was the first time a vehicle had come that close to the Fort since the last stragglers had arrived.

When Martin recognized the Jeep, his heart started to hammer in his chest. This was it, the invasion he'd been dreading, the consequences of his foolish sentimentality come back to end all their lives. He sent his two best shots—one of them was a woman, which he'd discovered when they'd organized a day's shooting competition—up into the sniper towers and went to the vestibule.

The Jeep was not in good shape. It had a big, ugly dent running down the passenger side, like it had been t-boned, and the windshield was starred with cracks. The exhaust pipe belched dark, ugly smoke. The Jeep pulled up in the parking area and sat motionless for a long time, as Martin's nerves stretched tighter and tighter. He almost gave the order to fill it with bullets.

Then the driver door opened and Albert's aunt stepped out. She didn't look good, either. Sick, maybe, and certainly moving slow. She was wearing a fleece jacket and jeans and heavy boots that flopped on her feet, so big on her that he could see they didn't fit from a hundred yards.

He held his breath while he waited for the other car doors to open, but they didn't. The woman stepped around the Jeep and stopped, resting her hand on the hood and breathing and staring at the vestibule. She took a deep breath and drew herself up and walked towards them, limping a little, boots flapping.

"Stop there," Martin said, cranking the gain up on the vestibule's speakers, loud enough to be heard on the front lawn.

She stopped and swayed slightly, staring around, then started walking again.

"Stop," Martin said again. She pushed forward. Her hair was coming loose from its ponytail, her face was sheened with sweat and lined with exhaustion. She put a hand to her stomach and groaned.

"Stop!" Martin said, and played his MP3 of a cocking rifle. She stared into the darkness of the vestibule with mournful eyes. Then she staggered in.

Martin did not have it in him to shoot a sick, injured middle-aged lady. Partly that was basic human decency—Martin was not a bad person, he knew that—and partly it was the fully rational calculus of maintaining his moral authority in Fort Doom.

"What do you want?"

"Albert died," she said. "There's so much sickness. It took him, then my boys. Her voice was hollow and flat. "They say it's cholera." She squeezed her face into a grief mask. "So many people are sick."

Martin felt his own guts clench, his own bowels turn to water. He had Cipro and other broad-spectrum/last-resort antibiotics, but he hadn't replaced them yet this year and a bunch of them were expiring soon. He'd read that their efficacy would start to fall off a cliff when that happened. After a deliberate bioweapon attack, cholera was one of the fears that kept him up at night. He had lots of guns, but you can't shoot germs.

"If you're sick you'll have to leave." He made his voice hard. She stared into the vestibule's camera, clutching her gut, trembling, sheened with sweat. He'd need to break out a bunny suit and bleach solution and power-wash the whole thing. She wasn't moving. "Go," he said.

She stared on, nearly doubled over now, chin raised, still

staring, or glaring maybe. Martin didn't let himself feel empathy for her. It was the grasshopper and the ants: he'd done all the work to make himself a cozy shelter from the blowing winter and she had done whatever she'd done instead—made a bunch of babies, watched reality TV, taken drugs, or crocheted. People who didn't think ahead were self-correcting problems. She was correcting herself, and it wasn't pretty, but it wasn't his problem, either.

Her chin trembled. She was holding back tears. "Please," she said, in a tiny voice that barely reached the mic.

There was motion behind him, people drifting into the hospitality suite, watching the interaction. Watching *him*. This was a leadership test, a moment of truth. He could shoot her dead where she stood. The additional fluids would not pose any extra hazard. He was going to need to power-wash and bleach no matter what. Would his people see that as a show of strength or a show of weakness?

"If you come back in an hour, I'll leave you some supplies down at the trailhead. We don't have much, but I can give you some food, some Tylenol, warm blankets. But I can't let a sick person in here. This isn't a hospital. You bring sickness in here, we could all get it. We could all die." The last word snapped her head back like he'd fired a bullet between her eyes. Those eyes, the eyes of a dead woman who knew it.

Slowly, she straightened up. She took a step backwards, hand still pressed to her stomach like she was gutshot. She backed out of the vestibule and then turned and walked in slow, careful—pained—steps to her car. She managed to get past the bumper before a cramp doubled her over. He saw her knuckles go white on the car's hood as she struggled to stay upright, then she straightened again and got in her wreck of a car, driving off slowly.

He waited until she was out of sight of the highest cameras, then he took a couple of deep breaths, put away the gun he'd had lined up with the shooting slit in the vestibule door, and stepped back into the hospitality suite with a carefully composed look of concern and confidence on his face.

"What a disaster. I really feel for her," he said, making a point of meeting the eyes of Lloyd, the physically strongest of the men in the Fort, then Saleha, the oldest person, then Giorgia, the hottest woman, who all constituted a kind of power center in Fort Doom.

Giorgia said, "I don't think I could have done that, Martin." He couldn't tell if it was admiration or recrimination.

"It was hard," he said. "But I'll round up as many supplies as we can spare. I wish there was more we could do, but you know, sickness in here—" He made a pained, disgusted face. "It would be ugly. Our safety has to come first. She'll have to figure out her own destiny."

Saleha said, "It's a waste of supplies. She's not going to make it. All you'll be doing is encouraging dependence. If she lives, she'll be back for more, I guarantee it."

Martin privately agreed and made a mental note of who nodded along and who looked like they thought Saleha was a monster for saying it.

"I won't give her anything we can't afford. It's the right thing to do."

Then he made a show out of breaking out a bunny suit from under one of the benches and fitting the mask and eye protectors, then lugging out the power washer. It was the right thing to do, but it was also a very showily correct thing to do. The kind of thing a competent leader would do, to keep his people safe.

He stuffed the bunny suit into a hazmat burn bag, packed

a tub of food—he thought about putting eyedrops in the jug of water, which would see off Albert's aunt, but in the end, he couldn't bring himself to be a poisoner, it was the most cowardly of all the ways to kill—and drove it down to the trailhead in an ATV. He had Lloyd cover him with a rifle from one of the towers, and kept his walkie on the whole way.

The next morning, the tub was gone.

ONE WEEK WENT by. Two. Three. The shortwave was full of news, all of it contradictory and impossible to understand. There was a "Provisional Arizona Republic," but if it was real, and not just some shitkickers with a transmitter, then it was a mess. The guy who styled himself the "Secretary of Communications" for the republic made Alex Jones sound calm and coherent, and he ranted for sixteen-hour stretches that *had* to be amphetamine-fueled. They certainly sounded that way.

Martin had appointed Gene to serve as quartermaster. Gene was a young man without much ambition. He'd been a junior trader and going nowhere, but he was easy to manipulate and sucked at lying, and Martin valued both of those traits. In his experience, they made for the very highest caliber of flunky. He wasn't going to dip into the supplies, and if he did, he'd out himself by turning into a stammering mess at the first hint of an accusation.

Gene made color-coordinated spreadsheets showing their rate of consumption of all their supplies, with excellent bar- and pie-charts for easy reference. The upshot was that they could eat off their stores for another two months if need be, but it would involve rationing and a lot of dinners of dried meat and vitamin pills and fiber supplements to keep everything moving.

No one wanted that, and besides, everyone was bored shit-less and starting to clique up and hook up and break up and generally go stir-crazy. So Martin decreed that they would hunt and scavenge for supplies to stretch out their stores, aiming for a minimum of fifty percent of all consumables coming from outside the Fort. They'd hunt game, of course— Lloyd could dress a steer or a deer, and the rest of them were learning, and Giorgia was an excellent cook who made every-thing from cowboy steaks to liver tagine from the animals they brought down.

The scavenging parties were a new one: the Fort was very remote, but Martin had mapped out all the nearby settlements: a couple of ranches, a gas station with an attached country store, a Nevada Highway Patrol substation. The scavengers took out the electric ATVs in silent mode by moonlight, dressed in charcoal gray with their faces blacked and their hands in black gloves, and scouted them with night-vision scopes before approaching the empty ones: the gas station, two of the ranches.

The gas station had been trashed and looted and someone had tried to blow up its storage tanks, but their fire-suppression systems had kicked in, leaving every surface slimed with cancer-ish residue. But the ranches yielded all kinds of loot: canned goods, root-cellars' worth of vegetables, blankets, outfits they played dress-up in, ancient board games, a box of card decks and an inlaid carousel of poker chips, photo albums that they pored over and laughed at and speculated on.

That killed another week, and in three days they were one hundred percent reliant on external sources for food. Admit-tedly, a lot of that came from the ranches, a nonrenewable resource, but as Andreas pointed out, if the shit continued to hit the fan, there would be a lot fewer people and that meant a lot more elk and such. Andreas also had some things to say about the kinds of delicacies that could be prepared from edible cactus, and ideas about how to figure out which cacti qualified.

There were more ranches, further away, and even a little town, with a Navajo gift shop and a gun store. Martin figured that if they put together a raiding party and outfitted one of the empty ranches as a base of operations, they could make incursions into these more distant targets without risking the ATVs' power cells or straying so far from the Fort that they couldn't retreat to it if someone needed emergency medical care.

There wasn't any good reason to go for the gun store, but everyone was excited at the prospect. Living through the visit from Albert's aunt and then witnessing the ruins of the general store and gas station had convinced them that they were smarter and better than the idiots out in the world who hadn't made the same kinds of preparation. When they tried to imagine what they'd do if they were stuck out there in the world while a group of smarter people were cozy in Fort Doom, it was easy to imagine a marauding force trying to take the Fort. The guns might come in handy—and besides, if they didn't get 'em, someone else would, and then the guns might end up pointed at the Fort. When you thought about it that way, it was practically a moral imperative.

They used drones to scout the run, doing several flyovers and then a couple of low flybys to get a sense of who might be in the area. They spotted some Mexicans outside of a neatly kept house, tending a garden and pointing with alarm at the drone as it buzzed them, but apart from them, nothing. Martin had chosen a truly remote place for his Fort, remote even by Arizona standards, where there was so much big sky and big country that you could go off the beaten path and see no one at all for days. Of course, if they'd traveled not much farther in the opposite direction, they'd be at the outskirts of Phoenix metro, and god knew what kind of chaos they'd find there. All the more reason to get the guns.

Planning the gun run was incredibly fun. Martin turned the hospitality suite into a war room, brought in a big whiteboard, tacked up aerial photos from the drones. They started calling the ranch "Forward Base Alpha" which was *really cool* to say. Getting close enough to the gun store—Big Tom's, it was called—to check out its condition in detail was hard: the drones had a range of just over a klick, and the terrain around Big Tom's was flat, with only a little low scrub, so there wasn't anywhere to shelter while the recon teams piloted the drones in. They just had to hope that they'd find it untouched, ready to be cracked open with Fort Doom's oxyacetylene cutting torch. Alan and Crispin were drafted to operate a cargo vehicle— Martin's armored pickup—to carry away the loot once the place was sprung.

Martin called the mission for a Monday—they used a big paper calendar, hung prominently in the hospitality suite, to track the procession of days and nights—and the night before they barbequed steaks and drank some of his very best old bourbon, including a bottle of twenty-year-old Pappy that Gene had carefully noted in his quartermaster's spreadsheet. There was enough for three glasses each, and Martin couldn't help but brag that each of those little shot glasses held $100 worth of liquor at pre-collapse prices. Who knew what it would fetch in the marketplaces of the new world when it emerged? He entertained a brief fantasy of presiding over a market stall in some fair town, surrounded by mercenaries with hair triggers, dickering over trade goods with princelings of the nearby fortresses. It was ridiculous, Frazetta stuff, but it was a hard image to shake.

*

THE MISSION WAS a catastrophe.

Brett didn't come back. He'd been on point when they scurried under cover of darkness to Big Tom's, wearing night-scopes. His backups, Alan and Crispin, had circled wide and were coming in from the other side, waiting for Brett to make his entry.

Crispin didn't make it, either.

Alan was the one who told the story, shaking and crying. The footage from his GoPro was shit, even with the night filters on, an uninterpretable blurrycam jumble.

Brett had crept to within a hundred yards, then crawled, then belly-crawled, inching through the parking lot of Big Tom's, trying to keep the few cars between him and the store, moving slowly and smoothly. Alan kept his rifle trained on the front door, Crispin moved in a rotation between several targets· windows, the roof, a blind corner. Every time he moved his scope, he whispered "clear" into the walkie he was wearing.

"Am I go?" Brett asked. He was breathing heavily.

"Go," Crispin said.

"Go," Alan said.

Brett got up in a runner's crouch and sprinted to the door. He flattened himself against the wall. They heard his breath rasping through the walkie earpieces. Alan wished he could be there with Brett. This was so fucking *cool*.

They saw a small red light go on, and pan over the door, then it winked out. "Locked. Good lock, too. Steel plating. OK, going to knock."

He rapped at the door. They'd debated this, but on balance they decided it was for the best. If there was someone inside, better to make contact this way then to come on them by surprise. It was a *gun store,* after all. He thumped. "Hello? Anyone home?"

They all held their breath. Brett's breath rasped in. "OK." A distant sound of velcro as he unholstered the Makita drill from his thigh and twisted in the high-speed steel bit. They saw the pinprick of light from the drill as he worked the trigger while holding the chuck to tighten on the bit, then he crouched and fitted the bit in the lock's keyway. They heard the distant whine of the drill, slightly out of phase with the walkies' staticky transmission. "Come on you little bastard," Brett whispered. Then: "Shit." He stopped the drill—sound of the broken bit falling to the ground, fumbling with a replacement—and then the whirr of the drill started again.

"All the way through. Switching to a bigger bit." The sounds of the chuck working, clink of the bits, rasp of Brett's breath, sound of Crispin chanting "clear, clear, clear" as he moved his rifle around.

"OK," Brett said, just as blinding lights went on all around the building. Crispin squeezed off a shot, reflexively (Alan thought) and then there were two more shots and Brett pitched forward. Through his scope, Alan saw the smoke rising out of the bullet hole in the door, and for an instant he saw the frayed edges of the thin metal that had been used to cover the firing slit. More shots and puffs of smoke rising from the parking lot. One of the broken-down SUVs lost its windscreen in a shatter of glass cubes that glittered in the incredible light.

"Brett? Brett?" Alan said. The blood oozing from around him was unmistakable, and Alan felt a sudden dose of cold grue as he realized how exposed he was.

He was about to get up and scramble back when trapdoors on the roof of the gun store flopped back in unison and four sharpshooters popped out, laying down suppressing fire as they got into position behind brick bluffs on the roof's corners. They wore shooting glasses and all tactical, faces grim but mouths open in wide grins, inaudible war cries as they fired into the night.

He heard Crispin die over the walkie, a meaty sound, a shout, two more, a gasp, then nothing. There was stickiness all over Alan's legs. He'd pissed himself. This was idiotic, a misunderstanding. They didn't want a fight. There was nothing to fight *over*. Fort Doom had lots of guns already, more than they could ever fire. This was a break from the tedium, a game. He moaned.

Had they spotted him? The sharpshooters were scanning the terrain slowly and methodically. He wanted to call out to them, to surrender, but he knew he'd be executed on the spot. He understood that this is exactly what they'd have done in Fort Doom if someone had shown up there, armed, drilling out the locks, covered by backup. He was going to die.

Alan had been a very successful property developer who had started off flipping distressed homes, then he'd made connections with the city planner's office and started getting inside dope on which places would face the least resistance if he wanted to tear them down and build high-rises, and he'd hustled up some money and started buying houses for cash, two or three in a row, on big old lots, family places going back generations. He'd specialized in having them demo'ed before anyone knew that anything was up, dozing them to the foundation slabs all in the same day, in and out before the first noise complaints could be followed up on. He called his boys The Wrecking Crew and paid top dollar if they could finish by sunset. The condos he put up paid for it all, mid-rises then high-rises then complexes. He understood the power of unrelenting speed. Sometimes, he'd pictured himself as a shark, never stopping, surging forward to snap up prey, moving from debt to payment to debt to payment, creaming off the profit.

He was not feeling like a shark anymore.

He tried to be a snail. A slug. Low-lying, slow-moving. So slow you'd never see him. He put his face in the coarse, cool nighttime sand, making himself as flat as he could be. Using his fingertips and the tips of his booted toes, he edged himself half an inch backwards, towards the trike he'd left parked twenty yards away. No one shot him. In his earpiece, he heard the sound from Brett's walkie, faint conversation from the sharpshooters, one word in three: *got him see him good shot motherfucker.*

Another half inch. Holding his breath, then breathing shallowly. A slug. A snail. Another half inch.

Another. Count to ten. Another. Scrape of the door to Big Tom's opening, bang as it hit Brett's corpse, slow slide and grunt as someone pushed the door and Brett's body along with it. *Fuckin' assholes* from the walkie.

Boots on concrete. Scuffle of the walkie being handled. "Hey, any of you assholes out there hear me?" Alan held his breath, stole his hand to the walkie on his belt, felt blindly for the mute button. Was that it? He was dying to breathe, and it would definitely come out as a gasp. A snail. A slug. He pressed the button. A soft click.

"Hello? I bet these sons of bitches have backup out there. Greg, you see anyone?" Muffled reply. "Yeah, OK." Scuffle. "Lizzy, kill the lights, would you? Nightscopes are useless with them on. Let's see what we got out there."

His blood went cold. The piss coating his legs turned to ice. Fuck. He inched faster. Faster. Conversation in the walkie earpiece, incomprehensible over the rasp of his clothes, the rasp of his breath. Faster.

Click.

The lights went off. Green blobs danced in front of his eyes, despite the long moments they'd been pressed into the dirt. He leaped to his feet and *ran,* sprinting for the place he thought he'd left the trike, not able to see, stumbling, and there was shouting behind him. A rifle shot, two more. He fell to the ground, sobbing but not hit. Up again, trying to zigzag, his pants stuck to his legs by piss, refusing to cooperate, and then he smashed face-first into the trike's roll bar, stars in his vision. He tumbled into the trike, flattening himself on the floorboard. A shot went into the trike's body, another ricocheted off into the desert. Flecks of dust rained down on him. The keys were in the ignition and he'd left it pointing out, part of the careful planning that had been so much fun to do on the whiteboard.

He turned the key, bent double over the trike, head down. Awkward foot on the accelerator and the electric brush motor engaged and the trike rocketed forward, nearly throwing him clear, knocking his foot free of the accelerator, and the trike stopped suddenly, nearly throwing him clear again. He scrambled into the seat and a bullet hole appeared in the windscreen ahead of him, which starred. He closed his eyes and whimpered even as he planted his ass firmly in the seat, sitting higher, head exposed, hands on the wheel, foot back on the accelerator and this time he was braced for the acceleration and the trike *leaped* forward and he opened his eyes and flipped on the headlights because he had to see where he was going and they had nightscopes, and he swerved back and forth, trying to make the movement random and unpredictable (in large part succeeding, because he was too shaken to steer in any fashion save erratically).

More shots puffed into the dirt around him, one close enough to spray him with hard bits of gravel that cut open his cheek. As the walkie faded out of range, he heard them hooting and swearing.

He drove and drove and drove, stopping on a deserted stretch of road with good sightlines in all directions, where he vomited until there was nothing more to come up except mucousy spit. He had a cooler on the passenger seat and he opened and drained a can of Coke, ate twenty milligrams of Adderall, and then fired up the bike again.

He drove to Forward Base Alpha first and opened the padlock they'd fitted to the door with shaking hands. Walking around the familiar ranch house with its shelves of supplies and stack of paperbacks and board games, as well as the overnight bag he'd packed, gave him a sense of absolute unreality. Only a few hours before, he'd been here with Brett and Crispin, laughing, going over the plans, trembling with excitement. Now he was trembling with terror in the room, bleeding, lightheaded, empty-stomached but nauseated all the same, vision out of focus, legs chapped with his own piss.

He dropped his pants on the floor and pulled handfuls of baby wipes out of a container and scrubbed at his legs and ass and balls, tossing the dirty wipes on the floor. He upended his overnight bag and found a spare pair of pants and pulled them on, then transferred the contents of his dirty pants' pockets. He changed shirts. He got his trike keys. He looked around the room. There was food. He should take food. A handful of pepperoni sticks, a box of energy bars, a six-pack of Gatorade. The Adderall sang in his veins, made him feel like the first time he'd drunk a cup of coffee, like superpowers were on their way.

He had a crazy, nearly irresistible urge to torch the ranch house. Something about it, haunted by the ghosts of the men who'd died that night, full of evidence of their idiocy. He could do it. They'd moved some gas supplies to the ranch to run the backup gennie for when the solar cells didn't top up the batteries. Splish-splosh, one match, *woompf.*

It would send up a plume of smoke for miles around, though. If the sharpshooters from Big Tom's were driving through the night looking for him, they'd see it. The ranch was halfway to Fort Doom. He wouldn't burn it down, then.

He got on the trike and drove.

THE SURVIVING RESIDENTS of Fort Doom watched Alan shiver and weep as he told his story, and Martin watched them watching Alan, trying to control his rage. The fucking *ineptitude* and the *panic*. Alan had driven back to Fort Doom, not knowing whether he was followed, whether there was a drone overhead or cars on his tail. The Big Tom's gang had been organized, ruthless, and, of course, fantastically well-armed. Martin could button up the fort and snipe at them from his towers, but what if they had heavy arms, grenade launchers, missiles, the kind of thing that an army might bring to a battlefield?

The odds were against it. Probably they had high-fived, buried the bodies, and celebrated with a big pancake breakfast. But what if they hadn't. One thing Martin had learned as a trader: small risks with huge downsides couldn't be ignored.

So he waited until Alan had told his story and everyone had commiserated and said kind words about Crispin and Brett, and then he took Alan back into his room, "for a drink."

Alan looked small and beaten, huddled on one of the armchairs in Martin's room. Martin poured him an above-average single malt on a big whiskey rock, the kind of thing that Alan used to celebrate his business triumphs with. Alan had had a lot of those, and they'd enjoyed plenty of boozy nights in some of the nicer bars in Phoenix together—there'd even been a fishing trip together in Bermuda, with deadly blender drinks the bartender called "Zac Attacks." The bartender was named Zac. Nice kid. Yale dropout.

"You going to be OK?" He forced concern into his tone.

Alan drank. "I guess so. I mean, yeah, sure. People have gotten over worse. Plenty of people. Especially these days."

Martin took a drink, watched him. He hadn't figured that Alan would fold up like this. Panic. Lose his shit, really. "That's good. Because you need to do something."

"What's that?" He reached for the bottle and refilled his glass. The whiskey rolled over the big cube. He rattled it against the edges of the heavy lowball glass.

"You need to make this right."

A puzzled look. Martin could see that the adrenaline and Adderall were wearing off. His eyelids were drooping, shoulders slumping deeper.

"You need to go back and make sure you didn't leave a trail."

"What?"

"You heard me, Alan. They follow you here, it'll be all the shit you went through, times a thousand. War, maybe. You fucked this up—"

"I—"

Martin raised his voice. He had the only soundproofed room in the Fort. "Shut the *fuck* up, Alan. You fucked up, asshole. You panicked. Jesus fucking Christ, don't you remember all those conversations we had about not carrying anything that could lead back to here or Forward Base Alpha, in case you dropped something, or were captured, or killed? Remember that, Alan? What was the point of all that if you were going to fucking run like a rabbit, leaving god knows what signs pointing here? What was the point, Alan, if you were going to endanger every single one of us with your panic, your reck- lessness, your *cowardice,* Alan?"

Alan withered under the words. Martin pressed him. "Well, Alan, what the fuck have you got to say for yourself?"

Alan's red eyes swam with tears. "Martin, I'm sorry—"

"That's just great, we'll put that on our fucking tombstones. 'Alan is sorry.'"

"What do you *want* from me, Martin?"

"Get out there and make it right, you dumb fuck. Go and backtrack your trail, carefully. Eliminate any sign you left behind you. Walk it if you have to. Every crossroad and at least a mile on either side. Bring a broom, bring a rake, whatever it takes. Take care of it."

"I haven't slept in—"

Martin rattled a bottle of Adderall in front of him. "Thirty milligrams should do it. You can sleep when you're done. Bring a bedroll and a pop-up tent, one of those little one-man Shift- pods. Don't fuck it up."

Alan dry-swallowed the round blue pill and heaved himself to his feet. Felix helped him pack, bringing him to the store- room and rousing Gene to play quartermaster, barking out a supply list at Gene and having Gene load it onto one of the intact ATVs, along with a spare battery for the trike.

He saw Alan off on his own via the big cargo door on the other side of the hill, moving the camouflage out of the way first. "Go," he said. "Come back with your shield or on it."

IT WAS NEARLY dawn when they heard the shot. Martin rushed to the monitors, reviewed the footage. It showed Alan's trike laboring up the hill to the front door, then Alan pacing for a while, then sitting in the trike's driver seat for a longer while, contemplating the emptiness and the desert and the night. Then, without any windup or hesitation, Alan drew his sidearm, put the barrel in his mouth, and *pop*.

That was the shot.

Martin waited until dawn, and then he got the power washer and went outside to clean up.

Later that day, he took out the trike Alan had been on. His tracks were obvious: he'd ridden down to the bottom of the hill, done a wide circle leading out to the highway, then turned around and come back. He'd never even tried to erase his trail.

Martin walkied into Fort Doom, told them he was going to go and check Alan's trail for signs pointing home. He still had all Alan's supplies.

It turned out Alan hadn't been all that obvious on his way home. Or maybe Martin wasn't good at reading sign. Either way, he found nothing between the Fort and Forward Base Alpha, and then he crept slowly and cautiously from Forward Base Alpha to Big Tom's and, finding no sign, went back to Fort Doom, arriving after sunset, tired and sore.

No one but Gene had seen any part of Martin and Alan's private discussion the night before, and Gene wouldn't talk. Martin made somber noises about trauma and bravery and sacrifice, and the need for all of them to know that they could always talk to him, to any of them, really, because they were all in this together, they were a unit now, a family, really, and they all had a duty to one another.

He used the excavator to trench out a shallow grave for Alan and then filled it in. He didn't mark the grave, and when Giorgia asked him about it, he told her it was to keep from giving any sign that there was any inhabitation near Fort Doom, and she nodded seriously and gave him a look of admiration that he called to mind that night as he lay himself down to sleep.

BOREDOM WAS UNQUESTIONABLY the worst part of the end of the world. Out there in the world, things were anything *but* boring, to judge from the shortwave broadcasts. The Provisional Republic of Arizona seemed to have gone off the air, but the CBs picked up scouting parties, and there were hams who'd crackle into life now and again, telling tales of military occupation and plagues in far-flung cities, wars and aerial bombing campaigns. There was a National Guard station in Provo that sent out a daily admonition for refugees to stay the fuck out of Utah, and there were so. Many. Preachers. Sin, sin, sin. Redemption, redemption, redemption. One of them claimed consistently that New York City had been nuked until the rubble bounced, but that didn't feature on anyone else's communications, so the people of Fort Doom concluded that he was full of shit. This offended their sensibilities—a couple of them had grown up in New York and most of them had worked for funds or banks with New York offices that demanded their presence every now and again, with late nights of expensive sushi and priceless whiskey.

No one had any appetite for more "missions," and after a brief deliberation, they decided that they would decommission Forward Base Alpha. Clearing out the ranch and bringing everything useful back to Fort Doom occupied a couple weeks, but then it was done and Gene had inventoried it and there was nothing else to do.

They'd formed several different kinds of couples and even a triple or two, and between the thin walls and the claustrophobic gossip, everyone had a pretty good idea of what it would be like to fuck everybody else. They'd all been sentenced to solitary confinement, in each other's company. Izzy had been an English major, and he made them all watch a video he'd brought on his laptop, a Broadway production of *No Exit,* and they all laughed at "Hell is other people," and then Izzy made a cross-stitch that said that and framed it and hung it in the hospitality suite. That's when Martin decided he needed to step in.

"We're going to have to start scavenging again. I know it's dangerous, but we've learned some hard lessons about being cautious. The good news is, we don't have to hurry—we're not desperate, yet. We find a place we want to check out, we can afford to watch it, for days, even a week, make sure it's safe before we move. That's a luxury we have because the cupboard isn't bare. But if we let the cupboard get bare, we lose that buffer; we'll have to rush into whatever situation we find, or start to go hungry. That's way more dangerous than going out now. The only thing worse than suffering the tragedy of losing Crispin and Alan and Brett would be for their deaths to be in vain, for us to learn nothing from them."

No one liked the idea, but everyone agreed that he was right.

MARTIN'S METICULOUS MAPS had plenty of possible scouting locations, further afield than the ranch houses. They had good luck with a family farm: it was inhabited, but the people there were willing to trade eggs and cheese for gemstones. Martin loved that: he had a lot of gemstones stockpiled, and in the wee hours of the night he wondered if he was kidding himself about whether anyone would want them. You can't eat gems, and converting them to useful goods required something like a functioning civilization. The fact that these stoic Latino farmers were willing to take a little bag of rubies and sapphires for five big wheels of cheese and a promise of four dozen eggs per week for the next month meant that they, too, thought that civilization would come back.

That was Martin's plan, after all: wait for order to reassert itself, then emerge with all the necessities for securing a place in it: trade goods, bearer bonds, cash money, and his wits, all backed by a loyal group of followers who knew how to fire every gun in Fort Doom's substantial armory.

Civilizations had risen and fallen before. Humanity needed to work together, but hell was other people. When the best people were on top, things worked: they convinced the rational, cajoled the stubborn, and, frankly, forced the rest. It was for the greater good. Put one of the losers, the takers, at the top of the pile, and they'd lead the rest into catastrophe. One thing had been very clear to Martin through all his life: the takers were steering the ship, and they were going to crash it.

Another farm proved to be looted and burned, which was scary. Then they found a town, strangest of strange things! Elfrida even had two stores where the storekeepers ran a ledger on a tablet, keeping track of what everyone took. They'd all agreed that they'd settle up "when things were back to normal." Martin was with the group that visited the town after the initial scout-out, and he forced himself not to laugh at "back to normal." The storekeepers' tablets had lists of things that people in the town needed: medicine, some construction materials, engine parts, controllers and other components for solar arrays. The tablets listed trade goods from all the people in town: everything from kitchen garden produce to frozen meat to clothing and female sanitary goods.

From his discussions with the storekeepers. Martin learned

that there were other little towns like this one, even some bigger places, where they were using solar power, local networking, databases on tablets, to keep track of who had what and who needed what and who'd taken what. The towns traded a little and kept notes on what was going on, who they'd met, and what to watch out for.

"What about protection?" Martin asked.

The shopkeeper, Pakistani or Indian and middle-aged, wearing a clean white button-up shirt and slacks, shrugged. "What kind of protection?"

"You know. Gangs, militias, that kind of thing." He thought about the word he was looking for. "Marauders."

The shopkeeper smiled. "We don't have that sort of thing. Thank goodness!" He smiled at Martin. Martin suppressed his disgusted headshake. Give it a month or two, this guy would be dead and everything he owned would be in the possession of someone stronger and a hell of a lot less naïve. Martin almost wanted to shoot the guy himself. Better a good guy like Martin should get all this guy's trade goods than some *marauder*.

"Well, if it ever becomes a problem, we might be able to help you," Martin said. "We'll check in every week or two, and you let us know if anyone's bothering you." That was how you started rebuilding, Martin thought: the strong protecting the weak, the weak giving the strong a tribute and deference.

The shopkeeper gave Martin a funny look and said he would, and then traded Martin a bunch of dried mango for some of Martin's powdered milk. There were kids in the town and they drank more than the local cows and goats gave.

A RADIO STATION started up, purportedly in Phoenix, all young people, with special guests who came on to talk about the abandoned houses they'd "liberated." Some were in neighborhoods where the Fort Doom residents owned property, places where there had been gates and guards and security systems. They all bristled at the thought that their homes might be invaded next. So many terrible things had happened since they took to Fort Doom, but this was what made The Event seem real: if the property rights of people like them were slipping away, then everything was up for grabs.

The DJs played recorded music and brought on live bands, and traded tips about the locations of clinics and hospitals, soup kitchens, and day-cares. It was surreal. They painted a picture of a radically depopulated Phoenix, full of empty houses and shuttered businesses, cold ashes from violence long past. Phoenix, populated only by the people who couldn't leave.

Summer was coming soon, and one DJ interviewed an emergency cooling working group, six eager HVAC hackers who were talking through ways to build neighborhood shelters where you could go to get out of the summer heat that was scant months away, plans for evaporative coolers that ran on cheap solar cells, with parts lists and depots you could go to get or give parts.

Through trade and rationing, the residents of Fort Doom had managed to live in relative comfort, but that didn't mean that life was easy. Some supplies were running low—peanut butter, fresh fruit, oatmeal—and the boredom was like a living thing, gnawing away at their extremities from the moment they rolled out of bed to the moment they lay back down. For all the joking about being in solitary together, there was a current of truth underneath it all, manifesting itself in snappish arguments and long sulks, factions, and epic binge drinking sessions. Gene inventoried the med supplies and discovered that most of their opioid painkillers were gone, and there was a witch hunt over who'd been getting high, but no one was ever conclusively convicted of the pilferage.

And there was Phoenix, and the radio broadcasts, and the news from their old neighborhoods, and there was James and Ray, who were simultaneously their best scouts and the biggest troublemakers, demanding to be allowed to go check things out, see how they were going. Giorgia decided to go with them. The residents of Fort Doom were about done with the end of the world and ready to go back to massages, steaks, cocktail bars, squash games, hard work, big profits, arguing on social media, ill-advised sex with interesting strangers, all the comforts of modernity. When they'd left Phoenix, it had been a thriving city, filled with TaskRabbits and 7-Elevens, Ubers and exclusive bespoke suitmakers and couture fashion boutiques. Surely some remnant of all that remained.

So he green-lit the mission, and they tuned into the DJs all around the clock, like it was a radio play about a much more interesting apocalypse than the one they were living through.

Warren had a joke, "Armageddon tired of waiting around," and he would bust it out all day. At first they groaned, then they chorused it with him, then they tuned it out.

But as the days after James and Ray and Giorgia left for Phoenix stretched out into a week, and as the DJs on the radio station reported on a wave of sickness that was passing through the city, thought to be legionella or listeria, and advised on treating people without antibiotics, keeping them hydrated and comfortable, they found themselves all making the same stupid joke. "Armageddon tired of this shit," they'd say. "Armageddon tired, too." No one laughed, not even Warren.

When the three finally returned, ten days later, they came with a bounty: canned fruit, chocolate, opioids, a stack of graphic novels and old porno mags from some small-town used bookstore. They'd traded away gemstones, a little ammo—for a caliber of gun that Martin had decided against keeping in the Fort, forgetting to get rid of the loads—and a huge bag of shitty weed.

They were greeted as returning heroes and regaled them all with heroic tales of adventures and narrow escapes, describing a Phoenix that changed block by block: first a long burn scar still smelling of smoke, then a perfectly kept neighborhood with rows of porta-potties every couple houses, solar shower bags on the roofs, people waving from the roofs and kids playing in a makeshift day-care under a shade sail on an apartment-building lawn. They'd tried to visit Martin's old complex, where several of them (including Ray) had homes, but some-one had fired warning shots over their heads from the guard-house. They'd tried shouting to the unseen defenders, but when another volley whizzed over their heads (lower, this time), they'd gotten the message and run off.

Still, everyone was excited by all the news, the picture of a city picking itself up from its knees, the pockets of normalcy. And Martin was glad that gemstones were still acceptable trade goods. He looked forward to the day when he could get his thumb drives out of his floor safe and start mobilizing his cryptocurrency assets again.

Giorgia and Martin had a drink in his room that night, after she'd had a hot shower and a whiskey. They'd had an on-again/off-again in the early days of Fort Doom, and apparently it was on again. Martin fell asleep spooned up to her, face buried in her shampoo-smelling hair, tired, sticky, and deeply satiated.

Leadership wasn't easy, but it had its perks.

*

GIORGIA GOT SICK the next day. Martin woke to her vomiting in his en-suite, groaning between volleys. With trepidation, he peeked into the bathroom, discovering her nude, bent over the toilet, backs of her legs streaked with watery stools that were pooling around her knees. The smell was incredible. He covered his mouth and nose and backed out and went and got a bucket and filled it with a mild bleach solution. He donned gloves and a mask and broke into a fresh package of kitchen sponges and cleaned up around Giorgia, giving her a hair elastic, even sponging the backs of her legs down. He emptied the bucket down the toilet between her spasms, and dissolved rehydration salts in distilled water for her. He got her turned around, seated on the toilet, with the empty, bleach-smelling bucket for what remained of the mucousy contents of her gut. She looked like hell and was running a temperature.

Martin didn't want to alarm the rest, but he went and got Ray and James and checked in with them to see if they had any symptoms. They all agreed—even Giorgia, between spasms— that they should turn Martin's room into an isolation ward, and brought in some cots. Gene packed a few boxes of supplies and brought in a mini-fridge on a dolly and some of their broad-spectrum antibiotics, including a couple of doses in liquid form, along with a hypo so they could inject Giorgia, who was in no shape to take anything orally or even as a suppository. They mixed it with some dramamine, which knocked her out. Martin instructed the other two to take turns waking her at twenty-minute intervals to sip at water, and change her bedpan as necessary.

James and Ray were sick by the next morning. Martin let them take care of themselves, getting more buckets and a chem-toilet so they wouldn't have to compete for the en-suite.

Martin had spent the night in one of the empty double rooms—
Gene had helped him clear out the surplus supplies—and had
started wearing one of his few remaining bunny suits to visit
the quarantine, checking in on an hourly basis.

A pall hung over the Fort, everyone speaking in whispers,
and the other residents were subtly avoiding Martin, edging
away from him when he entered a room. He spent the afternoon outside, walking the perimeter, checking the wiring in
the solar array and the sensors, repairing some of the crumbl-
ing mortar around the shortwave antenna. Normally, he liked
the solitude, but that day his thoughts ran around and around
in a loop that circled from anxiety about whether he was
going to get sick; to irrational resentment at James, Ray, and
Giorgia for bringing their pathogens home to Fort Doom; to
an even more irrational resentment of the rest of the Fort's
residents for their obvious suspicion that he was about to get
sick, too.

It was almost a relief when his guts spasmed. Not literally,
of course. The pain doubled him up like a kick in the abdomen,
and he knew in a flash he'd never make it back to the Fort,
so he yanked his pants down around his ankles just in time
to spare them from the torrent that sprayed out of his ass.
Moments later, he began to vomit.

Once the first wave had passed, he cleaned himself up with
bleach wipes from his day-pack and drank some electrolyte,
then put the bleach wipes in a baggie and snuck some of his
private stash of Cipro, which he'd been carrying around since
Giorgia first took sick.

He joined the other three in their quarantine. James was now
too weak to make it to the toilet, which meant that there were
two bedpans to be emptied. On the other hand, it also meant
that there was no competition for the two toilets. Martin made

it clear to Ray that the en-suite was his. Ray could use the chem-toilet. Ray didn't object. He was so weak and feverish, he could barely speak.

Giorgia died on day eight, her fever so high that she practically sizzled. Martin figured out that she was dead when he went to feed her a teaspoon full of water and found that her hot, dry skin had gone cold and clammy. Gene left a body bag outside the door of Martin's room (Martin had followed several online guides to outfitting the Fort, and body bags appeared on all of them) and he and Ray managed to put Giorgia's body into it, then they changed the sheets.

James died the next day. Martin couldn't struggle out of bed to help bag him at first, but then he did, and the two bodies were hauled away by the healthy survivors. They burned the bodies, along with bags of sheets and clothes that Martin and Ray passed out.

Martin started to rally the next day, and then, amazingly, so did Ray. They lay exhausted in their beds, drinking broth and electrolyte, then they took turns in Martin's shower, bundled up their filthy clothes and sheets and changed into clean pajamas, brushed their teeth, shaved. They agreed that they had better spend another day in the quarantine, just in case, and then they both decided fuck that, and went back out among the rest, weak and floaty. Martin had lost ten pounds and his skin was grayish and loose on his face, but he knew he would live. He was a survivor.

THE NEXT TIME, it was Saleha, Lloyd, and Izzy. None of them lived.

They buried them in the little impromptu graveyard, down the hill from Fort Doom, in the lee of its rise, where it couldn't be seen from the road. They didn't mark the graves, but they noted the GPS coordinates so they could put up stones later, when normalcy had been reestablished.

It wasn't clear how the infection had come back to Fort Doom, or even if it was the same infection. The septic tanks were full, though, and they'd had to switch to chem-toilets and empty them into a pit they'd excavated for the purpose, noisome and aswarm with flies.

Martin spoke over the graves, summoning his best words.

There had been an interruption in the radio programming from Phoenix, lasting for a long month, while infection burned through the city, but it was back on the air, with news about antibiotic supplies that were being manufactured in a reclaimed factory in Chandler. The original DJs were off the air and there was a memorial program for them.

BY CHRISTMAS, THINGS had settled into a routine. There wasn't so much time to be bored any longer, at least. Between hunting and careful trading forays and digging new latrine pits, the residents of Fort Doom had their hands full. It would have been much worse if the farms of Elfrida hadn't had such a lucky good year, a bountiful harvest they traded with Fort Doom for more gems, and when those ran out, humiliating and backbreaking stints picking in the fields. Martin drew the line at this, and discouraged the others in the Fort from it, but they didn't all listen to him. Pickers got paid in fruit, everyone else just got root vegetables, the only thing the farmers were willing to trade.

Sara picked for two weeks straight, coming back lean and brown and muscled, and conspicuously complaining about the fact that Fort Doom didn't afford them any opportunities for agriculture. Martin tried to shut her down by talking about the intrinsically vulnerable circumstances of farming, and she countered by snappishly reminding them all of the vulnerability of fucking starving to death.

No more boredom in Fort Doom, then, but still: plenty of tension. Martin decided that they needed to throw a party. Thanksgiving had come and gone unobserved, but they could still celebrate the extraordinary circumstances of their survival of The Event by trimming a tree, cooking a feast, exchanging small gifts.

Martin had packed a plastic tree in the Fort's supplies, thinking of how much fun it would be to surprise his guests on their first Christmas together. It had come as a package with candy canes and tinsel and ornaments. He awoke early on December nineteenth to assemble the tree in the hospitality suite, taking the opportunity to bag up the drifts of litter and sweep up the tracked-in dirt. When he was done, he stepped back and surveyed the room, expecting it to look festive and cheerful. But it looked sad and desperate, the plastic tree and its twinkling strings of LEDs small and artificial, the room still grimy, the sofa cushions stained and threadbare.

For the millionth time, he wished that the fucking crisis would end. *Armegeddon tired of this shit*. Which made him remember that Warren was dead, in a bag in an unmarked grave in the lee of the ridge.

Sara was the first one awake after Martin put up the tree, and she rolled her eyes at it and said she'd been invited to Christmas dinner with the other "farmhands" who'd picked that fall. But she helped make the name slips for the Secret Santa and rearranged the tinsel and ornaments to good effect. Martin had deliberately left the decorations clumped together to give other people something to fix, which was the most surefire way to create a sense of ownership over the project.

The kitchen still had a good supply of spices, and Martin had deliberately stashed three cases of cooking wine, and he asked Sara to see if he could figure out a decent mulled wine recipe with the materials at hand, and that got everyone kibbitzing, and then Fort Doom was filled with delicious smells and day drinking and wobbly good cheer.

That was lunchtime. By dinnertime, though, they had cheap wine hangovers, and the black dog stalked them, reminding them of the family members they'd left behind at The Event, of the dead from Fort Doom, of the chaos outside the armored door. Dinner was somber and quick, and no one wanted to hang around the hospitality suite after.

GENE HATCHED A plan to liven up some of their MREs and make a real feast out of the Christmas dinner, adding fresh ingredients and salted venison, plating everything with care, using real table linens and setting out candles. Martin gave the plan his blessing and went back to work on his Secret Santa gift: a leather cigar case with two of his dwindling store of Cohibas for Seth, one for him and one for a friend. Smoking cigars on the ridge while the sun set over the desert was one of the true pleasures of the end of the world.

Finally, on the twenty-fourth, with one day until the party, the mood shifted. The idea of a "Christmas spirit" was stupid and sentimental, but that didn't make it less real. They had it! Everyone was hiding in their own private spaces, making gifts, and when they weren't doing that they were making paper snowflakes, or cutting up clothes from the rag bag to make party outfits. Someone put a sprig of paper mistletoe over the doorway between the galley and the Hospitality Suite and they made a game of ambushing each other and kissing on the cheek. This game was considerably enlivened by the now-perpetual pot of cheap spiced wine.

Sara made her great-grandmother's Depression Cookies, which were flourless and used powdered egg and powdered milk and still smelled and looked great in the oven. They were decorated with icing and set on a conspicuous serving tray in the kitchen, with a DO NOT EAT THIS MEANS YOU sign, and they all stopped by to admire them and dare each other to violate the sign. It was the most fun they'd had in weeks and the best mood they'd felt in months, and Martin kept peeking in on them, reassuring himself that his plan was working, that he was the leader he thought he was.

THE DAY AFTER Christmas, they lolled around the hospitality suite in their pajamas, still full from the feast the night before. Seth stepped outside to enjoy one of his cigars and came back in, rosy cheeked, radiating cold and smelling of good, mellow Cuban tobacco.

They had hangovers, of course, fierce headaches that made them want to talk in low voices. As he sweated and grew a little nauseated, Martin wished he hadn't drunk so much mulled wine the night before, but comforted himself by recalling that they'd gotten through the entire supply of cheap wine and wouldn't be tempted for a repeat.

Seth was the first to start vomiting. It came on suddenly, too quickly for him to reach the toilet, and he left streaks on the floor all the way to the bathroom, awful smelling and all-pervasive.

When Martin stood to get the gloves and bleach wipes, his

head swam and he realized that he didn't just have a headache, he had a fever. He gingerly cleaned up the mess, then got the ear thermometer. It read 103°.

They were all sick. Maybe it was whatever had almost killed Martin the last time. Maybe it was something new. Fort Doom was out of antibiotics.

BY NEW YEAR'S, eight of the remaining twelve had died. The rest were too weak to bury them, though they did manage to drag their bodies out the front door.

Fort Doom was a charnel house. The septic tank had backed up again, so even when the survivors could muster the strength to get to the toilet, it wouldn't flush. The chem-toilets overflowed. They filled buckets, then knocked the buckets over as they reeled around with fever, fetching water and rehydration salts and headache pills.

Martin's fever spiked to 107°, and then he slept for a long time, waking only when his guts spasmed and tried to wring out whatever was left in them.

When his fever broke on January fourth, he discovered he was the last person alive in Fort Doom.

MARTIN NURSED HIMSELF back to health, crawling at first, then staggering around, drinking high-calorie meal-replacement powders and bouillon cubes in lukewarm water. He dragged the smaller bodies outside, rested a day and a night, then did the larger bodies. He cleaned.

Days went past and his fever returned, receded. The power failed and he got the backup generator working. He checked the CCTV cameras and thought about leaving, thought about where he could go. He was too weak to get far, and he'd be helpless.

Now that he was running on generator power, he had to conserve his propane stores, so he stopped boiling his water before drinking it. Now he dripped iodine into it and sucked it through a LifeStraw and hoped that that would be enough. The overflowing septic pits made him leery of drinking any more of the Fort's well water without treating it. He didn't know why the sickness had burned through Fort Doom, but that was his top suspect.

Then, one day, the fever came back and sat on him, burning him up, refusing to budge. His joints ached, his bowels twisted and knotted. He drifted in and out of lucidity, weak and alone. And scared. So, so, so scared.

The proximity sensors knocked him out of a feverish half sleep. Shivering, he crawled to the monitor, saw the cars surrounding the entrance to Fort Doom. Saw the passenger door to the lead car open. The other doors. Four figures. Three men. A woman.

Albert's aunt.

The terror was a searing counterpart to the fever chills. It got even worse when he realized he couldn't remember buttoning up the Fort the last time he'd ventured outside to dump his trash.

On the monitor, Albert's aunt pointed her finger at the doorway. Something about the way she pointed told him that he hadn't closed it. A moment later, he heard voices, far and growing closer. At first he couldn't make out their words, then he realized that was because they were speaking Spanish.

GRACIELA HAD LEARNED a lot since she'd gone back to Phoenix, so sick she thought she was dying. She'd learned first aid, and basic sanitation, and the kind of food hygiene you used in a pandemic. She'd learned the word pandemic.

She'd learned to assay the antibiotics coming off the little production line they'd built as part of the quality assurance process. She'd learned to take direction from the tech leads on the big water filtration plant they'd brought back online. She'd learned to read topographical maps, and she'd learned to lead the teams that sought out the sick to offer them aid.

She'd learned that she liked doing these things. She'd learned that rebuilding, caring, and fixing kept the sudden terrors and the creeping tears away. She'd learned that while nothing would ever bring back her sons, her husband, her nephew Albert, that the memory of the people she'd helped nurse from the brink of death would soften the sorrow she felt when she thought of her own dead. She'd kept count: one helped for each she'd lost; then two, then five alive for each of her dead. She'd stopped counting. There were two children who lived with her now, no one knew where their parents were. Lanae was six and Darnell was nine. When they smiled, it was like all her dead were smiling on her.

THE MAN WHO'D left her to die had left his door open. She knew he had guns. They all had guns, out here. She was pretty sure one of her guys was carrying, even though none of them were supposed to carry. Thinking of the way that the man had talked to her, had talked to Albert, had fired on them, she was secretly glad that they had a gun, too.

"Sir? Hello?" She had smelled these smells before, but they didn't get easier to take. Shit. Puke. Sickness. Rotting garbage. Dead people. One of the men came back from around the rear of the entrance to the bunker with vomit down the front of his own shirt. So many dead back there. She made sure her mask was in place and smeared some VapoRub under her nose.

"Sir?" She took a tentative step into the vestibule, over the mounds of trash bags, some torn open by animals. She was glad the bodies were hidden from her view. It was natural, what animals did to human remains, but it could be hard to take.

THEY TOOK SO long to leave. Martin bit down on his belt when the spasms hit, not making so much as a whimper. His panic room was little bigger than a coffin, just a crawlspace beneath the garage, filled with old gas fumes. He had a charged phone, though, and the local Wi-Fi, and could watch as they searched the Fort, watch outside as they built a pyre and burned the dead. That took so long. He whimpered into the leather of his belt.

But they left, eventually.

By then, he was too weak to move the heavy plate over his head. He pushed it as hard as he could, so hard he lost control of his anal sphincter and felt hot shit squirt down his leg. He pushed harder, panic rising in him. The fever ground at his joints.

Finally, he closed his eyes. He'd take a nap and try again. He'd regain his strength after a nap.

acknowledgments

My agent, Russell Galen, did a lot of heavy lifting to make this book real, as always going above and beyond. It means a lot, Russ, thank you. Tor Books supported me in so many ways on this, and the personal encouragement from my editor Patrick Nielsen Hayden and publisher Fritz Foy was especially welcome – and any acknowledgment for Tor would be remiss without a sincere thank you to Tom Doherty for his long services to the field and his support for me, personally. Thank you also to Tor's production team and especially the art direction people for making me part of the special, lucky lotto winners who get Will Stahle covers. Holy moly, those COVERS. Thank you to Macmillan Audio (Robert Allen) and Google Play (Chris Palma), who were incredibly supportive of my quest for audiobook excellence, and to Skyboat Media, who are a true pleasure to work with, and my readers. Thanks also to Jigsaw/First Look, Head of Zeus, and the folks at Heyne. It takes a lot of talented, dedicated people to make a book, and it's always a leap of faith. Thanks for inspiration to Matt Taibbi, the Electronic Frontier Foundation, Alex Steffen and the outquisition, and everyone who fights for justice: #blacklivesmatter, Alexandria Ocasio-Cortez, Erika Garner, Bernie Sanders, and the millions in the streets. This isn't the kind of fight you win, it's the kind of fight you fight.